Kate of Clyve Shore

Also by Lena Kennedy

Maggie
Autumn Alley
Nelly Kelly
Lizzie
Lady Penelope
Susan
Lily, My Lovely
Down Our Street
The Dandelion Seed
Eve's Apples
The Inn on the Marsh
Owen Oliver
Ivy of the Angel
Queenie's Castle

About the author

Lena Kennedy lived all her life in the East End of London and wrote with great energy about the people and times she knew there. She was 67 before her first novel, *Maggie*, was accepted for publication. Since then her bestselling novels have shown her to be among the finest and best loved of contemporary novelists. Lena Kennedy died in August 1986.

LENA KENNEDY

Kate of Clyve Shore

Three Stories

HODDER

First published in Great Britain in 1992 by
Little, Brown and Company

This edition published in 2012 by Hodder & Stoughton
An Hachette UK company

A CIP catalogue record for this title is available
from the British Library

eBook ISBN 9781444767469
Print ISBN 9781444767452

Hodder & Stoughton Ltd
338 Euston Road
London NW1 3BH

www.hodder.co.uk

KATE OF CLYVE SHORE

I

Pirates

If you ever find yourself in the town of Rochester, you will not fail to be aware of its ancient past. It was the site of a Roman walled city, and the Normans built one of their finest castles there, as well as a magnificent cathedral. The castle was destroyed in 1215 by King John's siege but the tall keep remains standing and will give you superb views across the windswept marshlands of Kent.

Inside the cathedral, on a windowsill and away from the brasses and oak pews, you may notice the carved wooden bust of a young woman. Her eyes stare out directly at her admirers and her bearing tells us that she was proud and spirited when she was alive and walking those Kentish marshes hundreds of years ago.

This is her story, the story which reminds us that however quiet and simple our lives, the march of history affects us all. This is the sad tale of Kate of Clyve Shore.

Young Kate was a most unusual-looking girl. Her face was wide at the brow and narrow at the chin. Her shiny black hair lay flat over her forehead and fell to her waist in two thick braids. Her tremulous bottom lip drooped until it resembled one of the luscious ripe strawberries that grow in the fields of Kent. She had white skin and full red lips but the most outstanding feature of her face was the gaze from her eyes. Her eyes were beautiful; widely spaced, deep-set and dark blue, they were the colour of a calm sea. And her gaze was hypnotic.

At the time of our story Kate had just turned fifteen years old. This sweet country girl had lived all her life with her family in a tiny thatched cottage out on the Kentish marsh just past the village of Clyve Shore. Beyond loomed the massive shape of Clyve Castle, where most of the villagers earned their livelihoods.

For as long as she could remember, Kate had travelled back and forth along the dry, sandy road leading to the castle while balancing on her head a heavy basket full of linen. Unlike older and more weary souls, Kate always stepped out briskly on her long shapely legs, her back as straight as a soldier's. The basket on her head contained the frills and furbelows of the gentlefolk who were staying as guests at the castle – white lawn ruffs to wear about the neck, and lace borders to be attached to the cuffs. Kate's mother, Meg, endlessly washed, boiled, starched and ironed batches of this finery day after day, until the rough walls of the little thatched cottage ran with steam.

Meg had once been a servant at the castle, as had generations of her family before her, but now she did all her work at home with Kate collecting and delivering for her.

The road to the castle cut through the pretty Kent

countryside – low rolling marshland which led down to the Thames on one side, and a dense forest of oaks on the other. But as she walked along in the golden sunshine, Kate was quite oblivious to all this beauty. She did not see the moorhens darting among the swampy reeds or the storks wading through the brackish water. Her ears were deaf to the rustle of the foxes and the sweet song of the thrush in the woods. For she was too busy day-dreaming.

And what dreams they were! Yes, one day she would find a rich husband, a young nobleman who would buy her fine clothes and jewellery, and take her mother and young brother away from that damp, steamy cottage which made her mother's cough so much worse. Pa, well, Pa could stay where he was, serving that old priest he was so fond of . . . then he'd be sorry. That would teach him not to call her daft, not to tease her for dreaming, for wanting something better than what she saw her mother had had.

Kate could see the young gentleman in her mind's eye – handsome, kind and brave. Yes, when he asked for her hand in marriage, she would accept immediately.

Ah, the sweet dreams of youth! Of course, Kate knew nothing of her real destiny.

The gates of the castle were closed now. Kate looked up at the thick, grey stone walls and tall turrets, to ignore the leering faces of the guards on the bridge that crossed the moat.

As she approached, the huge iron gates into the castle were opened by an old guard whose face was as red as the uniform he wore.

'Come on, get inside, Kate,' he said, giving the girl an impatient push. 'Don't hang about. Her Ladyship is waiting for that clean linen.'

George was a very old retainer, fat and blustering. Every day when Kate arrived, he greeted her in the same way. Now, cursing and swearing, he quickly barred the gates once Kate was inside.

Kate walked slowly across the dusty courtyard to the kitchens at the rear of the castle. On her way, she passed several soldiers sitting around playing dice.

'Hallo, pretty Kitty,' they called, catching her gaze and nudging each other suggestively. But Kate passed them all looking quite unconcerned. Her wicker basket remained firmly on her head and her long hips swayed provocatively.

Handing in the basket to the maid at the kitchen door, Kate then sat down in the courtyard, leaning her back against the wall. She looked at the scene around her.

The lawn stretched out in front, a brilliant green of well-watered grass kept short by the sheep that were let loose on it each night. Delicate lace patterns waved across it as the sun shone through the big cedars. Beyond, at the bottom of the hill, was a small lake of cool dark water, home of two pairs of majestic swans whose white feathers contrasted with the vivid plumage of the peacocks that strutted across the lawns in front of the house.

Kate watched quietly as the tall figure of Lady Evelyn Mortimer appeared in the garden with her companions to play quoits. They laughed and joked with one another, completely oblivious to the slight figure of the servant girl watching them so keenly.

How Kate admired Lady Evelyn! She was so exquisitely beautiful, so serene, so knowing.

As Lady Evelyn stood poised to throw the wooden rings, the young men of the party clapped and cheered. They were clearly all admirers, too.

Kate's brow wrinkled in a tiny envious frown. Lady Evelyn with her red-gold hair and velvet gowns, she had everything. How lucky she was to live in this grand castle and have such a fine wardrobe. She had everything she wanted and servants to do anything she ordered.

The only thing Kate did not envy Lady Evelyn for was her husband, Lord Mortimer. He was ancient, a disgusting, gouty old man with rheumy eyes and a bald head. He repelled her. Surely Lady Evelyn could have done better than him.

Kate's reverie was broken by a delicious smell of cooking coming from the kitchen. She sniffed hungrily. 'I wonder if I can get a taste,' she thought. She had not eaten since getting up at dawn.

She got to her feet and went down into the great kitchens where she found a hive of activity as a great supper was being prepared. On long trestle tables were platters loaded with good things. There were whole hogs' heads in the process of being decorated, large turkey pies, jugged hare and cold sweetmeats and marzipan shapes to please the palate.

The sight of all this delicious food made Kate stand and stare.

Her lower lip dropped.

'Get out of the way, Kate!' shouted the serving men, bumping into her in their hurry to carry the platters through to the great hall.

By the massive fireplace sat a very old man. His skin was brown and wrinkled from age and, possibly, from the smoke from the fire. He sat patiently, turning a spit upon which was roasting a whole lamb. As the spit turned, some of the fat fell crackling and hissing into the roaring fire but most of it was collected in a dish beneath.

By now the smell of the cooking was more than Kate could bear. She crept over to the fireplace. 'Give us a taster, Old Jem,' she whispered.

The grizzled old head turned slightly sideways and a brown claw reached out to snatch a piece of coarse white bread from the table. Dipping this into the dish of fat, Jem held it out to her. 'Here ye are, take it quick,' he said. 'Don't let her see you – she's around here somewhere.'

Kate murmured gratefully and retired to a dark corner to enjoy her tasty morsel while the hustle and bustle carried on all around her. Jem stayed in his place while a plump young boy heaped more wood on the fire and stood by with large bellows to blast the flames with air whenever it was necessary to restore them.

Kate ate her bread and dripping with relish, savouring the rich meaty juices running down her throat. When she had finished, she moved back to sit next to Old Jem by the fireplace and warm her hands against the great heat of the fire. 'Aren't you sick of turning that spit?' she asked.

Jem's old face cracked into a smile. His skin was crinkled like parchment. 'Nay, lass,' he replied. 'I've been doing it too long now. I worked here with your grandfather and your mother.' He smiled nostalgically. 'Your mother was a bright little wench, just like you, she was.'

Kate was not interested. 'You won't catch *me* staying here all my life,' she said defiantly.

Jem's gnarled claw patted her knee. 'Let's hope not, pet,' he said. He looked around quickly and leaned towards her. 'Listen, Katy,' he whispered, 'take heed of what I say. You must get back home as quick as you can.'

'What for?' Kate looked at him quizzically.

'The French pirates are out in the bay, that's why,' said Jem.

Kate snorted and tossed her black braids. 'Who's scared of a lot of old Frenchies?' she sniffed.

'Never mind the sass,' replied Jem. 'Get your backside off that stool and get home as quick as you can. Tom, the fisherman, saw them at dawn this morning, and I know those devils, they'll be ashore tonight.'

He glanced around again. Now the expression on his face had changed. 'Look out, Kate, here she comes!'

He dropped his head with its mane of iron-grey hair, and began turning the handle of the spit as though his life depended upon it.

A sharp brittle voice called out: 'Katy, where are you?'

There before her was the formidable shape of Mistress Wilkins, Lady Evelyn's housekeeper. Behind her stood a servant with Kate's wicker basked now filled with dirty linen. 'Tell your mother I want these by early tomorrow morning,' Mistress Wilkins said. 'And they must be laundered well,' she added. The woman's thick black eyebrows met in a scowl, and her hard blue eyes stared at Kate so intensely that the girl felt very uncomfortable. She began to shift from foot to foot, and her lip dropped.

'Shut your mouth, for goodness sake, child!' shouted the housekeeper. 'Really, Kate, are you as slow-witted as you look?'

With an impatient snort, Mistress Wilkins swept out of the kitchen.

Kate picked up her basket. 'Miserable old hag,' she muttered. 'Goodbye, Jem,' she called. Then off she went with another day's laundry.

The soldiers were still lounging about by the main gate. Old George held the small side entrance gate open only a little way, peering nervously out into the road as Kate slipped by. 'Come on, Kate,' he called. 'Hurry and get home before dark.'

'What's it to do with you?' retorted Kate pertly. She put down her basket slowly and hitched up her skirt so that she would not trip up on the rough country road.

'A little higher, pretty Kitty,' chanted the soldiers, laughing and nudging as they always did.

Kate stuck out her tongue at them, swept the heavy basket on to her head, and marched out.

It was a long and lonely road that led back to her home but Kate had made the journey so often that it held no fears for her any more. The sun had begun to set over the sea in a blaze of orange and yellow glory. Looking over towards the seashore, she could see the River Thames, a straight silver strip in the distance where it joined its mother, the sea. A white mist had started to creep over the marsh, hovering just a few feet above the water. She suddenly remembered Old Jem's warning about the French pirates, and quickened her pace. But within moments her day-dreams had caught up with her again as she imagined herself wearing Lady Evelyn's green riding habit and riding out on a prancing white stallion. On her head she had a green bonnet with a long green feather floating in the breeze.

Daylight was fast disappearing and the tall oak trees cast long shadows across the road. About fifty yards off the road was the Bull Inn, an establishment used chiefly by fishermen. As Kate went past, the place seemed much noisier than usual and certainly noisy for that early time of the evening. Suddenly she noticed a shape sitting by the side of the road.

'Who is that?' she wondered out aloud. It looked like the landlord of the inn.

That was odd. He was just sitting there with his eyes wide open.

Kate walked over to get a closer look and gasped as she saw the large knife sticking out of the landlord's back.

For a moment she froze in panic but then she turned and ran, clutching and holding on to her skirts. But poor Kate, she ran fast enough but she kept looking backwards over her shoulder so she was hardly aware of the four large men in her path until she crashed straight into them. Rough hands grabbed and pushed her. Kate almost fainted with fright. She caught glimpses of long beards and striped shirts but not much more as she was dragged struggling towards the inn. The linen from her basket was strewn across the road.

The men were foreign. They jabbered in a strange language as their rough hands pawed at her. She fought, kicked and screamed, but they showed no mercy, dragging her back towards the inn.

As they approached the building, two other men joined them. One of these was a giant of a man, and he spoke a rough kind of English in an accent that sounded vaguely familiar to Kate. 'I'll take the lass,' he said. 'She's bonny enough. She'll do well for the captain.' He said something to the other men that Kate could not understand and, with obvious reluctance, they let go. Now the giant caught her up in his great arms and carried her into the inn.

Inside, the place was a shambles. The giant stood Kate on her feet and she looked around with a bewildered stare. Windows were smashed, chairs and tables had been thrown around. The sawdust on the floor was sodden with spilled beer.

A man lolled in the windowseat drinking from a brown bottle. He was very slim and had the elegant air of a gentleman, but he wore the same rough clothes as the fishermen. His hair was red-gold, and around it he had tied a bright red kerchief. He had a pointed beard that was, Kate noticed for some peculiar reason, the same colour as Lady Evelyn's hair.

'What have you there, Jamie?' the man asked. His voice had the same familiar high-pitched into-nation.

'A braw lassie, Captain,' replied the giant. 'I just got her away from the men.'

'I'll take care of her,' the Captain declared with a charming grin. He leaned over and pulled Kate towards him. Holding her tight he began to force some of the potent brandy down her throat.

From then on, Kate knew very little of what happened to her. She was vaguely aware of being kissed and she remembered how good that felt and how nice he smelled. She remembered him carrying her to bed and the two laughing as he removed his boots. But after that she remembered nothing.

When Kate awoke the next morning she was alone in a big bed. She dressed quickly and slipped downstairs and out of the inn. Then she ran as fast as her slim legs would carry her home to the cottage on the marsh.

2

Lady of the Castle

The sun was high in the sky as Kate's mother Meg set off down the road towards the castle. She was a thin little woman but as she walked the wooden clogs on her feet made persistent echoing thuds down that dry sandy road. She pulled the old woollen shawl tightly around her frail shoulders. In spite of the sunshine she was feeling chilled. If only that damn cough would not keep her awake at night!

As she neared the castle she rehearsed in her head what she was going to say to Lady Evelyn, and what excuse she could give for the linen – much of it spoiled and some of it lost. She plodded along, her face pale and grim, her lips drawn tight with worry.

The villagers had by now all returned to their homes after sheltering in the church during the disturbances of the previous night. It was no new adventure for them to be raided by pirates, for it often happened. Pirates of all nationalities regularly raided that Kent coast. The flat lonely marshland made an easy target for the privateers. They all came, the Dutch, the Norwegians, and, most often of all, the dreaded French, nowadays led ashore, it was rumoured, by a young Scottish nobleman who had fled to exile in

France during the last bout of hostility between Scotland and England. The pirates never stayed long, just long enough to cause death and havoc in the small, unprotected Kent village. In fact, the villagers' only protection came from the church, which was guarded by an ancient priest who in turn was protected by Jacob – young Kate's father.

Over the years, many men had lost their lives during these raids, while defending their property and families. Many young girls were raped, and some even disappeared forever, to be sold as slaves, some said.

At least Katy had been spared that fate, thought Meg, in an effort to console herself. Even so, it would not be easy for Kate to find a husband now if the truth ever leaked out. Kent farmers were very fussy and would certainly not want a Frenchman's leavings. What chance did dull-witted Kate have of matrimony now?

'I had better not tell Jacob,' Meg decided. 'He'll like as not tell the priest, and I certainly don't want Kate shut up in a convent. What a religious old fool he is, with his bowing and scraping,' Meg thought scathingly of her husband.

As she walked along, she reviewed the situation and by the time she was nearing the drawbridge to the castle, Meg had sorted out many of her thoughts. She had decided that the only thing she could do was to speak to Lady Evelyn in private. Lady Evelyn was the only person with any sense about here.

Old George at the gate was very pleased to see Meg and he greeted her with a friendly smile. During her days as maid to the old Lady Mortimer, George had been rather sweet on her. When she had first come to the castle with her Ladyship she had been an attractive dark-eyed slip of a girl. George had been very taken with her and it had been a great disappointment to him when Meg chose the humpbacked Jacob for her husband instead of George himself.

'How are you, my dear?' he enquired.

'Quite well, George,' Meg replied. 'I wish to speak to her Ladyship.'

Meg had faded quite a lot this year and did not look at all well, thought George, as he shut the gate behind her.

'I want you to take a message for me,' continued Meg. 'I will not be bothered with that bitch of a housekeeper.'

George grinned, his thick grey whiskers sticking out like a brush. She was still the same little Meg, so full of spirit. 'Come with me, my dear,' he said. 'Her Ladyship is always pleased to see you.'

He led her all the way to Lady Mortimer's parlour. There was no one there and Meg stood by a straight-backed chair while she waited for her Ladyship to arrive. She would never sit down. It wouldn't be right, for a woman in her position.

She looked around herself. It was a pleasant room now, since Lady Evelyn had made her mark. Now the walls were covered with exquisite tapestries from France and fresh flowers had been placed in every available space. The old Lady Mortimer had made the place dark and gloomy with no happiness or spirit. This was all so different!

Lady Evelyn had come like a breath of spring to Clyve Castle. Lord Mortimer must have been turning sixty when he brought his new bride down from Scotland. What a change that had been. Lady Evelyn was now thirty, and a real beauty in her prime, while her husband was old and gouty, fit for little else but his brandy and bed.

Suddenly Lady Evelyn swept into the room. She looked so calm and collected, and she was dressed in the green riding habit that Kate often spoke about. She looked radiant. The glint of gold in her hair was almost the colour of the bright marigolds on the table.

'Meg, my dear,' she said with a warm smile on her face. 'What can I do for you?'

Meg's eyes filled with tears. 'I came to see you, My Lady,' she stammered, 'because the linen was spoilt last night and some was lost, blown away in the wind.'

'Oh yes, the raid,' replied Lady Evelyn. 'I heard about it. It is a bad business. We really need more protection on our coast. But tell me, what happened to Kate?' Lady Evelyn was renowned for treating common folk with kindness and respect.

She had already been told, thought Meg, looking down uneasily at her feet. 'The truth is, My Lady, that the pirates got her last night. It could have been a lot worse but the fact now is that my daughter is no longer a virgin.'

Lady Evelyn's white brow creased in a tiny frown. 'Oh dear,' she murmured quietly. She paused and then continued, 'I had better come down and talk to Kate myself. Now, don't worry about the linen, Meg. I'll send a man down to collect what you have retrieved and I'll see Kate in the morning.'

She placed her arm gently about Meg's frail shoulders. 'Go home now and don't worry. I'll bring something for that troublesome cough tomorrow.'

Early next morning Kate sat at the door of her cottage. She was wearing a rough blue dress and her black hair was covered by a white sun bonnet. In front of her there was a large wooden platter of blackcurrants which she was stalking and throwing into a big earthenware pitcher. She was preparing the fruit to make jam or wine to sell at the fair. Kate was very sulky. She kept digging her bare toes into the sandy path and irritably pushing the strings of her bonnet out of the way. She was feeling very resentful because she had not been allowed out and could not understand what all the fuss was about.

Inside the cottage her mother was resting. Kate could hear that continuous dry cough, which seemed to be wearing her mother out.

The clip-clop of hooves on the road broke the silence of the morning. Looking up, Kate jumped quickly to her feet. 'Mother!' she called as she ran inside. 'Here comes Lady Evelyn.'

Lady Evelyn's fine figure was dismounting from her white horse. Taking the basket from the fat boy who rode with her, she entered the cottage, stooping low in the doorway to avoid knocking her head.

As always, Kate stared open-mouthed at this lovely lady and said nothing.

'I'm sorry, My Lady,' cried Meg, feeling extremely flustered at being found in bed. It was a rough sort of bed, too, made up of just a few planks and a straw mattress and placed in the corner of the sparsely furnished room. In fact, the only presentable piece of furniture in the whole house was a carved oak chair which had been a wedding present to Meg from her late mistress.

Lady Evelyn sat down on this best chair. Turning to Meg she said reassuringly: 'Take your rest, it's Kate I have come to talk to.'

Regardless of this, Meg rose and began bustling around the room. 'Kate,' she said, 'go and fetch that pitcher of cold mead. Her Ladyship may like a cool drink.'

But Kate did not hear her mother's words. She just stood transfixed with fright. She knew that the moment had come when she was going to have to reveal what had happened at the inn.

Minutes later, tears streamed down her face as she reluctantly recounted the story. She became more and more distressed until she finally let out a great howl and threw herself on the bed and refused to speak any more.

Lady Evelyn's patience had by now run out and she stopped trying to cajole Kate into saying anything more about what had happened. She and Meg sat over a glass of mead discussing the situation between themselves while Kate lay prostrate on the bed.

'Can we be sure it was the Frenchmen?' said Lady Evelyn.

'They must have taken her by force, My Lady,' replied Meg. 'Kate is not one to be free with the lads, so I am sure it must be the Frenchmen.'

As her mother spoke, Kate suddenly sat up. 'But he was no Frenchie,' she exclaimed. 'He looked and talked like you, My Lady.'

The effect of this last remark on Lady Evelyn was astonishing. She jumped up and in one stride was across the room to the bed. She grabbed Kate's wrist and pulled her from the bed. 'Now Kate, my girl,' she hissed threateningly, 'you will tell me word for word what happened to you, or I'll call that fat boy in to give you a good beating.'

With Lady Evelyn holding her wrist in a grip of iron, a very frightened Kate told her every detail of what she remembered, starting with how she had found the land-lord of the inn dead and going on to describe how the four foreigners had torn off her underclothes.

'A big man called Jamie came to my rescue,' she continued, 'but he handed me to his captain saying I was a "braw" lassie.' Kate looked down at her feet in shame. 'Then the captain made me drink some vile liquor and began to fondle and kiss me.' She recounted this in a low whisper.

Lady Evelyn's face grew very pale and her lips were set in a thin line. She let go of Kate's wrist and returned to the chair. Her knuckles shone white as she gripped the sides of the chair. 'Did this man Jamie ever mention the captain's name?' she asked.

'No, My Lady, he just called him Captain,' whispered Kate. Thinking now that she had to tell the whole truth, she began to tell them more of what happened until Lady Evelyn held up her hand to quieten her.

Meg, who was weeping gently, was rather puzzled at her Ladyship's persistent questions about what the captain had been wearing.

'And did he wear a ring?' Lady Evelyn asked urgently.

After a moment's thought, Kate remembered that he had. 'It had a funny flower and an animal on it,' she said with a nod.

This answer seemed to satisfy Lady Evelyn. She rose to her feet and patted Kate on the shoulder. 'You are very young, my dear, and you will soon forget it.' She looked unusually weary as she made for the door. Before she left, she turned again. 'Make sure Kate takes that physic I have brought. And there's also something for your cough, Meg.'

After a pause, she added: 'If there is any more trouble, you had better bring Kate to me at the castle. I promise I won't let the priest have her.'

'God bless you, My Lady,' said Meg gratefully.

As Lady Evelyn mounted her horse again, Kate stood motionless and open-mouthed as questions raced through her brain. What trouble? Why should she go to the castle if there is any? And why should the old priest want her? Now she felt really scared.

3

Angus

That night, after dark, a huge lumbering coach pulled by two black stallions sped along the road to Rochester. Most local folk did not venture out after dark unless there was urgent need, for the roads were uneven and full of hazards at that time of night.

When Lady Evelyn had ordered the servants to prepare the coach, a whisper had passed around the castle household. What could be wrong? Where was she going? But no one dared actually to put the questions to her Ladyship, not even old George who was to drive the coach and who could be heard muttering to himself as he climbed on board and picked up the reins.

Lady Evelyn was already there, sitting patiently inside the coach. She was well wrapped in a fur-lined hooded cloak which revealed just a glint of her golden hair in the darkness. Her small white faced peeped out, her lips set in a hard line.

There was no question that she was worried, George thought. She definitely had something on her mind.

'Stop at the Bull Inn by the river,' she ordered before they set off.

Perhaps Lady Evelyn had suddenly taken a lover, thought George. Well, no one would blame her if she had. His Lordship had become such a decrepit old wreck and worsening every day it seemed.

Both servant and mistress were preoccupied with their own thoughts as the coach rattled through the night.

'If it was him,' Lady Evelyn was thinking, 'this is where he will be. If I know Angus, he will spend more than one night ashore.'

Within half an hour, they had pulled up in the cobbled courtyard of the inn. George turned the coach round while Lady Evelyn hurried inside and up the stairs. She needed no guide. She knew where to find him.

She pushed open the door, her blue eyes shining bright with temper. The young man was sitting sprawled in a chair with the giant Jamie trying to prise his heavy riding boots from his feet. He looked up at Evelyn in astonishment as she stood in the doorway.

'So it *is* you, Angus,' she said quietly.

'Evelyn!' he exclaimed.

'Leave us, Jamie,' she said sharply.

With a respectful nod, Jamie touched his forelock and left the room.

'Why, it's the lovely Lady Evelyn,' repeated Angus, trying to rise from the chair. He had obviously been drinking heavily.

Evelyn pushed him back into the chair. 'Sober up, you fool!' she hissed. Removing her cloak, she poured some cold water from a pitcher into a bowl. Then she plunged in a towel and promptly placed it on Angus's head.

Angus sat up abruptly, water dripping from the ends of his red-gold beard. 'Careful, sis,' he grinned. 'You know I don't like water.'

Now Evelyn smiled at him. Her smile seemed like a ray of sunshine through a storm cloud.

'That's better,' he said, staggering to his feet. 'Now welcome to my humble abode, dear sister.' Evelyn sat in the windowseat and gazed down at the winding shape of the River Medway flowing below. It had rained quite heavily recently and the swollen waters rushed past the green river banks. Evelyn looked back at her brother, Angus, who stood tall and gracious beside her.

Their youth had been spent in the wild Scottish Highlands. Then fate had parted them but Evelyn still adored her weak-willed brother. They shared the same love of life and laughter and both had a strong sense of humour, that Celtic humour which had served them so well in times of trouble.

The moonlight cast dancing patterns on the floor, and outlined brother and sister as they held hands. For a few moments they were silently caught up in their common past, back home in Scotland, laughing and chasing each other through the heather.

Then Evelyn slowly drew back her hand. 'Do you know why I am here, Angus?' she asked firmly.

'I've got a good idea,' he grinned at her.

Evelyn stood up. She was not going to be swayed by his charm. 'That was a monstrous thing you did,' she chided.

Angus grasped her hand with both of his and

chuckled. 'Oh, 'twas only a bit of fun,' he said jauntily. But then he saw the anger in her face and the smile died on his lips.

'Fun indeed!' Evelyn snapped, pulling away her hand roughly now. 'I suppose it is fun when a man is murdered and a young girl raped.'

Angus shook his head. 'Now, Evelyn,' he said, 'the lass came willing enough.'

'Willing?' she retorted. 'A simple-minded young virgin is all she is.'

Angus rubbed his beard ruefully. 'A virgin? You don't say! It must have been the brandy.' He smirked.

Evelyn gave a disgusted sigh and sank down on the seat. 'Really, Angus,' she said in an exasperated voice. 'This is not a laughing matter. What *am* I to say to her mother? The mother is a fine little woman, and the father is a servant to the priest. I dread to think what a fuss *he* will make if he learns what has happened.'

For a second Angus actually looked concerned. 'Has anyone recognised me, Evelyn?' he asked.

Evelyn sniffed. 'There's no fear of that,' she said. 'The son of a nobleman disguised as a villain . . .'

Angus looked ashamed. 'Don't quarrel with me, Evelyn,' he said quietly. 'This may be the last time we meet.'

Evelyn looked alarmed. 'Why, are you not returning to France?' she asked.

Angus shook his head. 'No,' he replied. 'I am going to take a chance and go home again. We are all needed now.'

'But Angus,' Evelyn said with a frown, 'if you stay they will have your head.'

Angus shrugged. 'Come now, Evelyn, we must continue the fight, you know that. And God knows I dream of the day when you return to Scotland with me.'

'But I am perfectly happy at Clyve,' Evelyn replied.

Angus suddenly glowered and banged his fists on the wall with great violence. 'But sister, how can you possibly be happy? I have never forgiven Father for tying you to that lecherous husband.'

Evelyn smiled and touched his arm. 'Hush, Angus,' she said soothingly. 'Kent is my home now and these people are my people. And Hugh is no bother to me,' she added.

'Oh, sister, a lovely woman like you bound to an old man!' exclaimed Angus passionately. 'I can't bear thinking about it.'

The atmosphere in the room seemed charged with foreboding as they locked their eyes on each other's. They were both thinking about the same thing and they knew it.

Evelyn pulled her brother to her and held him tightly. 'When Hugh dies I don't think I shall marry again,' she said thickly.

Tears had begun to trickle down his cheeks. 'And that will be the end of this unlucky family,' he said bitterly, 'because I shall probably die young.'

Evelyn wiped away her tears and slipped on her cloak. 'Get some rest, dear brother, I must go now. Old George will be paralysed with the cold out there.'

She moved towards the door and then stopped. 'I

still don't know what possessed you to guide our enemies ashore,' she said. 'What were you doing?'

Angus shrugged again. 'It was a favour for a favour, Evelyn,' he replied. 'The pirates had helped me so I wanted to help them.'

'Oh well, what's done is done. Take care, dearest brother,' Evelyn said, and slipped softly down the stairs to climb into the awaiting coach.

As George manoeuvred the coach out of the court-yard, Angus stood silhouetted in the window, his eyes awash with tears. Evelyn returned the look. It was an exchange they would cherish forever, for who knew when or if they would meet again?

4

Tom

For a while peace returned to the village. With its winding main street and huddle of timber buildings, Clyve Shore was a sleepy place. Some of the buildings were tall with overhanging gables, and were often found next to small shacks with whitewashed walls. And every one had rough beams tarred with pitch to preserve them from the winter gales.

This tiny port had grown up almost overnight, it seemed, a peaceful inland bay at the mouth of the Thames. It had provided a secure anchorage for trading vessels for generations, and a safe haven from the channel storms. It was well known as a good place to tarry before the ebb tide that helped navigate the river, the wide Thames that flowed right on from the City of London itself.

Kate was quite unconcerned about sea tides at that moment as she strolled down the village street. On her father's instructions, she was on her way to the priest's house to help him pick the soft fruit that was ready for harvesting.

Dressed in her blue Sunday gown and yellow bonnet, she carried an old serge tunic under her arm to put on while picking. She was very proud of her bonnet, having spent many long winter evenings embroidering the fine linen. It had a neatly stitched brim that made a halo for her heart-shaped face.

Her father had ordered her to come down to pick the fruit to help earn her keep. He had been complaining recently about his daughter not being married yet and the fact that he was still having to keep 'a great wench'. But then he was always fussing.

Her mother, on the other hand, who was usually rather relaxed, had suddenly become very anxious. She rarely let Kate out of her sight these days. She seemed to have been very upset about that evening when Kate had been with that nobleman. Kate couldn't think why. It was all a lot of fuss over nothing, she thought.

With her head held high, she picked her way daintily through the village. She was feeling quite exhilarated as she had ever since the strange night in the arms of her mystery lover. Yes, she felt very alive, very vital and, apart from occasional moments when she felt oddly queasy, she had never felt so well in her life. She had chosen this route rather than go through the woods because she did not think she should be expected to tramp through the bracken and climb stiles when dressed in her best clothes.

As Kate meandered along in her dreamy manner, the village folk called greetings from their windows, making Kate dawdle all the more as she was determined that everyone should get a good look at her in all her finery.

By now she had completely forgotten the reason for her outing, and her pace became slower and slower.

Suddenly, she saw Tom, the fisherman, sitting on the shingle beach carefully whittling some wood having just finished repairing his nets in readiness for a night's fishing in local waters. Tom was considered a very important man in the village. Apart from being physically the largest fellow around these parts, he was also the owner of his own fishing boat.

When Tom saw Kate approaching, he immediately dropped his knife and carving. He hoisted his whole six-foot-three frame to its full height and stood there in his rough fisherman's garb. 'Well now,' he called, showing perfect white teeth, 'if it isn't young Katy. What brings you to Clyve all dressed in your Sunday best and it being only Tuesday?'

Kate blushed and laughed coyly. 'What's it to you, Big Tom?' she retorted.

'Come courting, have thee?' persisted Tom with a chuckle.

'Maybe yes, maybe no,' replied Kate with a smile. She lowered her eyes and scraped the sand with her foot.

Tom burst out with a hearty laugh. 'Well, if you have, I'm just the man for you.' He fell in step beside her and they made their way towards the shore.

As they strolled along together they certainly made a handsome couple. Tom was a head taller than Kate and had healthy sunburnt skin, piercing blue eyes, and arms bulging with muscles. This contrasted with the slight figure of Kate with her pale complexion and jet-black hair. Tom placed an arm about Kate's slender waist and pulled her to him.

Kate responded by leaning towards him. She felt so safe and protected when she was with Tom.

'Let's get married, Kate,' said Tom. 'You know I've always been soft on you.'

Kate did not reply. She tossed back her head and gazed dreamily out to sea. She imagined a big ship that came in from across the sea . . . She could see the young nobleman who had taken her in his arms. The little white-topped waves rushed in almost to her feet; she was oblivious to everything around her as she lost herself in her dreams.

She was rudely awakened from her daydream as Tom's huge hand descended on her buttock. 'Wake up, Kate,' he said. 'You haven't heard a word I've said.'

'You saucy great oaf!' Kate fumed, pulling herself away. 'If you think I'm going to marry a fisherman and live in a tiny cottage all my life, you can think again.'

Tom sniffed. 'Hoity toity, little Kate,' he mocked. 'I suppose you think you are going to marry a lord and live in a castle.'

But Kate wasn't listening. She just picked up her skirts and ran off.

'Don't go, Katy,' Tom called.

But, in fact, Kate had just remembered the ripe strawberries awaiting her.

Later that evening Kate was thankful to return to the peace of the cottage and her mother's gentle smile. She was feeling very tired and disgruntled. Her serge tunic was once more under her arm, but now it was covered in juice from the berries. After leaving Tom she had spent the rest of the day toiling under a blazing sun, back-breakingly picking the strawberries while a stream of abuse was kept up at her from her father.

Now she sat down next to her brother Nicholas at the table while her mother fussed around them and fetched their meals. Meg placed a big bowl of rabbit stew on the table. Kate tucked in hungrily. Whatever else may be wrong, there was certainly nothing wrong with Kate's appetite.

'I've baked some nice little cakes especially for you, Kate,' her mother said.

Kate eyed her suspiciously. All this unusual fuss made her wonder what was brewing. 'What's wrong, Ma?' she asked with her irritating open-mouthed expression.

Meg smiled. 'You'll be pleased,' she said. 'Lady Evelyn has offered you a position up at the castle. You are to go up there tomorrow.'

Kate was delighted, it was a dream come true. She jumped to her feet and danced around the room, hugging and kissing her mother.

Meg laughed with her daughter and kissed her, but underneath she was sad, wishing that she knew of some way to explain to Kate the reason for her departure. But it would be impossible to convey this to that lovely young woman with a hypnotic gaze and the mind of a child. Meg's main concern was to get Kate out of the house before her pious husband suspected the truth. She would have to leave all the explanations to Lady Evelyn.

'Go to bed and get a good night's rest, Kate,' Meg said. 'Billy will be calling for you in the morning.'

'I don't need that fat boy to take me to the castle,' sniffed Kate. 'I can go on my own.'

'No, Kate,' exclaimed her mother. 'Just remember what happened the last time you travelled that road alone.'

The memory of the murdered innkeeper and of being abducted by the terrifying Frenchmen suddenly made Kate feel very subdued. Once more she became that sweet little girl. She said goodnight to her mother and brother and made her way up the ladder to her bed under the eaves.

Sitting up in bed nibbling her nails, Kate wondered what was going on. Why was she suddenly going up to live at the castle? Why did her mother look so anxious all the time? She stared down at her stomach and a curious expression slowly crossed her face. Nothing had happened this month. There had been no blood. Was this something to do with what the Captain had done to her? Could it be that she was with child? Looking puzzled and bewildered she moved to go downstairs to talk to her mother but the sound of voices stopped her. Father was home. She would have to remain silent. Besides, on reflection, Lady Evelyn might not want Kate at the castle if she thought she was expecting, so it was better not to mention the subject.

So the naïve young Kate turned over with a soft sigh and went to sleep.

5

Clyve Castle

Kate awoke the next morning to all the familiar noises. The wood pigeons cooed in unison from their perches in the oak trees. The blackbird sang as though his heart would burst, so intense was his song. The old cockerel in the yard sounded very excited, his incessant crowing rising across the fields where the sheep bleated softly in response.

Kate lay very still listening to these sounds and watching the sun's rays creep through the tiny slit of a window by her bed. Her mass of hair was like a black spray against the snowy white pillow. She stretched her arms and wondered what life was going to be like at Clyve Castle. 'Well,' she mused, 'it's the same old sun that shines upon me and her Ladyship. And under all her fine clothes and jewellery, Lady Evelyn's just the same as me. I don't suppose I'll look very different to her through those coloured glass windows.' Yes, she was feeling quite philosophical this morning.

But she suddenly realised that she was also feeling quite sad. This was her last morning at home. Tears pricked her eyes. Her mother was her main concern. Now all the chores which had been Kate's would have to be done by her mother. The poor old soul would get no rest at all, and undoubtedly her incessant cough would get worse.

All these thoughts rushed through her head as the tears began to trickle down her face. Her mouth set in an obstinate line. 'I can refuse to go,' she decided. 'And I won't care if I offend Lady Evelyn.'

Suddenly her mother's voice echoed up the stairs. 'Come along, Kate! It's time you were up and ready.'

Slowly Kate climbed down the ladder, still dressed in her long white nightgown. She slumped onto a chair and placed her elbows on the table. She looked very dejected.

'Whatever's the matter? Pull yourself together, Kate,' admonished her mother, impatiently.

'I'm not going,' the girl replied sullenly. Then Kate began to cry. She made a most unholy noise.

Meg's nerves had reached breaking point. With a furious scowl on her face, she grabbed Kate's arm and shouted: 'Don't be so stupid, girl! It's what you've always wanted. It's time you grew up and learned to be an adult.'

Kate looked at her mother in astonishment. At last some message had reached her brain. She knew now that there was no choice, there was no going back. She knew too that her mother definitely wanted her to go. Or, put another way, her mother no longer wanted her at home.

She got to her feet and went out to the yard to wash her face. Not one word did she utter. Kate just washed, dressed, and picked up her small bundle of clothes. Then she waited just outside the cottage door until she heard the whistling of the fat boy who had come to fetch her.

'Goodbye!' called her mother tearfully. 'Be a good girl.'

But Kate walked away from the cottage where she had been born without a farewell. Her heart felt hard.

The fat boy held out his hand to take her bundle, but Kate shook her head. 'I know the way,' she retorted. 'Be off and I'll make my own way.'

The fat boy was upset, for he was a pleasant, good-natured lad and had been instructed to escort Kate to the castle. 'I must walk with you,' he insisted. 'Lady Evelyn has said so.'

'Well, keep to the other side of the road,' snapped Kate. 'I'm going to the castle to be personal maid to her Ladyship and if I get any sauce from you I'll see that you get a good whipping.'

The fat boy dropped a few paces behind and began picking apples from the trees. He stuffed his pockets with them. Suddenly, he shouted: ' 'Tis more likely the scullery for you, girl. Folk do say that you're daft.'

Kate responded to this by spinning round and throwing the bundle of clothes at him.

By the time they had reached the castle gates, Kate's temper had left her. Old George greeted her with good humour. 'Welcome home, your Ladyship,' he chuckled as Kate swept past him.

As she continued through the courtyard and the gardens, Kate savored the powerful heady scent of the roses which grew so happily in the chalky soil of Kent. And there, by the biggest rose bush, was the tall graceful figure of Lady Evelyn gathering the blooms while the early morning dew was still upon them.

Lady Evelyn smiled at Kate and handed her a large flower basket. Kate quietly fell in behind and followed demurely while Lady Evelyn gathered the exquisite full-blown pink roses and buds. They passed through the gardens until they came to a very secluded rose arbour. There deep red blooms entwined with sugar-pink ramblers, and the air was heavy with the exotic fragrance of honeysuckle.

Lady Evelyn made her way to a stone bench and sat down. Kate followed behind and stood uncertainly beside the bench.

Lady Evelyn took Kate's hand and made her sit down beside her. Maid and mistress sat beside each other in silence, the peace and tranquillity of their surroundings shutting them off from the outside world.

'Do you know why I asked you here, Kate?' Lady Evelyn asked. Her eyes stared directly into Kate's.

Kate stared back. 'Because I'm with child,' she replied quickly.

'Did your mother tell you?' she asked.

'No,' replied Kate. 'She was too frightened of my father.' She paused. 'Oh, dear, who will marry me now?'

Lady Evelyn smiled. She was amused at this. She was such a strange combination, this slow-witted, immature child. Perhaps she wasn't quite as stupid as she appeared. 'There's nothing to worry about while you are here with me, child,' Lady Evelyn said consolingly. 'Once you have the baby, I'll find a good home for it.'

'I don't want it,' protested Kate. The full truth of her situation had suddenly hit her, and she was horrified. 'It was that Captain what did it,' she said, 'filling me with strong drink and taking advantage of me. I don't want the child.'

Lady Evelyn smiled sadly. The unborn child in Kate's womb had the blood of her ancestors in its veins. Suddenly she felt envious of Kate, envious of her fecundity. An idea she had been playing with for a few days suddenly became vivid. 'I'll take your baby, Kate,' she said. 'But no one must ever know. It must be a secret forever, between us and only us.'

Kate was happy to agree. She was completely unconcerned about the fate of her unborn child. She was much more concerned about how she might get fat and lose her pretty figure.

Lady Evelyn settled back on the bench with a satisfied smile on her lips. This had all been much easier than she had anticipated. Kate was most obliging. Lady Evelyn's shrewd Celtic brain began to make careful calculations. She had been a good wife to her husband and he trusted her. Now that his brain had become so addled with alcohol and age, it would be very simple to fool him. The servants were very loyal to her; they owed her their livelihood, but they also liked her, she knew that. It seemed that her chief concern would be old friends of Hugh and those of his kin who lived nearby.

Lady Evelyn twisted a long-stemmed red rose in her fingers and raised the flower to her nose. A smile appeared on her full lips as she looked off into the distance. Yes, her plan would work, she thought. Now that the girl was in her charge, nothing could stop it from working.

A month later the old grey walls of the castle were glowing like molten gold with the flares from the tallows. In the grand hall, a magnificent banquet had been laid out. The long oak table groaned under the weight of the roast boar, boiled chickens, baby lambs and roast geese. All around the long table, family and friends had sat down to dine. Everyone was curious about the fact that his Lordship had come down to join them. Even the servants were buzzing and muttering at this extraordinary occurrence.

His Lordship, Hugh Mortimer, sat bolt upright in his large wooden armchair. A tight corset was covered by a heavy red brocade suit and seemed to be supporting his frail, bony body. His thin, white hair was worn long and tied back exposing his aristocratic face and long noble nose. In his time, he had been a greatly respected nobleman, a favourite in King Henry's court and much rewarded by the monarch himself. Now, at sixty, he was an old man, all used-up, a ghost of the fine gentleman he had once been. His hands shook, spilling food and drink everywhere while the servants waited close at hand to refill his glass whenever necessary.

Lady Evelyn looked radiant. Rows of emeralds gleamed from her neck and dangled from her ears. She was lively and talkative, laughing and teasing, attentive and provocative.

She was the model wife in her full wide gown as she entertained her husband's family and friends. She wore a linen head-dress and veil over a small cap. Her gown was a rich red with a low square neckline with embroidered edges that matched the flared sleeves, hem and waist belt.

Halfway through the meal Lord Mortimer fell asleep. His head fell back against his chair and his mouth dropped open to allow loud snores to escape in a noisy rattle.

Lady Evelyn made a sign at the servants who discreetly carried her husband to his bedchamber. Lady Evelyn continued with her entertaining, quite unperturbed by the interruption. But after a while, she bowed her head to her guests and quietly begged to be excused. As she left, she dropped a couple of clear hints about her condition.

After Lady Evelyn had left the hall, the meal continued as the guests speculated enthusiastically about what they had surmised. There was much chuckling.

'Bless my soul,' cackled one old fellow. 'Evelyn has cuckolded old Hugh at last.'

'Well, I wonder who the lucky knight is?' shouted another.

A very handsome young baron from Sussex stood up angrily. 'I have great respect for Lady Evelyn,' he said. 'If she says she is with child by Hugh, then it must be true.'

The other guests stared at him. This young fellow was very defensive, they thought. Could *he* be the culprit?

Well, whatever the truth of the matter, they would all believe what they wanted. Then in good humour, they toasted the unborn infant with the very best Mortimer brandy.

Upstairs, in her chamber, Lady Evelyn brushed her golden tresses and smiled triumphantly at herself in the mirror.

When the guests had all retired to bed or left for their own homes, the servants cleared away the meal. Now there was plenty of gossip and speculation, for servants miss nothing and know all that's going on in the household.

'Well, since his Lordship hasn't left his bed for three months, 'tis quite a feat,' observed one.

' 'Tis a wise child that knows its own father,' muttered another.

'Her Ladyship is certainly a dark horse,' added a young maid. 'There's been no indication of her condition until now.'

Kate was in the kitchen helping to clear away the linen. She listened to all with interest, but she kept her mouth shut as she had been told to.

6

Migration

A sunny July passed into an even sunnier August. It was a good year for apples which now hung heavy on the trees. The corn had ripened and was ready for harvesting. Like nature, young Kate bloomed with health and ripeness. Plenty of good food and a restful life had done wonders for her. Statuesque in her full-skirted gowns, she even seemed to have grown taller. She was happy, much more alert, and more engaged with the world.

Lady Evelyn watched Kate sail across the garden like a galleon against the breeze. The girl's condition would start to show before long. Soon they would have to leave Clyve Castle.

And indeed, as the leaves on the beech trees in the forest turned to a glorious burnished gold and the migrating birds prepared for their long flight south, so Kate and Lady Evelyn got ready for their journey to the hunting lodge at Shorne.

Lady Evelyn had been ordered a complete rest, the household was informed. And no one was surprised.

'But why she's taking that slut of a girl with her, is beyond me,' said Mistress Wilkins, the housekeeper, in acid tones. 'She's a lazy little bitch who is more trouble than she's worth. Her Ladyship is taking no other servants, just that girl and old George. It's quite ridiculous!'

Mistress Wilkins was quite beside herself with jealous rage. 'Who is to run the household?' she demanded. 'There's no one at Shorne but that old crone Sarah.'

Old Jem, sitting by the fireplace, had heard enough. He turned his grey head towards the housekeeper. 'Shut thy jaw, woman!' he roared. 'I care not where the bastard is born. I'm just sick of listening to your rantings.'

At this sudden outburst, a shocked silence descended upon the kitchen. The servants averted their eyes and quickly got on with their chores. But most of them were impressed by Old Jem's boldness and courage.

It was ten miles as the crow flies to Shorne, but the going was very rough in that lumbering old coach. The chill of autumn was in the air and the dense forest was dark and gloomy as they passed slowly through. Rain dripped slowly off the leaves all around.

Kate was feeling quite fearful. She had never left her native village before. The coach swayed from side to side as old George tried to control the frisky horses with oaths and curses. The horses were particularly nervous because of the sound of the trees brushing against the sides of the coach.

Kate clutched the padded sides of the coach in her terror, while Lady Evelyn patted her knee kindly.

'Don't worry, dear, it is not too far now,' she said.

'I don't like it,' wailed Kate. 'It's frightening in this forest.'

'You will find it very pleasant when we get out into the open,' said Lady Evelyn reassuringly.

Eventually they did leave the forest and when Kate looked out again she could see the green marsh that stretched out before them, rich pastures with grazing sheep and the edges of another forest. Ahead of them, she saw the tall chimney of the hunting lodge that the Mortimer family had owned for many generations. In his youth Lord Mortimer had held many wild hunting parties here, with gangs of young noblemen who would hunt all day in the forest and then retire to the lodge for an evening of eating and drinking. But in recent years the lodge had hardly been visited and had fallen into disuse. The only occupant nowadays was Sarah, Lady Evelyn's old wet-nurse, who was living out her old age here in this lonely place. She was all alone with only a little help and company from a young girl from the cottages.

Now Sarah was there to greet the coach at the entrance. She was tiny, a little old lady in a black gown and a spotless white cap. Her round face was so small and wrinkled that it was barely visible under the lacy frills. 'Welcome, your ladyship,' Sarah said, dropping a deep curtsy.

Minnie, the maid from the cottages, was also present, and her moonlike face beamed a welcome.

A blazing fire was burning in the hall when they entered. This cheered Kate immensely. It made the lodge appear instantly hospitable.

After a few days Kate began to enjoy her new environment. The building was too isolated to attract visitors from the main road, and was almost impossible to reach in winter. Set on the edge of the forest, there was always a wonderful stillness in the air on windless days. But when the wind was up, it howled around the trees by the lodge and rattled their leaves in a wild caress. Kate always found such moments very exciting.

Lady Evelyn had laid her plans with care. All they had to do now was wait.

Old Sarah knew what was expected. She poked Kate's belly with her bony finger. ' 'Tis fine and bonny,' she chuckled. 'And 'twill be born in the New Year.'

Lady Evelyn was well aware of the dangers of childbirth. She asked anxiously: 'Do you think it will be straightforward? I would not like anything to happen to the child.'

'The bairn, you mean, or the wench?' cackled Sarah, throwing back her wizened face.

Lady Evelyn flushed. She bristled at the old servant's familiarity but knew that she needed Sarah. Lady Evelyn had known Sarah all her life. Sarah had nursed both her and her brother Angus. She knew all the family secrets and Lady Evelyn knew she would guard this secret with her life, so long as she agreed to the deception that was planned.

As Sarah left the room muttering, Lady Evelyn decided that she would take the old crone into her confidence soon.

Lady Evelyn spent her days with Kate wandering around the gardens of the grounds. The garden was now quite neglected but it was still very beautiful with its herbs and quince trees and little sunken gardens.

Lady Evelyn did her floral embroidery while Kate

sat and dreamed, trying to ignore the movements of the child inside her. But she could not.

Evenings were spent in the warm hall beside the log fire. Animal head and antlers, trophies from his Lordship's hunting days, hung all around the walls. In the autumn twilight the two women sat together making clothes for the new baby. There seemed little difference between lady and maid as they sat in that warm panelled hall. They were just two women with the same interest at heart.

Kate had noticed the beautiful pearl brooch set in gold that Lady Evelyn wore day after day whatever the gown, and one day she plucked up the courage to ask her what it was.

Lady Evelyn smiled wistfully and touched the brooch with her fingertips. 'It was given to me by a dear friend,' she said. 'I wear it so that I can think of him every day even though he is no longer alive.'

Kate listened attentively. Lady Evelyn sighed. 'Sometimes I wonder how my life might have turned out if certain events had not happened.'

The cryptic comment baffled Kate and she felt it wise not to delve any further into Lady Evelyn's past. But now she knew for certain that Lady Evelyn's marriage to Lord Mortimer had had no passion in it. All Her Ladyship's passion was spent. She never said another word about the brooch and neither did Lady Evelyn.

One evening as they sat stitching a silk tunic, Lady Evelyn reflected on the queer twist of fate that had brought her and young Kate to this old lodge. Evelyn came from one of the great Scottish clans. But most of her relatives had been killed over the years in wars and private feuds. Now her beloved brother, Angus, was the only kin she had left. Inside Kate's belly was another member of the clan, Evelyn's own nephew or niece. In other circumstances, Kate might have been her sister-in-law. It was an extraordinary idea.

Lady Evelyn's white hands hovered like butterflies over flowers as she worked at her embroidery frame with these thoughts running through her mind. She smiled gently at Kate who sat warming her toes in front of the fire. Evelyn had grown very fond of this young girl. Kate was lazy and very obstinate, there was no question of that, but in spite of it, Lady Evelyn had discovered untold depths of character in the girl. She was unhesitatingly generous in every way. And she was never spiteful or mean about anyone.

Suddenly Lady Evelyn leaned forward and asked: 'Is there anything you would like from me, Kate?'

Kate stared back at her blankly. She did not say anything.

Lady Evelyn, suddenly worried that she may have hurt Kate's pride, added hastily, 'I mean, just as a little present.'

'Yes,' said Kate slowly and deliberately. 'I would like your green riding outfit.'

Lady Evelyn stared at her in astonishment, and then she burst out laughing. 'But you do not ride, Kate.'

'When this lump has left my belly, I'll soon learn,' retorted Kate with a toss of her head.

Beneath Lady Evelyn's amused smile was a tiny

feeling of shock. Kate's comment had confirmed what Evelyn had suspected: that the girl had no maternal feelings towards her unborn child whatsoever. But then, she should not worry too much about that; it suited her purposes no end.

'What I really mean, Kate,' she continued, 'is that I am taking your firstborn child from you. I would like to give you something in return.' She waited for Kate's response.

Kate thought for a while and then said: 'I would like Nicholas my young brother to be educated at the King's School.'

'All right, Kate,' replied Lady Evelyn. 'I'll arrange it with the bishop. Your brother Nicholas shall be educated and when the child is born you shall have my riding outfit. And then, my dear, I myself shall teach you to ride.'

Thus Kate's unborn child was bought and sold.

It was not long before the snows came. Then the little hunting lodge was completely cut off from the rest of the world by a thick mantle of white. Kate sat in the windowseat, occasionally opening the window to throw breadcrumbs to the birds – blue tits, chaffinches and robins, their scarlet breasts vivid against the snow. The temperature was bitterly cold and in spite of the fires, the lodge was hard to keep warm. They dressed in as many garments as they could but their frozen fingers and constant shivering made Kate and Sarah bad-tempered with each other.

The even-tempered Lady Evelyn did her best to

keep the peace but it was not always possible, for the truth was that the maid and the old wet-nurse simply did not like each other. Kate's Kentish pride resented Sarah's haughty attitude, and the two women quarrelled incessantly. Sarah regarded Kate as a wanton hussy whom Lady Evelyn had taken pity on. As yet, Lady Evelyn had not divulged the truth to her.

Poor Minnie, the maid from the cottages, was fond of Kate but terrified of Sarah, so she had a very bad time between them. And even old George had started to complain about his lodgings over the stables. He said that the ice on the inside of the windows each morning was too thick to scrape off.

By the time Christmas had arrived, Lady Evelyn was beginning to feel the strain, and she began to long for her own comfortable home where everything ran smoothly under the strict rule of Mistress Wilkins. There Lady Evelyn was never bothered by hostilities between her staff, so in these circumstances, she barely knew how to cope. In an attempt to smooth ruffled feathers, Lady Evelyn decided that they should all have a party at Christmas. They had a great feast in the hall before a well-built fire – turkey, goose and salted ham with preserved pudding to follow. Even George cheered up at the sight of all the wine that he was ordered to bring up from the cellar and which he was then invited to savour.

Kate came down to dinner looking resplendent in a pale grey gown of Lady Evelyn's with side panels inserted to allow for her extra inches. She came down the stairs lifting her skirts with the grace and carriage of a lady, her glossy black hair piled high on her head and her creamy skin glowing above the low-cut gown. This lovely girl, not long past sixteen and soon to give birth to her first child, made her entrance like a grand duchess. Old George stepped forward and took her arm to escort her to the table. Watching her from the foot of the stairs, Lady Evelyn thought what a pity it was that the girl was low-born. She would have made a lovely bride for Angus and graced the brilliant gay court of King James of Scotland so well.

At the thought of her brother, tears filled Lady Evelyn's eyes. She had heard nothing from him since he had sent word that he was off on a secret mission to London. She briefly closed her eyes and gave a quick prayer for his safety.

It was a very happy Christmas feast they enjoyed at the lodge. They stuffed themselves on all the good food and wine. Never had they eaten so well! Everybody laughed and giggled as the alcohol took effect.

Suddenly Lady Evelyn noticed that Kate could hardly keep her eyes open. She was listing in her chair and looked exhausted. Lady Evelyn helped Kate upstairs, undressed her and tucked her into bed. The girl was asleep as soon as her head touched the pillow. Lady Evelyn stood gazing down at the pretty heart-shaped face with the thick dark lashes closed over the wide eyes. What would Kate's future be, she wondered, once she had relinquished the child? What could be in store for her?

Lady Evelyn then went to her own bedchamber and lay there listening to the wild wind outside of the house. She could hear great thuds as the snow fell off the branches of the trees onto the white carpet below.

Soon the New Year arrived. By now the snow had given way to storms and high winds but it remained bitterly cold. Floods made the waters rise to cover much of the low land.

One night as Lady Evelyn lay in her bed she suddenly heard a cry of pain. She jumped from her bed and dashed outside her room. Kate was standing by her bed doubled over in pain. The expression on her face was one of sheer terror. Soon the whole household was awakened. Lady Evelyn had trained them well. They knew exactly what to do and now hurried about on their own particular task. Minnie was up and down the stairs with pans of hot water, while old George, awakened from the stables, stoked the fires and prepared the grey mare in case of an emergency. Lady Evelyn walked back and forth with Kate, who was now in strong labour. Old Sarah laid out bowls and towels, and prepared the crib for the child's arrival.

Kate paraded up and down majestically, stooping and yelling every time a spasm hit her. All this had a strange effect on Lady Evelyn, who had had very little direct experience of childbirth. Each time Kate yelled, a terrible nausea filled the noblewoman, as if the pain were being transferred to her own body.

Sarah had taken over. She timed the pains and, with the help of Minnie, got Kate on to the bed. She told Lady Evelyn to leave and get herself a glass of brandy to steady herself. But Lady Evelyn had no intention of missing the birth. This was the most important moment of her life.

Soon a tiny head appeared, then, amid Kate's screams, the shoulders, and the rest was easy. Watching the head appear and seeing that it was covered in red-gold hair, Lady Evelyn was oblivious to the blood and Kate's moans. She staggered over to the window to hide her emotion. Red-gold hair! It was the mark of her great clan. And now she knew that, thank God, it was a boy!

As the storm blew itself out and the grey light of dawn appeared, the high-pitched wail of the baby filled the bedchamber and echoed around the lodge.

'By the colour of his hair, he could well be your own, Lady Evelyn,' old Sarah said. She was pleased with herself and her skills as a midwife. 'He's a right bonnie laddie.'

Kate lay back in the huge bed, sobbing and crying like a small child. Lady Evelyn crossed the room with the small bundle in her arms. She held the baby out to Kate. 'Look, what a lovely son you have,' she murmured.

But Kate pushed it away. ' 'Tis yours,' she said flatly, 'not mine.'

Lady Evelyn looked sad and cuddled the baby to her breast. 'We will share him,' she said. 'Now what do you think we should call him?'

'Call him what you will,' sniffed Kate. 'I didn't even know his father's name, anyway.' She looked at Minnie. 'How about some food? I'm starving.'

Lady Evelyn looked down at the baby's crumpled face. 'Shall we call him Robert Angus Hugh Mortimer?' she asked. In her mind's eye she could see her dearly loved Robert, the man to whom she had once been betrothed, before the English murdered him. As she thought of him, her hand fell upon the precious brooch pinned to her gown. Robert had given it to her on their last meeting. She had worn it every day of her life since then. She treasured it more than anything else. And then, of course, there was her brother Angus who had fathered the baby.

Kate was sitting up in bed sipping a mug of milk. She did not seem in the slightest bit interested.

The tiny babe opened one brilliant blue eye and seemed to look up at his aunt with a quizzical expression. It was the look of Lady Evelyn's old father when disturbed while dozing. Lady Evelyn smiled. So the spirit of the family lives. A family is like an oak tree and all spring from that one great trunk – branches, leaves and acorns. All have one definite purpose in life – to perpetuate the life of that trunk, the family. 'Dear God,' prayed Lady Evelyn, 'let me have this child and I swear to bring him up to make this a kinder world where all men stand an equal chance . . .'

There was a moment of tension later when the child began to whimper and Sarah told Kate to feed the child. Kate protested that she would have no milk but Sarah had been persistent. Firmly grasping Kate's breast, she set the child against it to suckle. As the child settled down, a strange look came over Kate's face. She gazed down at the child in wonderment.

'Good,' declared old Sarah. 'He won't need no wet-nursing.'

Thus another battle had been fought and won. Now for the final phase of cuckolding his Lordship.

7

The Heir of Clyve Shore

Sunbeams danced upon the polished oak panels as Lady Evelyn came down the stairs. The new baby was safely tucked up in his tiny oak crib and Her Ladyship was ready for the next part of her plan. Now an urgent message had to be despatched to Clyve Castle to let them all know that Lady Evelyn had given birth to a prematurely born son. Hugh would be delighted but his health would prevent him from travelling. He would probably send an emissary, possibly one of the old neighbouring lords.

Lady Evelyn felt quite excited by all this deception but she knew that she had to remain cool and calm in order to tie all the loose ends of the intrigue. The servants had now all been let in on her plan and sworn to eternal secrecy. They had willingly agreed to verify her story, so there should be no problem in that regard. On the promise of a good reward for his silence, old George prepared for the road, while Lady Evelyn retired to her chamber. She knew she could trust George implicitly.

As the old coach lumbered back along the road towards Clyve Castle, Lady Evelyn stood by her bedroom window and rocked the carved oak crib which had held so many of her ancestors before now. Inside, under an embroidered eiderdown quilt, the tiny golden-haired babe slept snugly. Lady Evelyn could not take her eyes off him.

Somewhere in the back of her mind Lady Evelyn thought she should have a conscience about what she was doing, but she was too wrapped up in the child to give it too much thought. No, the more she saw of this lovely child, the son of her beloved brother, the less important moral considerations became.

Because of the flooding caused by the New Year storm, George did not return for two days. Lady Evelyn was sitting up in her large four-poster bed cuddling her new treasure when she heard footsteps outside. They were unsteady, like the tottering footsteps of an old man. Surely Hugh had not come! She collected herself, ready to meet his eagle eye. But her fears were unfounded. Soon Kate came in to announce the arrival of Sir Clarence Cowley, a local nobleman who had hunted with Hugh in days gone by, and the old priest, Father Peter, from Clyve Shore.

Lady Evelyn's prayer had been answered. These two would be the last to suspect any treachery. Together the men bowed low.

Sir Clarence spoke for them both. 'We come on behalf of the Lord of the Manor to congratulate you upon the birth of an heir,' he said.

Lady Evelyn smiled graciously. Such fine words were music to her ears.

After the ceremony of baptism and blessing performed by the priest, the men were wined and dined, and then left to return to Clyve to announce the birth and baptism of the next Lord of the Manor.

Lady Evelyn went to Kate and kissed her. She held the child in her arms. 'He's ours, my dear,' she whispered. 'Let us unite in taking care of him. And while I live I will see that you want for nothing.'

Kate looked gravely at her and said: 'When are you going to teach me to ride?'

Lady Evelyn laughed at this. What an extraordinary young woman she was, with the simple mind of a child. But she nodded. 'Soon,' she replied, 'when we return to Clyve. But first we must get you and the baby strong.' She held out the child for Kate to suckle.

As the child settled happily at his mother's breast and greedily sucked, Lady Evelyn stared down at Kate and wondered how long she would remain so docile. Not very long, she anticipated.

As the weather improved, most of the household at the hunting lodge were quite content, but Kate was getting increasingly restless. Every evening she would dress in the fine clothes Lady Evelyn had given her and sit gazing moodily out of the window. A tiny frown line ran down between her blue eyes and she bit her lip petulantly.

Lady Evelyn put it down to homesickness. Either it would pass or they would be back at Clyve Shore soon enough. But when Kate confided that she was worrying about her mother, Lady Evelyn sighed. She knew that it would not be fair to keep the girl here for much longer. She ordered them all to prepare for the return to Clyve and to face the world.

In fact, word came the next day with a messenger sent from the castle to inform Her Ladyship that Lord Mortimer was not at all well. Father Peter had been called to the castle in the night and it seemed that His Lordship was fading fast. Lady Evelyn would have to return immediately.

There was a definite breath of spring in the air as the old coach left the hunting lodge. There was a faint hint of green in the forest and primroses and snowdrops at the cottage doors.

Both Sarah and Minnie had wept at their departure but Kate was quite scornful; she was impatient to be away to her home.

So they left behind the red brick chimneys of the house that now guarded their dreadful secret and prepared to face a welcome from the people of Clyve who turned out in full to greet Her Ladyship and her baby son back to Clyve Shore.

The villagers stood waving from the doors of their cottages and hovels. Children ran forward with little posies of wood violets for Lady Evelyn. Her Ladyship was quite overwhelmed by the loyalty of these simple folk. She pressed the flowers to her lips and smiled gratefully. She gazed down at the cooing child in her arms and a newfound joy filled her heart.

The gates of Clyve Castle were opened wide in welcome and the servants lined the drive. Lady Evelyn felt a surge of confidence. She was Lady of the Manor once more.

Before dinner that evening, she visited her husband. As she entered his bedchamber a strange feeling of melancholy came over her. She had never before felt afraid of Hugh. In fact, it had been her indomitable spirit that had made her marriage a success. But now her knees felt quite weak and she fought to keep her courage up. She approached the canopied bed but as she gazed down at her husband, she drew back with shock.

Hugh was propped up on the bolsters slowly gasping for breath. He seemed to have shrunk to half his normal size, and the shadow of death was upon his withered features. In the time since she had last seen him, the flesh seemed to have dropped from his bones.

Evelyn felt very sad. She had a soft spot for Hugh. He had been very kind to her in his way.

Father Peter sat in the corner of the room, quietly chanting and praying incessantly above the noise of Hugh's harsh breathing. As Evelyn tried to choke back her sobs, Hugh's knobbly hand reached out slowly and touched her hair. Evelyn raised her eyes to his and saw in them a strange expression. She felt as though his eyes could see all the way into her very heart.

There was no doubt that this old man was about to enter the valley of death. He whispered hoarsely to her: 'Take your son, Evelyn, and leave this place. He will return once I am gone, and your child's life will be in danger.'

Evelyn gasped and pulled away as fear gripped her by the throat. 'My God, he knows,' she thought. Hugh's hand now lay still on the coverlet and it stirred no more.

Father Peter slowly stepped forward from the shadows and began to recite the last rites over Lord Mortimer.

As Lady Evelyn left the death chamber, she noticed a young, fair-haired lad assisting the priest. It was Nicholas, Kate's brother. Evelyn reminded herself to arrange for the boy to be sent to the King's School, as she had promised Kate.

Later that day Evelyn lay in her bedroom reflecting on her past life with her husband. She had to thank him for taking her away from the bloodshed of the clans, and she had found great peace and happiness here at Clyve. Hugh had loved her, she knew that, and she had been very fond of him, too, in spite of all his philandering and his fondness for drink. Her problem now was what to do should Hugh's son from his first marriage return from exile once he learned of his father's death.

Old King Henry VII had recently died and his only surviving son, Henry, had succeeded him at the age of eighteen. There had been much rejoicing among the people, for the tall handsome Henry was popular, and his subjects looked forward to enjoying the reign of a man whose ambition was to be the most magnificent and triumphant prince in Europe. Little did they know how much they would have to bear of the cost of such a vision. But in the meantime, there were amnesties for men who had been exiled under Henry VII, and many young men were welcomed back to court under Henry VIII.

It was highly likely that Hugh Mortimer – an ambitious young man with friends in the right places – would be one of them.

Slowly Lady Evelyn's mind cleared of doubt. No,

Hugh could not possibly have known the truth – though he probably thought she had taken a lover. Now her only thought was to protect her son. It was now she realised how much he filled the emptiness in her previously childless life. As far as she was concerned, he was *her* child and she would do anything to protect him.

Kate entered the bedchamber carrying the boy, who smiled and looked around for his mother with his bright blue eyes. The women bent their heads together, clucking and cooing to amuse the child. The problems of the day and the dead old man were temporarily forgotten.

Lord Mortimer's body lay in state in the Baron's Hall surrounded by candles and flowers. The castle was filled with visitors who had come to pay their last respects. Those who did not stay at the castle stayed at the priest's house, which had been built and improved by Lord Mortimer over the years.

War had reduced the great families and there was much talk of Lord Mortimer's son and heir, young Hugh, being allowed to return from exile and claim the estate for himself, now that his father was dead.

Mingling among the mourners was a small, brown-faced man who pottered about helping with the chores. It was Kate's father, Jacob. His face had a blank expression but that masked the way his mind was ticking over rapidly, as he thought that life did have its compensations. The Good Lord he had served so well all his life had taken his wife to her rest last winter but here he was now with his daft wayward daughter as

Lady Evelyn's maid-companion and his son to be educated. For Lady Evelyn had informed Jacob that morning of her intention to see that his son was educated at the King's School. For Jacob, this was a dream come true. He would devote his life totally to the old priest. The cottage on the marsh stood empty and desolate but Jacob was quite content now that he had at last found the peace he had been searching for.

As he was jostling to and fro among the crowds, he kept hearing snatches of conversation.

'Apparently he's been seen in Paris,' said one.

'That young Hugh, he's a bit of a rake,' said another.

'Yes, he'll be home for sure,' added a third.

This was Lord Mortimer's son Hugh they were discussing.

'Wouldn't want to be in Lady Evelyn's shoes if he does return,' the gossips continued. 'He'll ferret out the mystery of the child, all right.'

Kate had been sad to return to Clyve Shore to find her mother buried in the village churchyard. For a moment she had felt quite bitter towards Lady Evelyn for depriving her of those last days with her beloved mother. But Kate was not one to bear grudges and Lady Evelyn was not to know that the wracking cough that had plagued her mother for so long would gather strength and kill Meg off within days over Christmas.

But in the churchyard Meg lay, until the day Nicholas her son would be in a position to exhume her and then reinter her with her husband in front of the altar of Rochester Cathedral.

8

The Beggar

As a burst of pale sunshine lit up the woodland, the tall trees stood outlined against the sky. The slow funeral procession bearing Lord Mortimer's body came down the winding lane. Children in their best white linen trousers and skirts stood lining the route in solemn silence as the funeral cortège passed by.

It took twenty-four men, six at a time taking turns, to carry the coffin. The last six were Lord Mortimer's closest kin. The coffin was followed by two noblemen, Hugh's closest friends. And they in turn were followed by a long line of mounted men. Last came a coach containing the ladies. A fife and drum band led the way, the mournful music rising above the sound of sobs and shuffling feet.

The mass was long and dreary. The church was draped all around in purple silk. No candles or flowers were to be seen. The bright uniforms of the guards were the only splash of colour.

Lady Evelyn was feeling weary and worried as she knelt in the Mortimer family pew. Her heavy black widow's weeds made her neck ache. She felt quite worried because the baby Robert had been left with a maid as Kate had insisted on attending the funeral.

Through her lowered eyes Lady Evelyn glanced sideways at Kate. She could see that the girl was trying to look solemn but at one moment, when two of the more elderly pall-bearers collided in front of the altar, her shoulders shook with barely suppressed giggles.

'Oh dear,' sighed Lady Evelyn. 'Whatever shall I do with Kate? She's as skittish as a young pony.'

Soon the praying and the pageantry were over, and the body of Lord Mortimer was laid to rest forever in the massive granite vault that held all his ancestors. It was also the vault where Lady Evelyn was expected to be laid to rest, when her turn came.

Outside the church, the villagers knelt on the grass to pay their last respects to their master. The castle entourage passed by and the sun glinted on the bright trappings of the horses, as the procession re-formed to return to the castle.

On the journey back in the coach, Lady Evelyn found herself thinking about what the future would have in store for her. The sight of the Mortimer family vault had sent shivers down her spine. She did not feel like a Mortimer at all; too much Scottish blood flowed in her veins. One thing she was sure of was that if young Hugh, the prodigal son, did return to claim his inheritance, she would return to Scotland with the baby Robert. After all, he was Angus's son, and to Evelyn the welfare of her clan was of paramount importance. But she had not heard a word from Angus in months. She sat gazing ahead.

Suddenly, she sat up as she noticed a beggar sitting by the side of the road. Beggars were not an unfamiliar sight but this one made her heart miss a beat. He had a thick red beard. Otherwise, his face was covered by the thick woollen hood of his cape. But Lady Evelyn knew that it could only be one person – Jamie, Angus's friend. She sat back in the coach and smiled. That meant that Angus was close by.

Lord Mortimer's will was read later that evening. It held no surprises for Lady Evelyn. The entire estate was to be placed in the care of Hugh's old friend and neighbour, Sir Clarence Cowley, until such time as young Hugh returned to claim it as his, or until Robert came of age, whichever was the sooner. There were other small bequests: Lady Evelyn had been left all the Mortimer jewellery and most of her dowry.

After most of the guests had left, and those who were staying had been settled in their bedchambers, Lady Evelyn looked from her window out into the dark night. She was sure that Jamie would soon appear. Sure enough, she soon heard a rustling in the bushes followed by a low whistle. And suddenly he was there, his huge bulk framed in the doorway. How he had managed to slip in through the castle gates was a mystery to her, but security was of no concern to her now.

There stood Jamie, his hood down to reveal his bonnet awry on his red head and his blue eyes twinkling. ' 'Tis Jamie to see you, and how are you, lassie?' he said.

Lady Evelyn and Jamie sat in her bedchamber talking in excited whispers as Jamie tucked into cold beef and spiced ale that Lady Evelyn had got for him from the kitchens.

Lady Evelyn first urged him to tell her all the news about Angus.

'Well, lassie,' said Jamie, wiping his beard with a large freckled hand, 'the news is not good. Angus has been taken prisoner and is in the Tower.'

Evelyn gasped, her face paled and she swayed with shock.

'I have brought ye a letter from him,' Jamie added anxiously.

Evelyn snatched the letter and read it as though in a trance:-

> *Beloved Sister,*
> *It is my misfortune to inform you that I am a prisoner here. I've many compatriots to keep me company, but nevertheless I don't intend to stay in here for long. I need help.*
> *Jamie will explain to you.*
> *Now burn this.*
> *Always with you,*
> *Angus.*

Jamie tried to console Evelyn. 'He's been in worse trouble than this before and come out of it,' he said.

'How on earth did he get caught?' she asked.

'Well,' explained Jamie, 'he was having a drink with an old friend—'

'You mean he was in bad company?' Evelyn interrupted.

'I wouldn't say that, now,' said Jamie loyally. 'He has been arrested for piracy, but he's not been put on trial yet.'

The two sat in silence for a while thinking about Angus's predicament. Then, as Jamie picked over the remains of his meal, Evelyn scrutinised him carefully. Sitting there, with his thick strong legs astride, Jamie seemed ageless. He looked the same now as when she had watched him go off to war with her father and brothers. He had shared the hell of French and Spanish prisons with them and now here he was ready and eager to give his life to rescue Angus from his present incarceration. And he knew that she would help him in any way she could.

'Will you stay overnight, Jamie?' she enquired.

Jamie shook his great head. 'No, lass,' he said. 'I'll be away before daybreak. But first I've got a task for you.'

Under Jamie's instructions, Lady Evelyn wrote two letters. One was to a bishop who had always been a good friend to Lady Evelyn's family. He lived in Walsingham Abbey. The other letter was to a distant relative who lived on the Lowland borders. She requested safe conduct to the Highlands, for herself and a servant. She was willing to pay well for a safe and secret journey home to be arranged.

Tucking both letters into his sealskin sporran, Jamie next requested a gown, a long cloak and a hat. Angus planned to travel disguised as a woman. Jamie also needed money and a ring with the Mortimer crest, which he would return once he and Angus were safely over the border. With his fine bones and colouring,

Angus would easily get away with travelling under his sister's identity. The only problem with the plan Angus had worked out was that it might spoil Evelyn's own chances of escaping with Robert should the need arise. But she knew that she had to be unselfish. Her life was not at stake and if Angus were brought to trial it would be the end for him. She wished Jamie a safe journey and he slipped away into the night.

9

Kate and Tom

A few weeks later, Lady Evelyn was overjoyed to get a message that her brother Angus was on his way home. It seemed that it had been quite easy to bribe the guards to facilitate his escape from the Tower. Angus was not important enough as a prisoner for them to resist the financial incentives Jamie offered them. So after many sleepless nights listening for the dreaded noise of horses galloping through the night, Lady Evelyn was able to feel relatively reassured of her brother's safety and slipped back to her usual routine at the castle in a much better frame of mind.

It was summer. Robert was now six months old and a delightful child. He always seemed happy and content, and his sturdy limbs kicked and frolicked in his crib. He also seemed to have a powerful personality. And he could dominate the whole household with his temper.

Evelyn was happy with her child but recently a remarkable change had come over Kate. It seemed to start when the baby had started to drink from a cup instead of suckling at her breast. Kate instantly seemed to lose all interest in the child. As a result, there were often sharp words exchanged between Lady Evelyn and Kate. But the girl would not change her ways.

Kate had taken up riding and proved to be naturally gifted at it. She would disappear in the mornings on the little bay mare that Lady Evelyn had given her, and was often not seen again for the rest of the day. During these absences Lady Evelyn felt at her wits' end. She was responsible for the child and his welfare, yet she seemed to have so little control over either. Since she herself was still in mourning for her husband, Lady Evelyn seldom left the house, so what Kate did all day was a complete mystery.

One morning Evelyn watched Kate ride off on her pony. Watching her she thought that the girl was getting rid of her country mannerisms. She now had much more of the bearing of a high-born lady. And Evelyn had to agree that in the green riding habit, with the wide velvet hat with the curled feather, she looked magnificent. Her skin was glowing and she held herself upright in a confident pose. Yes, she was confident now.

It suddenly occurred to Lady Evelyn that Kate had taken a lover. That would explain the frequent absences and the glow on her cheeks, as well as the dramatic loss of interest in Robert.

She smiled at the thought. Well, well. She decided there and then to discover what Kate did on these mysterious expeditions.

So one morning, after Kate had gone, Lady Evelyn ordered the groom to saddle her stallion, Fleet. Fleet was very pleased to have his mistress back again after all these weeks of gloom. He snorted excitedly and galloped through the gates like the wind.

Not far from the village Lady Evelyn passed her old retainer George. He had just recently left her employ and retired to a small holding on the edge of the village. George now sat outside the door of his new home – more of a shack than a cottage – looking very different without his scarlet uniform. He looked smaller and older but also remarkably content. Old George was ecstatic to see his old mistress and to have her stop at his home. He wanted to show her the crops he had grown as well as his noisy brood of chickens.

Lady Evelyn was quite happy to admire his home and chat to the old man, for she knew that he would soon open up about Kate. And indeed he did.

'I'll tell 'e where she'll be right this minute, My Lady,' he said with a chuckle. 'I'm surprised that you don't know.'

'If I knew I wouldn't be asking you,' Lady Evelyn snapped.

'Well,' George continued. 'If you look down there by the shore just behind the black barn, you'll see the little pony tethered.'

'Yes, but where is Kate?' Lady Evelyn asked impatiently.

'She's either in the boat or else in the cottage with Big Tom. He's got a mite daring since his father died.'

Lady Evelyn looked askance. When she imagined Kate had a lover, she had not thought he might be a fisherman. This was not at all what she had in mind.

'Do you mean to say she spends most of the day with Tom the fisherman?' she asked.

'I do,' replied George. 'And she can no more help it than that bitch down there,' he added, giving his dog a poke with his foot.

'It will have to stop,' said Lady Evelyn sternly. 'Something must be done about it.'

'Well,' said George, 'he's very fond of the lass, is Tom. He always has been.'

'They must be married,' insisted Lady Evelyn.

'Perhaps I shouldn't say this, My Lady. The lass might take your orders, but I very much doubt if Tom will. He's a strong-willed lad and very proud. He's not doing too well these days with this new tax on nets. He probably doesn't even earn enough to keep a head-strong lass like Kate.'

'But I provide well for Kate and plan to continue to do so,' said Lady Evelyn.

'Maybe,' sniffed George, 'but he's got some funny notions, has Tom. And I don't think he'll humble himself to any gentry.'

'Are you trying to say that he's a rebel?' cried Lady Evelyn, annoyed that a fisherman could turn down any help she gave.

George shrugged and said no more.

Lady Evelyn mounted her stallion, mumbled her goodbyes and rode away at great speed. At first her face was dark with fury but by the time she was near-ing the castle a smile had returned to her lips. 'After all,' she reflected, 'Kate was no bargain. It would have cost a pretty penny to dispose of her in high society in any event.' But she still found it astonishing that some rogue of a fisherman would find it beneath his dignity to accept a dowry for Kate. Lady Evelyn was still smiling as she rode through the gates.

A ragged beggar was standing in the drive, wearing the tattered remains of what was once a kilt.

As Evelyn glanced in the man's direction, a little skin bag landed in her lap. She snatched it up quickly. 'Go to the kitchen, man, and you'll be given some food,' she called.

Hurrying to the privacy of her room, she opened the bag. Oh joy! she gasped, for inside the bag was the ring she had given Jamie and a hurriedly written message that Angus was safely over the border. Lady Evelyn clasped the ring to her breast and walked to the window. She felt so happy, so relieved to know for certain that her dear brother was safe at last.

Glancing out across the courtyard, she saw Kate come flying up the drive on her pony, her long black hair flowing in the wind.

'Here comes my next problem,' she thought ruefully. She would tackle her in the morning.

Kate came down to breakfast the next morning looking dishevelled and very disgruntled. Generally she was in a thoroughly bad humour.

After breakfast, the girl got on with the chores of washing and feeding Robert, but Lady Evelyn noticed how short-tempered she was with the baby. She would not respond when he wanted to play and slapped his hand when he started to cry.

'Whatever is wrong with you, Kate?' asked Lady Evelyn. 'If you cannot treat Robert better than this we had better find you a place in the kitchen.'

At the sharpness of Lady Evelyn's tongue, Kate burst into tears. 'Oh, My Lady,' she cried, 'you and I have shared too much to keep secrets from each other. It's Tom, the fisherman. I love him but he won't marry me.'

'Of course he'll marry you if he loves you,' replied Lady Evelyn, impressed by Kate's openness.

'No, he won't,' replied Kate. 'He wants to go to the deep sea.'

'But there's many a good man at sea while many a good woman waits on the shore,' parried Lady Evelyn.

'I know,' wailed Kate, 'but I'll be old and ugly when he returns.'

Lady Evelyn was silent for a moment. Then she said, looking alarmed: 'You haven't told Tom our secret, have you?'

'Oh no, My Lady,' said Kate, once more respectful.

Lady Evelyn nodded. 'That's all right, then,' she said with relief. 'I shall speak to your lover and we'll make a beautiful bride of you. *Then* he can go off to sea.'

Later that day the two women rode out together, their friendship better for the confidence they had shared.

In the little bay of Clyve Shore, ships of all nationalities dropped anchor when wild channel storms drove them to seek shelter. Tall white-sailed merchant ships were moored beside squat Thames barges, and all the captains and their crews drank together with the local fishermen.

Lady Evelyn and Kate left the dockside behind and struck off towards the marsh. They rode carefully over the soft ground. They jumped the dykes, their mounts sailing high in the air. Kate rode very well now, and with such perfect ease and confidence.

Soon the small fishing shack came into view. Behind it was the great black barn that sheltered the sheep in winter.

'It's very lonely out here,' observed Lady Evelyn. 'I can't see you living out here on your own when Tom is away.'

But Kate did not reply. Her eyes and attention were on Tom who had just come out of the door of the shack.

'Tom!' she called. 'I've brought Lady Evelyn to see you.'

Tom slowly ambled towards them. Lady Evelyn watched him with interest and wondered whether his slow deliberation was insolence or merely part of his usual make-up.

Tom held her stallion while she dismounted and she then gazed up at his great height. He towered over her! He certainly was a very handsome man. He was extremely tanned and had a mop of black frizzy hair, pulled back and plaited, as was the fashion with sailors.

Lady Evelyn's jaw was set. She stared at him with her vivid blue eyes, and prepared to do battle. But as Tom gazed at her with eyes as green as the sea and as steady as the rocks in the bay, it was Lady Evelyn's that dropped.

'Good morning, Tom,' she said. 'I would like to have a little talk with you.'

'Certainly, My Lady,' replied Tom. 'Would you like to sit out here or come into my humble abode?'

'That seat there will do,' said Lady Evelyn, pointing to a wooden bench just outside the door. 'What I have to say will not take long.'

As she sat down, she was acutely aware of Tom's penetrating stare. She met his eyes. 'I have come to know of your intentions regarding Kate,' she said firmly.

Tom nodded thoughtfully. Then he said: 'I think that is a matter for Kate and me to decide.' His reply was distinctly cold.

Lady Evelyn was taken aback for a moment but then she took a deep breath and returned to the fray. 'I took Kate from her mother at a very tender age,' she continued. 'As a result I feel very responsible for her.'

'That is not how I see it,' Tom replied quickly as though he had prepared for this conversation. 'Kate still has a father living and if I want to marry her, I'll ask him.'

The man was indeed insolent, decided Lady Evelyn. 'Don't be foolish,' she said. 'You know he cares for nothing but the church. He could not care less about what happens to his daughter.'

The fisherman and the noblewoman glared at each other. Clearly neither was going to back down.

But suddenly Kate threw herself at Tom. 'Oh, Tom, *why* can't we be wed?' she cried into his chest.

Tom looked embarrassed while Lady Evelyn looked irritated.

'Be quiet, Kate,' she snapped. 'Let's talk this over sensibly. Go and fetch a jug of cider.'

Kate did as she was bid.

When the girl had disappeared into the shack, Lady Evelyn patted the seat beside her and said: 'Come and sit here beside me. This matter is very important to me even if Kate is not my kin.'

Tom refused the offer to sit with a shake of his head. 'I beg your pardon if I speak out of turn, My Lady, but I believe the gentry have far too much say in the affairs of us ordinary folk. But quite apart from that, living up at the castle has given Kate ideas above her station and anything I can offer her now would not be enough.'

'Nonsense,' replied Lady Evelyn. 'Kate is still the sweet simple girl she always was.' She felt slightly ashamed that she was not being completely honest with him, but by now she had conquered all her scruples in her efforts to hold on to the baby Robert. She would not be beaten now. 'If money is the problem,' she continued, 'then Kate will be well provided for. She will have a generous allowance from me.'

'When I marry *I* will do the providing,' replied Tom scathingly. 'Kate is my woman, but until I can support her she will have to wait for me. Next week I am heading for the deep sea, and I swear to God that as soon as I have made enough to give us a good start I will come back for Kate.'

His stubborn expression showed that he was not to

be shifted. 'Oh dear,' thought Lady Evelyn. She was not getting anywhere.

'Well, Tom,' she said aloud, 'since I cannot persuade you myself, I'll leave you and Kate alone to discuss your future. But let me have just one last word: take heed that no harm comes to her.' She thought it her responsibility to warn him, knowing Kate as she did.

'Have no fear, My Lady,' Tom replied. 'Kate will come to no harm with me. Kate will remain as pure as the day she was born until the day we marry.'

Lady Evelyn's eyebrows lifted perceptibly but she said nothing. 'Very well.' She rose to her feet and took hold of her horse's bridle. 'I'll bid you good day.' Then she mounted and rode away, leaving the marsh and the golden horizon to Kate and her betrothed.

Tom was a very handsome man, she thought, and a very strong-willed one at that. He had made a big impression on her, even if he was a bit naïve about Kate's purity.

The moment Lady Evelyn had left, Kate had a tantrum. She turned on Tom, kicking, screaming, crying and cursing him. But Tom just sat back and smiled. He said nothing. Meanwhile, she shouted, she cried and she appealed to him.

Finally, Tom put his arm around her and kissed her. 'Come now, lass,' he said gently. 'Calm yourself down. When I return from the sea we will be wed and I will get you a fine house.' Tom had been quite content in his fisherman's shack, but he certainly wanted something better for Kate.

Kate relaxed and snuggled close to him. 'I will wait

for you, Tom,' she murmured, 'but if only we could be together for a while before you leave . . .'

Tom shook his head. ' 'Twill only make it harder for us to part,' he replied solemnly. He pulled her to him passionately. 'I have sold my father's boat and am leaving my home tomorrow because I love you and want better things for you and for our children.'

Kate smiled. She was happy to hear these words. She snuggled closer and they sat together watching the sun go down, both a little frightened of what tomorrow might bring.

Away to the Deep Sea

Tom slowly closed the door of the shack for the last time. He was leaving this place with much regret. A lifetime had been spent here. He touched the door latch with affection, remembering the day when he had found it on the beach.

At twenty-two he was quite old to be leaving home to seek his fortune in the wide world. Until he fell in love with Kate, he had loved his lonely life and had made a reasonable living in a small way, fishing in the bay and working on the farm when the weather was bad. But now the new owner had taken away his boat and there was no turning back.

With long strides he took to the road, thinking of Kate, of how he had twisted her long dark hair in his hands. When he returned in six months, Kate would be his forever.

Then for no apparent reason, his thoughts turned to his mother. She had been a small fair woman whom his father had been very protective towards. The village folk had always claimed that she was not right in the head because she would not go to church, but instead spent her time reading and muttering words from the Bible. She had been unusual in being able to read and had taught her son Tom to read as well.

There was quite a bit of ill feeling against the church during that time. Since King Henry's father had turned a blind eye to the excesses of the clergy, many people – common folk as well as gentry, merchants and artisans – embraced the teachings of John Wycliffe. Wycliffe had lived one hundred years before and he had caused a stir by criticising the sacramental doctrines and ritual practices of the church. Although Wycliffe died for his belief – dragged to London and burned at the stake – his followers, the Lollards, remained in force throughout the country. They were linked by itinerant preachers and religious beliefs based on communal Bible study. Early printed books about the saints' lives and religious books in English gave ordinary people a chance to think about the contents themselves, without interpretation by a priest. These were religious writings that meant something to these people, and they were very threatening to the church itself. If they were caught, these followers of Wycliffe were burned as heretics.

Tom's own grandfather had been burned at the stake, and the villagers used to say the perhaps his mother had never recovered from that experience, but, as Tom grew older, he had realised that she was not insane at all. Instead he knew that she was just very courageous and liked to think for herself.

When he remembered what she used to tell him and how they would talk for hours about equality and the inequalities of life, his chest burned. How angry he was about the way common folk were treated and how poor people had to pay taxes to the rich! He raged even more. Yes, his mother had instilled in him a desire to find a better life somewhere else, and to work towards a better life for his own children.

Entering the village, he went into the tavern to enquire about a ship. He was informed that he would get his keep and threepence a week, payable at the end of the voyage.

There was no problem finding a ship to take him. Few men wanted this kind of life so there was always a demand for willing souls. There was no guarantee of riches at the end of any voyage or any indication of how long a trip might last. But the chances were that some foreign prize would be bagged and that Tom would return with plenty of booty.

The recruiting bo'sun in the tavern gave him all this information, and big, strong, simple Tom took it all in carefully. He was then taken down to the great ship and put to work right away helping to load up the food stores for the voyage.

Other people too were already boarding the ship – notables – knights in shining armour and their heavy snorting horses. Watching them from the quayside, Tom realised that this was no merchant vessel but actually a naval ship preparing to invade France. Such a realisation was of great excitement to him. He lapped it in greedily.

Soon Tom was well ensconced in the life at sea. He was popular with the rest of the crew and enjoyed getting drunk and singing with them. The memory of Kate's tear-stained face gradually faded into the distant past.

After the ship had discharged the knights at Calais, it pulled out again and set sail for other waters.

Tom loved the life and within a year he was a hard-swearing, hard-drinking Jack Tar. Most of the others on board had felt the weight of his great fists. Gradually, as the seas took their toll, Tom rose in rank. He was very reliable and a dreaded fiend with a boat hook or cutlass, treating the enemy as though they were the mackerel he used to gut in his own small fishing boat.

After several months, Tom had risen to the rank of Bo'sun and was regarded as a great asset to the Navy. As time rolled on, Tom became the most feared and hated man on the ship. On dark nights the long boat would slip in to dock at little seaside towns on the Devon coast. Members of the crew would then become the press gang, forcing men to join the ship in order to replace the dwindling crew as its members died from pestilence and ill treatment at sea.

The press gangs swept into taverns where young farmers were having a quiet evening drink, they accosted lone men in the road, and they took young lads just returning from taking their sweethearts home. All were carried into the night and onto the boats never to return.

One night they returned with four 'recruits'. One sat cursing and holding his head. He had a cut on his temple from which blood was oozing. Two of the men lay unconscious while the fourth sat upright on the bunk. He was an old man with bright, intelligent eyes. He was there murmuring prayers when Tom came along.

'Who picked up this old bag of bones?' Tom roared.

'Better chuck that old bastard back on land, for all the use he'll be.'

The sailors moved to carry out Tom's orders but Tom suddenly had a change of heart. The old man's reaction was most unusual. He showed no sign of fear at all. This bothered Tom. He narrowed his eyes apprehensively at the thin old man with white hair. He noticed that he wore the long dark robes of a priest. 'Where are you from?' Tom yelled.

'I come from Kent,' the old man replied in a clear voice. 'My name is Peter Hayes.'

'Welcome,' said Tom, holding out his hand to the man. 'I'm a Kent man myself.' Peter Hayes took it and grasped it warmly.

They set sail immediately and soon old Peter was put to work in the galley. In no time at all he had become very popular with the whole crew. They were interested in what he had to say. He taught of a God who believed in love not war, and a world where all men were equal. And he read them stories in English from an old battered Bible he always carried around with him. Tom loved them. They were just like the stories his mother used to read him from her Bible, so many years ago.

One year later Peter died aboard ship. He was much mourned, and he was buried at sea. Tom very proudly read from the old book, an English Bible, which Peter had told him to keep when he was gone. Peter's brief presence in the lives of the rough men on board ship was to make a mark on them forever. For Tom it was as though he had been in touch with his dead mother.

He felt a deep gratitude to old Peter whose beliefs were so close to his own.

For all Tom's enjoyment of life at sea, the fortune he had reckoned on making had so far not materialised. All he had gained was a deep religious belief which would bring him only trouble in his native land, and a great deal of blood and tears. He had thought of writing to Kate. No other woman had ever taken her place, but life was lived for each day on a warship, so the letter had never been written.

The old king had been dead for several years now and – contrary to their early hopes – the young war-mongering King Henry cared little for the common folk. He was very involved with the wars with Scotland and France, squandering all the wealth that his parsimonious father had accumulated. The outrageously extravagant court bred discontent among the over-taxed people. And it was a very easy thing for the idealistic and big-hearted Tom to get involved.

The ship was lying in a Devon harbour. The officers, who had money, had gone ashore, leaving the sick and wounded to care for themselves. Shortage of food and pay and appalling conditions made many men desert ship and try to make their way back to their homes.

Also leaving the ship was a group of young men who had embarked at Calais. They were gentlemen and quite dandified, having spent much of their time in the English-occupied port. They were the sons of enemies of the last king, great men who had died for their beliefs, having sent their heirs to safety. But now with the new king on the throne they were flocking back to seek favour at the Royal court.

The festering wounds of the exhausted and wounded sailors below did not worry these young men. They were busy parading and preening themselves.

'They're more like women than men,' muttered Tom morosely. 'In my opinion, England is better off without the likes of them.'

One particular fellow made an impression on him. A thin, mean-faced young man with a short, clipped beard. Everywhere he went, two young pages followed him like lapdogs.

Tom mentioned this fellow to the officer on the watch.

'That's young Hugh Mortimer,' replied the officer. 'He comes from your part of the country, I believe.'

'I thought he had been exiled for killing a man in a church,' exclaimed a shocked Tom.

The guard shook his head. 'They've all been pardoned, and are creeping back now. But if the old tub springs a leak, they'll soon go overboard.'

The young men were rowed ashore and that night the local inn was alight with candles and merrymaking.

Tom and several shipmates sat disconsolately on the harbour wall. Tom had asked the captain only that day about paying the men off. Many had been away from their homes for two years. But the pompous captain had ignored Tom's request and made excuses, before going ashore with the gentlemen, to eat, drink and be merry.

So these tired, hungry, battle-weary men sat through

the night, listening bitterly to the sounds of merry-making – the shouting, cheering and laughing.

Tom sat silently whittling a stick, while another young sailor leaned against the wall of the tavern savouring the smells of food wafting outside from within.

Suddenly, the door of the inn burst open, and the mean-faced Hugh Mortimer dashed out. He shoved the young sailor aside, shouting: 'Get out of the door-way, you dog! Make way for your betters!'

As the lad fell to the ground, Hugh Mortimer stood over him and held his sword at the boy's throat. 'Shall I run you through?' he asked to the amusement of his friends, who had come out to see what was going on.

The next moment, Tom's great fist had struck Hugh Mortimer in the mouth. He fell backwards, his arms splayed, spitting blood and teeth. The young noble-man went down like a pole-axed ox.

The fury and bloodshed of the battle that followed was such that it was talked about for years to come. The frustrated sailors rushed into the affray without a care for their lives. Knives were plunged deep into drunken bodies. The alarm was sounded and soldiers came rushing from the inn. The survivors were captured and taken away by the military, but in the mêlée Tom made his getaway. He had not served his country for two years to be locked away. But now he was a fugitive from justice.

To get home, he had a long trek across three counties before he could reach the shores of Kent. The great fortune he was to have made had eluded him. And now his freedom was in jeopardy.

11

The Return of the Prodigal Son

The last two years had been kind to Kate and Lady Evelyn at their home in Clyve Castle. The little boy, Robert, was now a lively, bright two-and-a-half year old. He was not very big but he was extremely sturdy. He also seemed very advanced, as he ran about chattering and conversing in a very grown-up manner, for he spent all his time with adults and rarely played with other children.

This lovely spring morning Lady Evelyn and Kate were playing hide-and-seek with Robert in the park. Kate would pretend not to see the child's golden head peering from behind a tree, then Robert would be unable to contain himself for any longer and he would dash out shouting: 'Here I am!' He would throw himself at her, and together they rolled and laughed in the soft green grass.

These boisterous games belied the extraordinary change that had come over Kate. For Lady Evelyn had successfully moulded her into a well-dressed, well-spoken lady. She could easily be taken for a gentlewoman. And many a young man in the town would turn to look at her admiringly as she passed by. She was very different from the young girl who had willingly given up her firstborn in exchange for the good things in life.

Nowadays, Kate seemed rather sad and pensive when rocking young Robert to sleep. During these moments, she was thinking about Tom. Why had he not returned to marry her? Had he been drowned? Why had he not written? Was he never coming back? If he did return would they have children of their own? Or would she now spend the rest of her life in the service of Lady Evelyn and caring for a son who called her Katy? Her bottom drawer was all stitched and prepared and a beautiful wedding dress had been created and made by herself and Lady Evelyn. All these things were now packed away in lavender.

At these thoughts, big tears rolled down Kate's cheeks. 'Oh, Tom,' she sobbed, 'if you are alive, please come back to me, my darling.'

While Kate was weeping in the nursery, Lady Evelyn was receiving a visitor, Sir Clarence Cowley, now guardian of the Mortimer estate. He was shown into a room off the great hall, one that Lady Evelyn had turned into a private study for her own use.

Sir Clarence had great admiration for Lady Evelyn. He himself had had two bad marriages, and his only offspring was a wayward daughter. 'I'm sorry to bring you bad news, Evelyn,' he said, kissing her hand.

Evelyn tensed herself. She had known this tranquil life could not last. How was it to be shattered now?

'I have come to give you warning,' continued Sir Clarence. 'Young Hugh Mortimer is back in England.'

Lady Evelyn shuddered. 'Yes,' she nodded. 'It was

to be expected. I have made my plans against this day. It is very good of you to come all this way to warn me.'

'Will you move to the lower house at St Mary's, or will you return with me to London?' Sir Clarence asked.

'Neither,' replied Evelyn. 'I shall return to Scotland.'

Sir Clarence looked concerned. 'But it will be a long hazardous journey for you, particularly with a young child,' he said. 'Why not wait until times are more settled?'

'No,' she replied, 'my mind is made up. It has been for a long time. If there is to be trouble I would rather be with my own kind.

'Thank you for all your help, Sir Clarence, you have been a good friend to Robert and myself.'

Sir Clarence could see that Lady Evelyn was not to be persuaded otherwise. He said his farewells and left, leaving Lady Evelyn to prepare her own departure.

After Sir Clarence had gone, Evelyn sat down on a stool and thought hard about what she had to do. First she had to get a message to Angus in Scotland. She would send a man to London where a friend could be found. These were dangerous times and storm clouds were gathering. But whatever happened she could not stay here at Clyve Castle to be at the mercy of her stepson. And if she returned to Scotland, Robert would be able to take his place among her own family.

A messenger was hastily despatched to London, and Lady Evelyn anxiously awaited the reply. Her quick mind was already thinking ahead. She decided that she had to persuade Kate to come with her. And who knows, when Angus saw what a beautiful woman Kate had grown into, well, anything could happen . . .

After their meal that evening, the two women sat sewing together. Lady Evelyn decided that there was no time to lose in broaching the subject. 'Kate, dear,' she said quietly, 'you and I have been together for over three years now, and the time has now come when we must leave this place.' As Kate looked up at her in astonishment, she explained, 'My stepson is returning.'

'We'll go back to the lodge, then,' said Kate quickly.

'No,' replied Lady Evelyn, 'that wouldn't be far enough. We still have our secret to guard, and this man is an enemy. We must return to my home in Scotland so that Robert may be brought up safely.'

Immediately Kate jumped to her feet. 'I cannot leave here, My Lady, how would Tom ever find me when he returns?'

'Don't be hasty, Kate, dear,' urged Lady Evelyn. 'Think on it. Scotland is a fine land, and Robert will be in his rightful place.'

'No,' snapped Kate adamantly. 'I shall stay here and wait for Tom.'

Well, if the girl won't come, I'll have to go alone, thought Lady Evelyn. Angus would send an escort for her. But still she felt uneasy. She had grown so close to Kate that the thought of deserting her now was abhorrent. As they sat there, they suddenly heard the clatter of hoofs on the stones in the courtyard as horsemen galloped up the drive. Then there was the clanging of a night bell. The butler, Wilkins, unbolted the main door. Lady Evelyn felt very nervous. She gripped the sewing in her hand so tightly that her knuckles showed white. She felt Kate standing next to her, both staring down into the great hall.

Then they heard a terrible sound as a shrill voice cried: 'Wake up! The master of the house has returned!'

Through the great oak door strode the dandified figure of Hugh Mortimer, followed by three very young men. He wore a vermilion velvet cap, and a short coat of matching colour, with a large fur collar.

'I'm too late,' thought Lady Evelyn, panic-stricken. Swallowing hard, she formed a stiff smile on her lips and walked calmly out into the hall to greet the young man. 'Welcome home, Lord Mortimer,' she said coolly.

Hugh removed his cap and bowed low. His eyes looked mocking. 'Well, well, the lovely Lady Evelyn,' he said smoothly, 'as beautiful as ever.'

'Take off your cloak and let me order you some refreshment,' Lady Evelyn said icily.

But Hugh was not listening. He had just caught sight of Kate who was hovering at the bottom of the stairs. He could not miss the gaze in those huge eyes. 'Come here and greet your master,' he called.

Lady Evelyn frowned and looked very annoyed. 'Go and tidy yourself, my dear,' she called. 'I may need you.'

As Kate hurried away, Hugh watched her with narrowed eyes. 'Who is the dark beauty?' he asked.

'She is a village maid, my companion,' replied Lady Evelyn.

Hugh then introduced his own companions to Lady

Evelyn. 'This is my cousin Richard,' he said. The eldest of the three stepped forward and kissed Lady Evelyn's hand. 'And these are just a couple of young pups.' Hugh waved in the direction of the young boys.

Lady Evelyn felt oddly agitated. She did not understand these fancy young men, who were so effeminate in their dress. It took all her patience to be polite to them. 'Is there anything you need?' she asked, turning back to Hugh.

'Well,' replied Hugh with a laugh, 'all I want is some wine and some pretty women.'

The next two hours were agony for Lady Evelyn. Kate had returned dressed up in a gown and looking very pretty. Now Evelyn felt that she could not retire until Kate was safe in her bed.

Kate sat at the table, her face flushed with wine as she listened to the men's stupid patter. She was clearly very flattered as they proclaimed over her beauty. All this made Lady Evelyn extremely worried. For in spite of her sophisticated air and dress, Kate was still really very naïve. Evelyn prayed that Hugh Mortimer would be more interested in the young boys and leave Kate alone.

Eventually the drunken party broke up. As his companions staggered off to their various chambers, Hugh turned to Lady Evelyn with a distinct sneer on his lips. 'Goodnight, My Lady,' he said. 'By the way, I am looking forward to meeting my young brother tomorrow morning. Father was a bit old in the tooth when he begat him, but then the Mortimers do seem to go on forever.'

Lady Evelyn visibly paled. She caught her breath and forced herself to smile as she watched Hugh climb up the stairs to bed.

Later that night, Lady Evelyn sought out the butler. He was at the top of the stairway lighting the candles. 'Wilkins', she whispered, 'stop whatever you're doing and fetch your wife to my room.' This was to be her last evening at the castle. By the morning she would be gone.

When the Wilkinses returned to her chamber, Lady Evelyn told them her plan.

Lady Evelyn took off her glittering dinner gown, placing her precious pearl brooch on the bed as she did so, and put on a travelling outfit. That was all she could take. Then Mistress Wilkins helped her gather what she needed. Only a few bits and pieces were essential: the Mortimer family jewellery and Robert's garments.

As soon as her stallion was saddled and ready in the courtyard below, Lady Evelyn said her farewells to the Wilkinses. She told them that she had left enough money for them, and that if they did not wish to stay at Clyve Castle then Sir Clarence Cowley would house and employ them.

She crept along to Kate's room and gently shook her awake.

'What's wrong?' asked Kate sleepily.

'Everything,' replied Lady Evelyn. 'I am leaving within the hour. If you are coming, you must make haste and get ready.'

'I'll not come,' said Kate stubbornly. 'I'm going to wait here for Tom.'

Lady Evelyn swallowed hard. She had no choice but to be cruel. 'Your lover is dead, Kate,' she said flatly. 'He will never come back.'

But Kate merely burst into tears and turned over in her bed, hugging the pillows.

'I'll be back in half an hour,' continued Lady Evelyn. 'If you are coming with me, you'd better have your door open and be ready. I'm going to get Robert ready for the journey.'

In due course Evelyn returned to Kate's room but the door remained closed. 'Farewell, Kate,' whispered Lady Evelyn through the door. She suddenly felt very sad, and she choked back tears as she crept away.

Within minutes Lady Evelyn was out in the court-yard and mounted her stallion, Fleet. The child Robert was safely tucked up in a special harness against the saddle and under her cloak. Fleet's hoofs had been muffled with cloth tied around them at the fetlocks, so she rode out of the castle without making any sounds that might have woken the visitors.

It was a very saddlesore Lady Evelyn who arrived later that day at a house on the hill at Greenwich. This was where Jamie's sister, Jessie, lived. Jessie was housekeeper to a serious man who spent his time studying the stars. Since he was always looking up at the sky, he never noticed the comings and goings of Jessie's countrymen.

Lady Evelyn was exhausted. She had travelled forty miles nonstop. And Robert was very bad-tempered and grizzly. It had been a terrible journey, fraught with danger. Evelyn was usually a courageous woman but that night she had been afraid at every corner that a highwayman would pounce on her. Her weariness had made her depressed, and although she had a very good reason for returning to her homeland, she knew that she was gambling on a lot. And she had a lot to lose. All she possessed in the world now were the clothes she stood up in, and her jewellery. But that was what would buy her journey home.

Jessie was now a welcome sight. A tiny woman in a white apron, she was quite a contrast to her big brother Jamie. She did not seem to be totally surprised to see Lady Evelyn, and ushered her and the child into the house as quickly as she could, clucking like a mother hen.

Lady Evelyn rested for most of the next morning to regain her strength. From the adjoining room she could hear Jessie amusing Robert. It was time to get up again and think about her next move. She washed and dressed and went to join Jessie and Robert. As she walked out into the corridor, she almost crashed into the massive shape of Jamie, who was just coming up the stairs.

'Welcome, lass,' he said with a broad smile. 'It's a pleasure to see you again – and well, too.'

Lady Evelyn gasped with joy. 'Oh thank God you've found us!' she cried. 'I thought you must have gone. I was ready to set off on my own for Scotland.'

Jamie shook his shaggy head. 'No, there's no need for you do that, lass. I'm here to escort you and the laddie home now.'

Excitedly, they sat and talked for a while as Jamie

filled Evelyn in on what had been happening. Angus was safe across the border, as she knew. Apparently the young king was no longer very popular, and nobody trusted him. Jamie told Evelyn that a party of noblemen were travelling north the next day to join the border war. She would be able to travel with them. As they would be calling at many fine homes on the way, she would probably have a very enjoyable trip. She would certainly be safe.

Lady Evelyn felt overjoyed. Her intense anxiety dissolved as she heard all this news. She felt certain now about what she was doing, more reassured about Robert's safe future, and absolutely thrilled at the very real possibility of reaching home soon.

She suddenly remembered Kate and wondered what the girl was doing, all alone at Clyve Castle. As her mind wandered, her hand instinctively moved to her chest. Evelyn gave a little gasp and looked down with an anguished look on her face. Her brooch! It was gone! Panic seized her as she leaped to her feet and scanned the floor of the room.

'Whatever's the matter?' asked Jamie.

'My brooch, the brooch Robert gave me years ago. It's gone.' Poor Evelyn was close to tears. Then she slapped her hand over her mouth. 'Oh goodness!' she exclaimed. 'I must have left it at the castle. I took it off when I was changing last night. I must go back for it. I cannot be parted from it.'

Jamie placed a large hand on her arm and shook his great head. 'No, lass, you cannot go back now, you would be killed by Hugh Mortimer.'

'But what can I do? That brooch means everything to me . . .'

Jamie looked her sternly in the eye. 'More to you than your life, or that of young Robert?'

Lady Evelyn looked away and nodded. 'Yes, you're right, Jamie, I must remember what is really important now . . .'

Jamie smiled. 'Perhaps we'll be able to retrieve your brooch one day,' he said kindly.

12

Kate All Alone

When Kate opened her eyes the next morning she sensed something was different before she had even fully woken up. Then she realised what it was. There was silence, no sound of Robert greeting her with his childish prattle as he pawed her bedclothes and climbed on to the quilt. Well, she thought, Lady Evelyn had done as she said she would, and left at daybreak.

Kate momentarily wondered if she would ever see her child again. Then she thought of Lady Evelyn's parting words. A deep sense of gloom gripped her. Her Ladyship was probably right about Tom being drowned . . . and yet Kate did not feel that she wanted to flee, to leave the castle. On the contrary, something seemed to be compelling her to stay.

Her thoughts drifted on to the new master of Clyve Castle, Hugh Mortimer. Why did Lady Evelyn not like him?

She washed and dressed quickly, paying extra special attention to her raven-black hair. She did not know why. Then she went out into the corridor, where she saw the two young boys from the night before, sniggering and whispering together.

Kate felt a frisson of irritation at the sight of them.

As she passed them, she cupped her hands around their two sandy heads and knocked them together. As the youths reeled in pain and astonishment, Kate glided past with a set look on her face. She was suddenly angry that her quiet life had come to an end.

Downstairs the remains of last night's merriment was still on the table. She strode down into the kitchens, and found the servants standing around gossiping.

'Lady Evelyn has ridden away. And the Wilkinses, too, have left as if the devil were after them,' they told Kate.

'Stop standing about jabbering!' yelled Kate. 'I want my breakfast. And clear up that mess in the hall.'

Kate's position as Lady Evelyn's companion had given her seniority over the other servants. Her voice of authority made them jump to obey her orders. Thus, in her simple way, Kate restored order to the excited and disrupted household.

Then she automatically set herself about the tasks that Lady Evelyn normally did. When Hugh Mortimer came down to the hall, he found the place spotlessly clean, with fresh flowers everywhere.

Young Hugh was not in the slightest bit surprised to learn that Lady Evelyn had left the castle and was on her way to Scotland. But he was rather surprised that she had left the lovely Kate behind.

Later that day, Hugh's guests departed. Hugh spent the rest of the time touring his estate. When he returned, Kate did her utmost to please him. She conversed pleasantly and tried to make him comfortable as he lounged about in the great hall. Hugh had no qualms about casting lewd glances in her direction. And as Kate went about her chores, he took every opportunity to brush against her. Kate found to her surprise that she was not annoyed by this behaviour. Indeed, she rather liked it.

Later that evening Kate wandered into Lady Evelyn's chamber and was surprised to find that she had left all her beautiful gowns behind.

Suddenly she noticed a small object lying on the bed. She picked it up and saw that it was Lady Evelyn's pearl brooch, the one that she had always worn. How very strange that she had left if behind. She must have just taken it off and forgotten it in her haste. Well, she thought, I'll keep it for her . . .

Now her attention turned to the gowns before her. With a smile on her lips, Kate slipped off her working clothes. She certainly could not resist the chance to try one on. But as she lifted up a red velvet gown and held it against her slender body, a shadowy shape leapt suddenly from the corner. Rough hands grasped her white thighs from behind, then hot lips pressed against her as she felt herself dragged down to the bed.

Kate did not cry out. She did not struggle. For she was lost. The healthy young body that had waited so long for her lover finally succumbed to Hugh Mortimer's drunken demands and violent lovemaking.

Afterwards Kate had no regrets, and the next morning she felt as if she were glowing. It was the most wonderful thing that had ever happened to her. After that time, it happened again and again. Night after night Hugh pulled her down on the bed and threw his drunken body at her. As for Kate, she could not have enough of him. She kissed him and bit him, as he did her. And so a very sordid love affair was born. Pure animal passion brought the two together.

Hugh grew fond of Kate in a sadistic sort of way. He enjoyed tormenting her – pulling her to him or rejecting her, according to his mood. But Kate was content, sexually and otherwise. And she thought very little of Lady Evelyn, Robert or even Tom.

Sixty or so miles away, a young man walked slowly along the road to Clyve. Many of his old friends would have not recognised him. He had grown a long dark beard. His shoes had worn out and his feet were now bound with rags. His shoulders stooped with weariness. No one would be expected to recognise this wretch as Tom the fisherman.

He had just reached the top of the Hog's Back, and the town of Guildford lay before him. In a few more days now, with luck, he should be home. In the meantime, he would find a barn and rest up for a while. Fellow travellers on the road had told him of a very generous farmer who, in return for a bit of work, would give a welcome rest and shelter to travellers.

It had been a difficult journey, evading the King's men who were rounding up all deserters. But Tom had had plenty of company on the road with so many soldiers and sailors trying to make their way home.

He had seen many dreadful things in his travels, and was now a very bitter man. But he carried his small Bible with him everywhere. It gave him a certain comfort.

At last he reached the farm where shelter could be found. He greedily gobbled up the warm meal placed in front of him. The next morning, having learnt that Tom could handle horses, the farmer set him to ploughing. Walking up and down the strips of land, controlling the heavy horses, Tom felt wonderfully content. Yes, this would be the life for Kate and himself. He imagined a community of God's people living together in harmony and working the land together, living and dying for each other, each man being equal with the next. As he thought of these things, he pressed the Bible to his chest for comfort. He felt he could see his mother and sense her presence.

He returned to the farmhouse with very mixed feelings. The farmer told the men that those that wished to leave were free to do so when they had finished their tasks. All he required from them was one day's work for a night of rest and a good meal. The farmer turned to Tom: 'How about you, sailor? Will you stay a while longer, or are you away?'

Tom hesitated, and then replied: 'I would be glad to stay a few days longer, as I still have a long journey to the north of Kent.'

'Certainly,' said the farmer, who was called John Little. 'And I'll pay you well for your ploughing.' He was well pleased with Tom's hard work.

So Tom worked there for the rest of the week, and felt much better. He had worked hard for his money, but the main reward was the satisfaction he had of doing a good day's work. At night he spent much time making other weary travellers comfortable an reading stories from his Bible to the little children.

The people came to love and trust him, and even began to come to him with their problems. For the first time in many years Tom felt really happy. He had soon decided to go to Kate and ask if she would return to this place with him where he could be happy.

When the few days were up, John Little bade him farewell, and gave him a letter to deliver to his brother in the hamlet of Allhallows, not far from Tom's own home.

As Tom made to leave, John Little said: 'By the way, Tom, I hear you are one of us.'

Tom looked at him in puzzlement.

'You read from that vernacular Bible, don't you?' continued the farmer.

Tom nodded.

'How is that?' asked the farmer.

Tom proceeded to explain how he had come by the Bible, telling about his life at sea and Peter Hayes.

'May I see it?' asked the farmer, and Tom held it out to him.

After reading the writing inside, John Little looked up, his eyes blazing with joy. 'This Bible once belonged to my uncle,' he said.

Through this coincidence, Tom had made a friend for life. John Little told him that his brother would give him a good job, and then he invited Tom to spend his last night with his family in the farmhouse and tell him and his wife of the last year in his Uncle Peter's life.

They were confused, at first, they said, for they had been given to understand that Peter Hayes had died in prison. They could not understand what he had been doing on a boat at sea.

'Well,' replied Tom, 'it's the evil system we live under.' Then he explained about the press gangs, and how he and the rest of the crew had been disappointed with a bag of bones like old Peter, but then they had all come to love and respect him. Then Tom told them about his own early upbringing and his mother's teachings. It had him feel very happy to talk to Peter Hayes' relatives like this, and to find that they were such good, kind people. He knew that Kate would like them too.

The next day Tom continued his journey. It took several days. When he rested, Tom sat by the hedgerows reading and learning from his Bible, though he knew most of it by heart already. Following the farmer's directions, Tom came one day to the farm of another believer. There was a barn at the side of the road, which he made his way to. Inside Tom found many footsore travellers, all tired, hungry and ragged. The owner, Japhet Miller, made everyone welcome here. Japhet had kept faith with his friend, Peter Hayes, and always did his best to help the poor and weary.

When Tom made himself known to him with word from John Little, they spent many long hours into the night talking of Peter Hayes and the belief they all had in this faith of theirs. Peter's preachings against the behaviour of the church and priests had brought the wrath of the church down on him. Eventually he had left his home and disappeared, Japhet explained. But he had willed the land he owned to his niece. She had carried on his work of helping the poor and guiding them towards God, just as Japhet was doing here. As the jigsaw fell into place, Tom saw the path he wanted to follow.

Japhet was impressed by Tom's interest. 'We ask very little,' he said, 'just that we can live together side by side in peace with God.'

These, of course, were Tom's sentiments exactly.

There, under the stars, the two men shook hands. Solemnly they declared: 'To the freedom and glory of God.' Then they knelt down to pray, thinking of Peter Hayes.

13

Lady Evelyn's Journey and Kate's Downfall

Lady Evelyn left the comfort of Jessie's home at daybreak the next day. The dawn sky cast strange shadows over the heath, making a grand view of the city with its harvest of church spires. Her party was taking the road north, the old Roman road, Watling Street. And at one point she gazed back at the City, wondering if she would ever see it again.

Robert rode with Jamie now, all wrapped up inside his cloak. He was thoroughly enjoying himself, and trying to join in with the singing of the horsemen who galloped behind them. At first Evelyn had been worried about these men. She thought they might draw unwelcome attention to themselves. But Jamie had reassured her that they would surely need them when the journey got really tough later on. She only wished that she had Robert's brooch with her. She felt curiously vulnerable without it.

That first night they stopped at an inn at St Albans. As she tucked Robert into bed, the child chattering all the while, Evelyn suddenly had doubts about whether she was doing the right thing. She had felt almost overwhelmed by feelings of homesickness for Clyve Castle. And she missed Kate, her companion.

Pulling herself together, she lay down on the bed and rested for a while. Later, she arose and freshened herself before going down to dine with Jamie.

Downstairs, she was surprised to find that Jamie had company. Two men were talking to him. One was an older man; Jamie introduced him as Rupert McShane. He was very handsome and courteous. The younger man, Donald Fraser, could not hide his obvious admiration for Lady Evelyn. Throughout the evening, Evelyn found that his gaze was so intent she had to drop her eyes to avoid his look. The two men joined them for dinner. They were both very entertaining and witty conversationalists. Their company helped to ease the strain Evelyn had been feeling, and she realised that she had not enjoyed herself so much in years. She also had to admit to herself that she found Donald extremely attractive.

These men, Jamie explained, were to join their party. Knowing this, Evelyn felt that the journey north seemed much less daunting. It had been a long time since she had enjoyed such welcome masculine attention, and she liked it.

They started out again the next morning, laden with fresh supplies. A pony was found for Robert. He was already at home in the saddle and he needed a mount of his own for so long a journey. Jamie was always close at hand should he fall. Evelyn had begun to relax and feel quite confident. Despite the possible dangers, it all seemed very exciting all of a sudden, particularly since Donald Fraser had chosen to ride with her for most of the way.

One night they stayed in the beautiful city of Lincoln, after riding through Sherwood Forest in the day. It was exquisitely beautiful, with its great spreading oaks, and squirrels jumping from their branches. Occasionally a young deer appeared, to be chased by an excited Robert.

Lady Evelyn felt wonderfully at peace, now after all happy with the decision she had chosen to make. Had she known what lay in store for her though, she might have thought otherwise. She hardly thought of Kate during these days.

Meanwhile, in Kent, life was not smiling on Kate so benevolently. She had become quite obsessed with Hugh Mortimer but he was not kind to her. He left her for days at a time to go into town, and would return dishevelled and dirty, and in a terrible mood. He became increasingly demanding of Kate, and her lovely young body was covered in weals and bruises. Although he seemed gentle and sweet to her each morning, she was now becoming quite afraid of her lover.

One morning, after a particularly bad night, she arose early and dressed herself in a pretty blue cotton dress and underskirt, and a wide straw hat. She felt a great longing to get away from Hugh and the castle. She collected a basket and decided to go and pick mushrooms.

Once outside the castle gates, she inhaled deeply, drawing the clean salty air deep into her lungs. She looked quite innocent and demure as she made her way along the dusty lane, but inside her head, her mind was in turmoil. What was she doing here? How had she allowed herself to get into this situation? How she missed Robert and Lady Evelyn! Why had she not gone with them? They were so far away. So far from here. Kate had never been to Scotland. The only place she had ever known was this corner of Kent where she had been born. Now Lady Evelyn had gone and she felt as though a part of her had disappeared. She had no one to advise her. She never saw her father who still lived up at the priest's house, nor her brother, who had moved away from the village long ago, and she greatly missed her dead mother.

She found a patch of golden chanterelle mushrooms and began to gather them with care. But the melancholy thoughts would not go away. Kate sat down by the roadside, suddenly feeling too forlorn to think about mushrooms. What was she to do? Suddenly, she realised that she was quite near to where old George lived. She got to her feet and set off again with a bit more lightness in her step. At least he was someone she knew.

Arriving at George's shack, she pushed open the door. In spite of the loveliness of the day, George was sitting in front of the fire. Hearing the door, he looked up and said: 'Well, if it isn't little Kate. What brings you to these parts?' His wrinkled face looked even older than she remembered it.

Kate held out the basket of yellow mushrooms.

'I thought you'd forgotten all about me,' George grumbled.

Kate ignored him and sat down next to him before

the fire. In spite of his grumpiness, she knew that George was pleased to see her.

The shack was dirty and untidy, as was George himself. It seemed such a shame, Kate thought, when she remembered how clean and smart he used to be. She offered to clear up the cottage a little for him, but he declined.

'No, lass, leave things where I can find them,' he said with a shake of his head. Together they sat in silence before the fire. The only sound came from the crackling flames and the wheezing of George's asthmatic chest.

'Are you hungry, girl?' George suddenly asked, breaking the silence.

Kate nodded. 'I've had no breakfast,' she replied.

The truth was, she was very hungry. Although she had drunk plenty of wine lately, she had eaten very little.

George pottered about and in a few minutes had placed a bowl of porridge in front of her. 'Now, lass, tell me what's troubling you,' he said kindly.

At this, Kate burst into tears. Pushing aside the bowl of porridge, she laid her head in the old man's lap. As George put his arm around her shoulders to comfort her, Kate's dress slipped off her thin shoulders, to reveal the weals and bruises.

'I thought so,' muttered George. 'He's a mad bastard, that young Hugh. What's bred in the bone comes out in the flesh.'

Kate cried herself out, with George stroking her black hair. As he comforted the girl, his thoughts went back to the time he had begged Kate's mother to marry him. Then it had been he who had shed the tears. How different life would have been if she had said yes … Still, there was no point in dwelling on matters such as that any more, he thought. This child needs help now.

After Kate's sobs had subsided, George said: 'Come now, Kate, come and help me feed the fowls.' So together they went outside and scattered the grain for the chickens and ducks, and gathered the eggs. Then they sat together outside the shack drinking cider.

'You've got to get away from here, lass,' said George.

'I've nowhere to go,' replied Kate. 'Besides, sometimes he's very kind to me, and I love him.'

'Rubbish,' shouted George. 'What you have for each other is animal instinct, nothing more.'

'I don't know what you mean!' cried Kate.

'You're as innocent as a babe in arms,' bellowed George. 'That young man is mad and will do you harm. There's bad blood in the family, and he's clearly got plenty of it.'

He then regaled her with horrific tales of the behaviour of Hugh's ancestors.

Kate's nerves, already on edge, could stand no more. 'Oh be quiet, George,' she cried. 'It's all very well you saying this, but where can I go?'

'Well, you can't stay here,' replied George. 'Folk would talk, what with me being on my own. But it's a certainty that if Lord Hugh don't do for you then Big Tom will.'

Kate wailed and jumped up with a cry. 'My Tom is drowned, he's dead,' she yelled. 'Don't torture me any more!'

'I don't think he is,' replied George. 'The King's men have been in the village looking for him.'

Kate stared at him in astonishment. Then she bit her lip and picked up her basket. 'I don't believe you,' she hissed, and marched out of the door.

Old George smiled. That was more like the Kate he knew. With a bit of her spirit back, she might prove more of a match for that Hugh Mortimer.

On the journey back to Clyve Castle, Kate thought about what George had said. If Tom really was alive and returned he would kill her if he found out Hugh Mortimer had been her lover. She was mortified. Imagining what might happen made her feel quite frightened. She realised that she had only been so willing with Hugh because she had believed that Tom was dead. She suddenly felt quite unclean and had an urgent need to go to church. It was crucial for her to seek forgiveness.

She made her way to the church, stepping through the graveyard with its masses of white crosses. Reaching the door, she grasped the heavy iron ring and turned it. As the door opened, she momentarily panicked. But fighting the urge to run away, she stepped inside the cool building. As the smell of incense enveloped her, she dropped to her knees and poured out her troubles to the great spirit above. The sun glinted through the colourful glass windows. The old faded tapestries of the martyrs hanging from the wall seemed to surround her and give her great comfort.

'Forgive my sins, and send my Tom home,' she whimpered. She vowed that this was her church and her village and she would spend the rest of her days making amends for the bad things she had done. At last, when she arose from her knees, she felt at peace with the world. She had seen the light.

It was with a much lighter heart that she left the church and headed back towards the castle. She felt much stronger and confident. Her courage had returned.

She stopped and rested for a while in the orchard, leaning against a tree. There she thought about her son and how one day he might be master of this huge estate. She thought about Tom and how if he had come back and married her she might have had another son by now. For some reason, she thought, too, of her brother Nicholas, whom she had not seen for a long time. In fact, she never heard from him at all nowadays.

When she arrived at the castle, Kate was surprised to see an unfamiliar carriage in the drive.

'Who has come?' she enquired of the groom who was trying to steady the four foam-flecked horses.

' 'Tis a lady from France, Miss, to see the master,' replied the groom.

Kate stared with hostility at the grand scarlet-and-gold carriage. Whoever could it be?

As she entered the hall, Hugh called to her. 'Where have you been hiding from me all day, Katy?' He seemed in a happy mood.

Kate stared at him, acutely aware of a small shiver running down her spine.

'Come, Kate,' he continued, 'I want you to meet my guests.'

At this authoritative tone, Kate's resolutions collapsed. Once more, she was completely under Hugh's spell.

With a gay laugh, Hugh swept her into a side room and presented her to the owner of the fabulous coach. The woman was tall and thin in unusual clothes – not at all like English fashions. She wore a tall jewelled head-dress with a fine veil, and a long, trailing brocade gown with a fur trimming. An embroidered vest was tied under the bust. She looked most impressive.

The two women looked at each other frostily.

'My dear Catherine, please may I introduce you to Kate. Kate, this is the Countess of Lautrec, who has come all the way from France.'

The women narrowed their eyes at each other. The Countess pursed her lips. Then she turned and burst into French, chattering to Hugh and waving her fan in Kate's direction.

Kate felt very uncomfortable and grew more and more furious, her face flushed red. Hugh leaned against the great fireplace, enjoying Kate's discomfort.

'*Elle est belle, n'est-ce-pas?*' he said, nodding in Kate's direction. 'Absolutely beautiful, eh?' The Countess had a sneer on her lips as Hugh spoke these words.

Unable to bear it any longer, Kate picked up her skirts and stormed from the room. As she left, she heard Hugh saying to the Countess: 'So you will not accept the girl into your household?'

'Certainly not!' the Countess replied. 'Why, she is most insolent. She's clearly a bad-tempered little bitch.'

Hugh was chuckling. 'I agree that she is a tempera-mental girl, but I've grown very fond of her,' he said.

'I should like to see her settled somewhere before I go to London.'

'Take care, Hugh,' the woman warned. 'Influential friends have gone to a great deal of trouble to get you a place at Court. You don't want a baggage like that to spoil this opportunity for you.'

By now Kate had crept back nearer the door to hear the conversation better. What were they saying? She heard Hugh's next sentence and bit her lip.

'Well, perhaps you're right, my dear Catherine,' he said. 'As always . . . well, I'll have to think about how I'm going to deal with her.'

Kate's face was white with rage as she heard this exchange. How dare they! Well, she would show them both that they couldn't just laugh at her like this, or discuss her future as though she were some tiresome dog! No. She decided she would dine with them later as though nothing had happened. That way, she may find out some more of what was going on.

She bathed and dressed very carefully. Picking through the garments in Lady Evelyn's wardrobe she found it hard to decide which dress she would look most beautiful in. She settled on a purple gown she had never seen Lady Evelyn wear. It was, in fact, somewhat unfashionable, but Kate knew nothing about fashion. She brushed her black hair until it gleamed, and tied it back with a purple ribbon to match the dress. Then, for some unknown reason, she suddenly decided to wear Lady Evelyn's pearl brooch as well. Taking it from the jewellery chest, she pinned it on the bodice where it nestled between her breasts.

As she came into the hall to dine, the eyes of every one of Hugh Mortimer's guests were on her. They were all intrigued by this beautiful girl with the long shining mane, sulky expression on her face, and dark shadows under her eyes. She sat down and ate a huge meal with plenty to drink. All the while, she could not take her eyes away from the French Countess. The Countess's face was thick with cosmetics. Her neckline was very low and she seemed to be weighed down with many heavy glittering jewels.

The meal proceeded peacefully enough, and Kate sat watching the Countess closely, noticing how she flirted and chatted with the men. The bobbing up and down of her white head, the flashing of her rings, and her incessant chatter began to irritate Kate enormously. There was a great buzzing in her ears as the wine had gone to her head. Suddenly she found herself getting resentful. Why should this woman monopolise Hugh? She, Kate, was the mistress in this house . . .

Kate got to her feet and then made her way rather unsteadily across the room to where Hugh sat engrossed in conversation with his guests. Kate stood there for some minutes before being noticed. She stamped her foot and rapped on the table in front of him.

'If you are going to London, I am going with you,' she shouted.

Hugh looked up at her. He looked deeply shocked. But the Countess reached over and tapped Kate with her blue fan. 'Now then, my dear,' she cooed, 'don't be a naughty girl.'

This was all that was needed to set Kate off. She reached out and grabbed the wig from the Countess's head. The Countess screeched and tried to stop her. Thereby an amazing brawl began. The great hall had seen nothing like this before. The two women went at each other scratching and hissing like she-cats.

Hugh grabbed Kate and yanked her away, while two other guests grabbed the hysterical Countess.

Hugh dragged Kate towards the stairs calling for the servants to help him. The Countess's bodice had come apart in the affray. As she struggled to free herself from the men's restraining hands, she lost her balance and ended up sprawled on top of a fat gentleman, her large breasts exposed for all to see.

When Kate saw this, she roared and laughed hysterically. She was still laughing when they locked her in her room. But after a time, her laughs subsided and turned to tears. Eventually she fell asleep.

At daybreak she awoke cold and miserable. Recalling the night before, she felt quite frightened. She wondered what Hugh would do with her. Would he have her imprisoned? He was bound to punish her in some way. She suddenly felt frightened in a way she had never felt before. She felt utterly alone and vulnerable, waiting to find out her fate . . .

It was very quiet outside when the door suddenly burst open. There stood Hugh wearing a hat and a long cloak. He had a riding whip in his hand and he looked very cruel. 'By rights I should use this whip on you,' he said menacingly, 'but you are really not worth the bother.'

Kate was cringing in the corner as he spoke. She felt devastated by this remark.

Behind Hugh stood two men. Hugh turned to them and said: 'When I have left, turn this slut out. On no account is she to be allowed to return.' He turned on his heel and strode away down the corridor.

Kate ran to the door and followed him. 'Don't leave me,' she screamed. 'Beat me! Kill me! But please don't leave me behind.' She lunged for his cloak and hung on as he strode away. Hugh tried to shake her off but Kate hung on, following him outside to where his horse was saddled and ready. Hugh mounted with Kate still clutching him in desperation. He lifted his boot and kicked her away, and as he did so, his spur caught her face.

Kate fell to the ground clutching her head as Hugh clattered away shouting orders at his men behind him. On the ground, Kate watched him go. Blood poured from the wound and spattered the gown she had not taken off since the night before. She still wore the pearl brooch between her breasts. Now she could see Hugh's two henchmen coming towards her. Jumping to her feet, she ran to the gate and crossed the bridge as fast as she could. She heard the gates clang behind her, and the sound of mocking laughter.

She ran and ran, and kept on running until she came to the edge of her beloved marshland. There she threw herself down into the long grass to hide.

14

Tom's Return

Tom felt quite sad to leave the home of Japhet Miller and his wife. In a very short time he had come to admire this man as much as he had admired Peter Hayes. Japhet had clarified to Tom the messages Peter Hayes had tried to convey. These were the abolition of narrow-minded faith, and freedom for all men and women to think as they pleased rather than as the law of the land instructed them to.

Feeling that he now knew where he belonged, Tom began his journey home to Kate. He did not know what lay in store for him in the future but he did know that if Kate still loved him he would not have a care in the world.

He was soon across the border and carried on swinging across the heath to Rochester. Just outside the city gates, the body of a man swung from the gibbet. The sight of this carcase swinging slowly in the wind reminded Tom that he had to take great care. He hoped that by now the King's men thought him dead.

Deciding to avoid the town, he struck off alongside the great wall towards the marsh and home. It was a long way round but in spite of his years away Tom could recall every twist and turn in the path that led to the village of Clyve. It was beginning to get dark and over the flat land a white mist was rising, hiding the moor hens in the reeds and giving off an eery light.

Kate had laid low all day. She thought it would be safer to leave when it was dark. Now she made her way to the town. She was miserable. Her face throbbed where she had been cut. She was exhausted and her spirits were very low.

The light was bad now and Kate felt quite spooked. Along the path, she suddenly heard footsteps. She was terrified, her heart fluttering like that of an animal in a trap. Crouching down by the side of the road, she peered out through the long grass. Through the mist she could just make out a very tall man coming towards her. He had a long cloak and was walking in a weary fashion. She stared at him trying to hold her breath. Her heart was pounding in her chest. Who was it? Could it be Hugh coming back to hurt her? Surely not? Yet he looked strangely familiar. Kate was terrified.

The man came closer and closer. To her horror, he seemed to slow as he neared her. He seemed alert to any danger and detected movements in the grass. Then the man stopped.

'Who's there?' he called. This was the moment of truth for Kate. The voice was unmistakable! Kate could hardly believe it, but she leaped to her feet and dashed from the grass.

'My darling, my Tom! You've come back!' she cried. Tom grabbed her in his arms and swept her up. The next moment he was smothering her with kisses.

Kate felt faint with joy. This was the exquisite moment of reunion that she had dreamed of so often over the last few years, until she had believed he was dead and given up hope of it.

Once their passionate kissing had stopped, they walked on together hand in hand and made their way to the fisherman's cottage they had both left almost three years before.

Tom was smiling broadly. He was delighted to have found his darling again. She looked exactly the same, dark with her blue eyes and long black hair. He did not notice how dishevelled her gown was, or even the gash on her cheek or the tears mixed with the mud on her face. He had feared the worst but he had found his love waiting for him.

The little cottage was looking somewhat neglected and battered by winter storms. But it was still standing, waiting for them. Tom kicked open the door and led Kate inside. He swept the sand up from the floor and wiped the dust away from the bed. He then gently laid Kate upon his bed, which he had slept on as a boy.

Kate held out her arms to him as Tom sank on top of her with a gentle moan. The outside world was lost to them as they moved as one in time with the lapping of the waves on the shore.

A rosy down crept over the sea to find Kate and Tom still sleeping like two tired children in a locked embrace. As the sun warmed his face, Tom awoke. He gently extricated himself from Kate's arms and swung his long legs over the side of the bed. Kate slept on. Tom tenderly covered her with a sheepskin. Then he went down to the beach and collected some driftwood for a fire. Ten minutes later he had a fire going in the grate. The cottage was coming back to life, and Tom was beginning to feel complete again. It would not take him long to get the place ship-shape now.

Kate was still sleeping when Tom set off across the fields to the nearest farm for eggs and milk. The farm was just a small one with only a few cows and goats, and a flock of hens. It belonged to the Filmer family. Danny Filmer had been a childhood friend of Tom's. Together as boys they had dug for lug worms and fished off the shore. They had remained friends as adults. Tom wondered how he was.

As Tom approached, two dogs came tearing up to him, barking loudly. At the sound of their barks, a young man appeared from behind the barn. He stared at Tom and then gave a shout. The two men ran towards each other and put their arms out to embrace. Their strong hug was one of a longstanding friend- ship. Danny drew Tom towards the house. 'Mary,' he called. 'Come out and see who's here.'

Turning to Tom, he said, 'We had given you up for dead.'

Mary soon emerged from the house. She had been a shy young milkmaid when Tom had left. Now she had a child hanging onto her skirt and was clearly expecting another. She looked delighted to see their longlost neighbour.

'Welcome back, Tom,' she said with a smile on her pretty face. 'It's wonderful to see you again.'

'How's life been treating you?' asked Tom, as they settled on the wall outside the house.

'Well,' replied Danny, 'my father died last year, so now the house and farm are mine. And I leased some land from the church.' He pointed to the freshly planted fields.

'That's fine, Danny,' cried Tom. 'What more could a man ask than a bonny family and his own piece of land to work?'

'Except that it belongs to the church, Tom,' said Danny, with a frown. 'I practically had to go down on my hands and knees to the Bishop to get him to lease it to me.'

'But that marsh is free grazing land,' said Tom with a puzzled look on his face. 'All our lives we ran free on this land.'

'I know,' replied Danny, 'but that was before the church had it fenced off. Now we have to pay to use it.'

Tom shook his head sorrowfully. 'That does not seem just,' he murmured.

'Quite,' replied Danny, shaking his head. 'Times are very hard now. What with these taxes and tithes, it's very hard to produce enough for a family to live on.'

Danny jumped down from the wall. 'But that's enough of our troubles. Come inside and have something to eat with us. It is good to see you.' He held out his arm in a gesture of welcome.

But Tom was now feeling furious. 'Why should a man work himself to death to keep those pot-bellied old priests wealthy?' he burst out.

'Ssh, Tom,' whispered Danny, 'you never know who may be listening.'

Mary had prepared a meal and they sat down to enjoy their food.

Just before Tom left with milk and eggs, Dan said: 'Are you married yet, Tom?'

Tom smiled. 'Not yet,' he said quietly. 'But I may be before long.'

When he returned to the cottage, Kate was still sleeping. Tom cooked her breakfast and the smell of eggs woke her. Kate sat up in bed and at first looked around with a disgruntled expression. Then she saw Tom. She leaped naked from the bed and threw herself at him.

After they had kissed again, Kate slipped on her dress – the only garment she had now – and ate her food. Afterwards, she warmed her toes by the fire and brushed and re-braided her long hair. She looked as happy as a contented pussy cat. But Tom thought something about her was different. Kate had changed. He realised that she now wanted to be fussed, while the Kate of old would just as likely have given a kick as a kiss.

As he watched her doing her hair, Tom pondered on this. It slowly dawned on him that the reason she was now like this was that she was now used to being made love to. He felt very sad at this realisation, but at the same time thought that it would be unfair to pry. After all, he had been away for a long time. A phrase from the Bible sprang to mind: 'Let him who is pure among you cast the first stone.' No, he decided, he did not want to know. They were together again, and that was all that mattered.

After Kate had cleared up the meal, Tom suggested that they go fishing to catch something for dinner. Although Tom no longer had a boat, he still had his nets. He spread his nets out in the tide, while Kate tucked up the long skirts of her dress and ran about collecting mussels. These she laid out on the sand.

After a while, Tom noticed that she was sitting down and looking somewhat disconsolate. He sat beside her and pulled her to him.

'What's the matter with you, Kate darling?' he asked. 'You loved me well enough last night.'

Kate cuddled up. 'Oh, Tom,' she wailed. 'I love you deeply, but there are things I should tell you—'

But Tom cut her short by putting his fingers on her lips. 'Hush, darling,' he whispered. 'As far as I am concerned, our lives together began last night. I want you, and I need you so badly that nothing you tell me could change that. It's always been you and it always will be for me.' He clasped her to him in a passionate embrace.

Kate went to him with all the love and passion she had within her and together they made love on the sand.

Later, when they were spent, they gathered in the nets and collected their haul. Then they cooked their catch over an open fire on the beach. Peace and contentment surrounded them. 'We shall go and see Father Peter tomorrow,' said Tom, 'and see about getting married.'

Kate looked concerned for a moment. She could visualise the piercing gimlet eyes of the old priest.

Seeing her hesitate, Tom squeezed her hand reassuringly. 'Kate, my love,' he said, 'I feel as you do about these old priests, but if we want to marry there's nothing else we can do.' He then showed her his little Bible and told her how things might be better and fairer one day.

'But, Tom,' Kate cried, 'if you are found with this Bible on you, you will be accused of being a heretic.'

'No,' he replied. 'Educated men are now reading this Bible. It's not just for the priests any more.'

But Kate was not reassured. She was afraid that they would be captured and sent to prison. Some heretics were even burned, she had heard.

'All right,' said Tom, placing his Bible back in his pocket. 'Tomorrow we'll go and see the priest.'

The next day they made their way to the priest's house. The huge iron knocker echoed through the place when they lifted and dropped it. The door was opened by a young man in a cassock who asked their business. Then he told them that Father Peter was not able to see them as he had been taken ill and had gone to the monastery with his servant, Jacob.

Kate breathed a sigh of relief. The young man knew nothing about her. And what was even better was that her father had gone too, so she would not have to face his accusing stare either. Her father's eyes were even more accusing than those of Father Peter.

Tom was quiet and seemed a little surly. He was surprised by how Kate suddenly relaxed and chatted to the young priest quite happily. The priest explained that the banns would have to be called for the next three weeks and they would be expected to attend the services. He was only there temporarily, until Father Peter returned.

Kate looked very happy on the journey home, but Tom continued to be quiet and withdrawn, thinking about how the religious freedom he had learned from Peter Hayes was in jeopardy.

While Tom was thinking along these melancholy lines, Kate was thinking about the lovely white wedding gown which was still at the castle, and all the beautiful linen she and Lady Evelyn had worked at for so long. Dare she mention the Hope Chest to Tom?

15

The Hope Chest

Kate squatted before the fire stirring a steaming pot. Tom had gone to the farm for milk and eggs, and she had been left to prepare the meal. She stared gloomily around at the shabby dwelling. It had been built by Tom's father some fifty years before. It had rough stone walls and simple basic furniture. It suddenly seemed very depressing to her. Her thoughts drifted to images of all the lovely things Lady Evelyn had had at the castle, and her mind settled once again on the Hope Chest. How those grand possessions would brighten up this place! Now her mind was made up. When Tom came back she would ask him if it were possible to get the chest.

Through the little window, Kate could see Tom coming home. How handsome he looked, she thought. After just two weeks at home, all traces of his weary journey had disappeared. Kate sighed; the thought just would not go away. She did not want to upset him but she desperately wanted that Hope Chest.

Tom strode through the door confidently and placed a jar of pickles on the table. It was a present from Mary.

'Mary would like to come over to see you, Kate,' he

said, 'but she's very heavy with child at the moment. I told her you would go to visit her.'

Kate sniffed angrily. 'How can I go looking like this?' she snapped. 'I look like a beggar in this old dress.' Then she burst into a fit of tears.

Tom held her close and stroked her hair. 'There now, my lovely,' he said soothingly. 'I didn't dream that you were so unhappy. Tomorrow I'll get a job in the fields and will buy you a new dress.'

Kate stopped sobbing and looked up coyly at him. 'There's no need for that, Tom,' she said. 'I have plenty of clothes up at the castle.'

At this, Tom drew away from her stiffly. 'If there's anything of yours at that castle, that's where it will stay. That life is over. You must cut yourself off from those people forever.'

'But Tom,' Kate protested. 'All the clothes and linen are mine. Lady Evelyn gave them to me. And there's a beautiful white wedding gown which we made, ready for the day when you would return and we would marry.'

But Tom would not listen. He marched out of the cottage and angrily slammed the door.

Kate watched him stride to the seashore where he stood for a long time gazing across the water. No, she could tell that he was not to be swayed on this issue. She decided that she had better not mention the castle again.

The next morning, Tom said: 'I'd like you to go and stay with the Filmers until we are married.'

Kate looked horrified. 'Whatever for?' she cried.

'Now that the priest knows of our plans,' replied Tom, 'he may come down here to see us and nose about.'

'Fiddle, faddle!' retorted Kate with a sneer.

'Look, Kate,' said Tom softly. 'It's only our good name I'm thinking of. We are going to settle down here to live. And village gossips have long memories. I have great plans for us, Kate. We'll have a son and a beautiful daughter.'

Kate's eyes suddenly glazed over in a dreamy expression. 'I once had a son,' she said wistfully.

Tom stared at her and looked puzzled. 'Don't be silly, Kate. What are you talking about?'

Kate said no more on the subject and she gave in to Tom's pressure. It was agreed that she would go to stay at the farm until the wedding, and the next day Tom would go to Allhallows, to John Little's brother, to get a job.

Mary made Kate very welcome, but the girl turned out to be of little help to her around the house, choosing instead to play most of the day with her young daughter.

When Kate went to church to fulfil her obligation to attend each day until her wedding, Mary and Danny discussed her. 'Tom hasn't much of a bargain there,' said Mary. 'She's very pretty, but a little simple, I think.'

'She always was, right from a child,' agreed her husband. 'And I don't suppose living up at the castle helped.'

'I just hope that Tom doesn't regret his decision,' said Mary.

'Oh, I'm sure he won't,' replied Danny. 'Tom always does the right thing.'

Meanwhile, at the church the rest of the congregation had left but Kate stayed to look around. She had always enjoyed the peace in the church, and she loved the bright frescoes on the walls where the Martyrdom of St Edmund was depicted. Now she knelt before a statue of the Virgin which was surrounded by candles and bright flowers.

Slowly she felt overwhelmed by the atmosphere. She sank back on her heels and started to cry. As she cried she began to pray to the Virgin. 'Please, Holy Mother, let me be married in my beautiful white gown. I promise to be good and never sin again.'

The young priest had been waiting to speak to her at the back of the church. Watching her kneeling before the statue, he could see the anguish on her face.

'You seem very distressed, my dear,' he said gently, as Kate finished her prayer and got back on her feet. 'Can I help you at all?'

He was a very sympathetic man, so Kate told him of her Hope Chest and the many hours spent preparing it. She said she could not go back to the castle as she had been a servant there and fallen sick. Now the soldiers at the gate would not let her in again. She told him that George was the only one who knew where the chest was.

The priest listened to her tale of woe with patience. Finally he nodded. 'I'll see what I can do to retrieve it for you,' he said.

'Thank you, Father,' said Kate with a curtsy. 'I'm very grateful for your kindness.'

The next day old George appeared driving a donkey cart along the road from Clyve. He stopped to unload the cargo at the Filmers' farm. It was a heavy carved oak chest and an oak chair which had been left with old George, a present from her father. It was her mother's old chair. Now the sight of it brought tears to Kate's eyes. She positively bloomed with happiness when she opened the chest, for there was all the linen for her bottom drawer!

'Oh, George!' she exclaimed. 'You did it, you got it all for me!' She flung her arms around the old man's neck and hugged him.

'I would not have faced those ruffians for anyone but you,' muttered George gruffly. But he looked pleased by her appreciative response.

Mary Filmer admired all Kate's linen, and from then on Kate worked hard in the house from dawn to dusk. It was as though she had been given new heart.

While Kate was gloating over her trousseau, Tom's long legs were carrying him across the fields to Allhallows, fifteen miles away. It was early morning and dew still lay fresh on the meadows.

As he strode along, he took great gulps of the clean salty air. There was nothing like Kent on a fine early morning, he thought, looking at the tall golden ears of ripe corn, the apple-laden trees in the orchards. How fine, he thought, to be a landowner and come up over this ridge every morning, and be lord of all you surveyed. But men would not be slaves forever, maybe the day would come – who knows.

Richard Little lived in a large farm overlooking the saltings, the small backwater that ran in from the sea. Richard was very different from his benevolent brother John. He was well-dressed and confident, but quite reserved.

Tom followed him into the front room of the house which overlooked the river. From the window Richard could keep an eye on the comings and goings of all the ships that passed. He read his brother's letter without comment. Then he looked up. 'So, you've finished with the sea,' he said, 'and want to work ashore.'

'Yes,' replied Tom with a nod, 'and I'm getting married soon.'

'Very commendable,' Richard said, looking Tom up and down. 'You look like a trustworthy sort of man,' he said. 'I'm not as philanthropic as my brother, I'll tell you that. I'm a born farmer but I'm in shipping for profit. Not many settle in these wild parts and labour is always hard to get. I usually send to town for labour when I need men.'

'Slave gangs,' muttered Tom without thinking. Then he bit his lip. He needed this work, so he had better not say too much.

'Call it what you like,' Richard said. 'I do not like exploiting poverty any more than my brother does. That is why I need a good overseer. I've several herds of sheep and cattle to care for, and judging by this letter my brother seems to think that you may be the right man for the job.'

Tom stood quite respectfully listening to the farmer as he continued. 'I want the labour gangs supervised properly. And I want no more children dropping dead on my land. If you want the job, I'll pay you well, and you shall have a cottage on the marsh.'

Tom was overjoyed by this news. Richard was clearly a humane man. It would be possible to work for him. And he was offering a cottage for him and Kate. It seemed too good to be true.

He bowed his head respectfully. 'I'm most grateful, sir, and will serve you well.'

'One final thing,' said Richard. 'I understand that you share our religious beliefs. I hope you know that there is always an element of danger.'

Tom nodded. 'Of course,' he said. 'But I believe passionately too.'

'Right,' said Richard, 'now we know where we stand. Serve me well and you'll not regret it.'

On Tom's journey home he thought about how much his luck had changed since he had met old Peter Hayes. Perhaps the man had been a saint. And the prospect of settling a score with the rogues who sent young children to work in the fields from dawn till dusk gave him great pleasure.

16

The Wedding

The wedding of Kate to Tom the fisherman was the talk of Clyve village for many a day. It was a great occasion. A line of young maids walked behind dressed in pretty flowered dresses and carrying sweet scented posies, while the bride herself looked magnificent in a pure white gown.

Tom had not liked the idea of the reclaimed Hope Chest very much but Kate had whined and wheedled her way round him to get him to accept it.

Their new cottage on the marsh soon looked very smart with the embroidered chair covers, curtains and bedspreads. There was no denying how pretty it looked, so Tom finally had to give in to her.

The children decorated the Filmers' barn with flowers for the celebration. A barrel of ale was presented by the local inn. The village fiddler played and the Morris dancers danced all afternoon. There was plenty to eat and drink, and the wining and dancing went on well into the night. Everyone from Clyve Shore was there. Tom was a popular fellow and everyone was happy to see him happy with his bride.

The two love birds settled in to their cosy home on the wild marsh. Old George gave Kate some ducks and chickens to tend, while each day Tom rode his new bay mare across the marsh to keep an eye on the land of his benefactor.

Matters were much fairer now. The workers had their money divided equally between them, instead of it going into the pockets of the rogues who had marched them from the towns. Women were allowed to rest in the shade at certain times of the day, and the children were well-fed and not allowed to work too many hours.

Tom made many friends but also a few enemies, pious men and women who mischievously whispered tales to the priest. But none of these bothered the happy couple. Tom cared for nothing but Katy, and she, rather houseproud and bossy, loved her Tom as dearly as ever. She kept some sheep and began to spin their wool and then weave fine cloth to make clothes for herself and Tom. She became very skilled.

The days and months passed. By the time Kate was with child, two years had gone by. But Kate was as fresh and lovely as ever, if a little bit plumper. Life could not be better, she often thought now.

One day when Tom was working and Kate sat weaving at her loom, she heard the sound of a horse galloping up to the cottage. Putting down the shuttle on the warp, she went to see who it was.

Outside she saw a large man dismounting from a sweaty horse. He had bright red hair and looked vaguely familiar. As he turned to walk to the cottage, Kate felt very alarmed. Something about the man reminded her of something long ago.

'Good morning,' he called. 'I am sent by Lady Evelyn Mortimer.'

'Lady Evelyn!' Kate was astonished. 'Now I know who you are.'

The man nodded. 'That's right, ma'am,' he said. 'James McManus. I've come on a mission all the way from Scotland and Lady Evelyn asked me to find you and tell you that she is well and that her son Robert is thriving.'

Kate invited the giant Scot inside her cottage. She gave him a refreshing tankard of elderflower wine which he drank while he told her all the news from the north.

He said that Lady Evelyn was well but that her brother Angus had died in the bloody battle of Flodden, where many brave Scottish men had fallen, including Donald Fraser, Lady Evelyn's companion, and King James of Scotland himself.

'Lady Evelyn was devastated,' Jamie said. 'She threw herself into good works, helping the distraught wives and orphans of those men who died. But she was a broken woman. She has recovered somewhat but is still a little low. With Donald and her brother gone, she feels very alone and harks back to when her betrothed Robert was alive. She told me that it would mean everything to her if she could have back in her possession a brooch which Robert once gave her. She left it behind in the rush when she escaped from the castle to go north.'

Jamie paused. 'I thought that you might know about it, since you remained behind. I have prayed all the way down from Scotland that you would be able to lead me to the brooch, or perhaps let me know of its whereabouts . . .'

Kate got to her feet. 'It gives me much pleasure to be able to help you, sir,' she said gently. She disappeared into the corner and rummaged around in the chest. Then she came back and handed Jamie the exquisite pearl brooch. 'I have kept it for her, sir. It was one of the few items I took from the castle when I escaped. I knew then that it was very precious to Her Ladyship. That's why I have kept it safe.'

Jamie laughed. 'What a relief!' he exclaimed. 'I need go no further. I was all prepared to march up to the castle and challenge that rogue Hugh Mortimer.'

Kate smiled. 'Hugh Mortimer is universally hated around here,' she said. 'Or at least so my husband says. Lord Mortimer has been appointed one of King Henry's commissioners and amuses himself by collecting the taxes with terrible violence. My husband says that the people are going to rebel against the taxes like never before if Lord Mortimer is not careful.'

Jamie got to his feet and tucked the brooch into his leather jerkin. 'Well, I had better be getting back to Scotland now that my mission is over. Thanks to you, it has been easy to serve my Lady Evelyn.

'By the way, Her Ladyship sends word to you to say that she hopes you will come and visit one day. She is very fond of you, you know.'

Glancing down at her belly, Kate blushed. 'Thank you, sir,' she said. 'Perhaps when my child is a certain age we will be able to travel to see you all in

Scotland. And I should like to see Robert again,' she added quietly.

Jamie smiled. 'Oh, he's a fine laddie. He's a keen shot and a fine horseman. He'll be a match for the English one day.'

'Oh, perhaps there'll never be a need for him to fight,' said Kate, surprised by how much she suddenly cared about Robert's welfare.

Watching Jamie ride away, Kate felt quite strange. Jamie's unexpected visit had stirred up all sorts of feelings within her that had lain dormant for years. And Robert, *her* son. The baby within her made her now acknowledge that she *was* Robert's mother, even if she never allowed herself to be so in the past. Yes, she would go and visit Lady Evelyn one day, and meet her fine strapping son Robert . . .

Outside Kate's small domestic world, there were stirrings in the air. Much of the old common land around the village was being taken over by the church, which exerted its power over the ordinary people in a bullying fashion. At harvest time the church sent men to collect the tithes to maintain the church, in all its glory – or, more likely – to keep up the extravagant lifestyles of the men of the church. Far from being devout men of prayer, they wined and dined to excess, and certainly did not observe their vows of chastity, even in the monasteries. In the meantime, there was also growing discontent with the Roman church and the Pope himself. The King wanted to get rid of his Spanish wife, and was battling with the church to do so. But the

King, too, was taxing the people to pay for his own extravagance and wars.

The young priest who had helped Kate had recently been replaced by another priest who was very unpopular with the villagers.

There was a great deal of trouble in Clyve that autumn concerning the tithes. Men sent to collect the tithes were beaten up by the farmers and when the sheriff came to arrest them, they had mysteriously disappeared. These people used Tom's old shack and barn to hide until Tom rowed them out into the Channel to board one of Richard Little's ships. They they set sail for the Netherlands where they were free from persecution.

In spite of the beatings meted out to them, these were kind, gentle people, who called each other brother and sister. They hated the Church of Rome and were happy to escape to a new land where they could worship as they pleased.

Kate knew of Tom's work and the meetings he held in the black barn but she did not involve herself in it. She was too busy awaiting the birth of her child. She continued to weave fine cloth and look after her animals and tend her vegetables. Tom approved of this. He did not want Kate involved in his dangerous work.

November came, and the coast was buffeted with wild storms. Some of the dykes collapsed and water flooded part of the land.

Kate was throwing grain to her chickens in the blustery wind when in the distance she heard the sound of horses' hooves. She stood listening as they came nearer, and soon she could see that they were made by soldiers. Now she could hear the clinking of their armour. What on earth would bring soldiers to Clyve? But to her horror and amazement, they turned towards the cottage. Three knights rode up the path towards her.

Kate was terrified. She shrank away and gasped when she saw the leading knight was none other than Hugh Mortimer. Why was he here? Had he come to persecute her?

Hugh Mortimer laughed loudly at the sight of her. 'Well, well, if it isn't my lovely Kate,' he said with a sneer.

Dismounting, he walked towards her, his armour clanking as he moved. Lifting his sword, he placed its tip on her stomach. 'And whose little bastard have we here?'

Kate shrank to the ground in terror but said nothing. 'Now, where's that heretic husband of yours?' Hugh demanded menacingly.

'He's not here,' stammered Kate. Her heart leapt in her chest. Oh no, Tom's activities had been found out.

Hugh Mortimer ignored her. Gesturing to his men, he ordered them to search the cottage.

Kate started to cry as she heard the two men crashing around the house, smashing her precious furniture as they threw it about in their search for Tom. She was still weeping when they finally came out.

'He's not in there, my lord,' said one.

Hugh shrugged. 'Never mind,' he said. 'Then I

don't doubt we'll find him in the tavern.' With a mocking salute to Kate, the men rode off.

After a while, Kate picked herself up off the ground. The cold wind howled around her. She had to think fast. Of course Tom would not be at the tavern. He was hardly a drinking man. No, he was probably at the black barn giving a Bible reading. While Hugh Mortimer and his men were looking in the tavern, with any luck they would also stop to refresh themselves as well. So she might have a bit of time yet. She had to get to Tom and warn him of the danger he was in. If they caught him they would certainly burn him as a heretic and rabble rouser.

Kate began to run across the muddy marsh. In her panic, she stumbled and often fell. In many places she had to wade through freezing black water, and crash through the sharp reeds which whipped her bare legs. The child inside her weighed her down but she struggled on, panting and gasping. The wind blew hard against her face as the skies darkened. Thick grey clouds were gathering above her and soon blinding rain started to fall.

Kate was hardly aware of the elements. The one thought in her mind was to reach Tom and warn him. She struggled blindly on, gasping for breath and strength. Then, stumbling on a mound of peat, she lost her footing and fell.

In the village, the men were gathering up every pitchfork and shovel they could muster. Lord Mortimer, now a favourite in the King's court, was coming to collect the King's taxes, they heard. They were sick of paying out what little they had to finance the King's wars and high living. No, this time, they would resist in every way they could.

Thus, as the storm clouds gathered over the sea, these darker ones gathered in the village. No, the villagers had had enough. The Lord of the manor was not going to have it all his own way. Everyone was gathering at the Filmers' farm. These men were ready to fight to be free of the tyranny of taxes.

Since Hugh Mortimer had also taken it upon himself to root out the heretics of the church as well as collect taxes for King Henry, he was facing an angry and combined opposition. The villagers were united, whatever their faith and now they were all ready to fight the common enemy.

Meanwhile, Kate had been right about Hugh Mortimer and his men. Having reached the tavern, they did stay to drink their fill for a while. When they had finished, they looted the bar.

This fortuitous delay had given many village families time to make their way to the black barn and comparative safety. And now, in the narrowest part of the road, Tom and his followers waited. A trip rope had been set across the road, and on each side of the hill were parties of poorly armed but brave men. Armed with his sturdy sailor's knife, Tom crouched with them. Earlier, when he knew that the trouble was starting, he sent a lad in a wagon to pick up Kate and Mary Filmer and her children, and then bring them to the barn. They would be safer here than at home.

Now, like his men, Tom pulled his jerkin tighter round his chest and pulled his cap down over his ears as the wind grew stronger. Tom looked up at the sky with a worried expression. Where was Katy? Now the temperature was dropping further.

Hugh Mortimer and his men left the inn, shouting and swearing. They carried lighted torches through the village, ready to ride out and hunt down their quarries. The rain had ceased now but the wind was howling as loud as ever. As they passed a small cottage, one of his drunken men threw a flaming torch at the thatched roof. It blazed up immediately with a roar. Then they galloped on towards the narrow neck of the road.

The first horse and rider came down with a crash as the horse's legs got tangled in the trip. His mount grunted with fright as it struggled to get up off its back. Those riding behind tumbled down on top and fell too.

Taking advantage of the confusion among Hugh Mortimer's followers the men from the bushes leapt out. These hard, embittered men fought desperately with their feeble weapons. God was with them, and their weapons seemed to find the right spots.

Tom emerged from the bushes and strode boldly into the road. Singling out Lord Mortimer, he grabbed him by the shoulder and sank his sailor's knife deep into an unprotected part of his neck. Hugh Mortimer sank to the ground without a murmur.

The battle did not last long. Once they had seen that their leader was dead, those who were still standing jumped onto their horses and fled in panic back to the protection of the castle.

As Tom and the villagers began to attend to their wounded, someone noticed the ominous orange flames coming from the direction of the village.

'Our homes!' he shouted. 'They're on fire!'

They all ran to the village in the hope of saving their homes, but it was no use. The pitch that tarred the cottages fed the flames and in no time every cottage was ablaze. The storm-driven wind whipped the flames into a roaring fury and soon the inn and the shops and even the surrounding cornfields were ablaze. Some villagers fled to the church which by now was also ringed with the lapping flames. The heat was so intense that the stone walls were cracking. Inside it felt like an oven.

Tom and the others worked all night long to try to put out the fire and save what they could. By the morning, a very weary band of men made its way back across the marsh. Black soot covered their grey, exhausted faces. The wind had dropped by now but it remained bitterly cold and misty. A heavy pall of smoke hung low over the village.

The men and women trudged along carrying the few possessions they had been able to save, and leading their children by the hand. They had lost almost everything. There was nothing left of Clyve village. Only a charred church with cracked walls was left standing.

The procession of villagers walked slowly back to the black barn where some of the older women and young children had remained hidden. The storm had ripped off part of the roof and the sand had been driven in. To stay dry they had climbed up to the hay loft and nestled down there in the warm hay. They had passed the time by listening to Mary Filmer reading stories from the Bible, trying not to think of their menfolk and fathers out there in the storm fighting that raging inferno.

Now the men had started to arrive back. They were worn out and covered with soot and grime. Tom was looking round anxiously for Kate. He wore no shirt and his body was caked with sweat and blood. His eyes looked panicked as they scanned the crowd of people milling about.

At last he found Mary and hurried to her. 'Where's Kate? Is she not with you?' he asked anxiously.

'Oh, Tom,' Mary replied. 'No, she's not here. I was hoping that she was with you.'

'I thought she would be coming with you, in the wagon I sent,' said Tom. 'I've been trying to convince myself all night that she was safe. But where can she be?'

'Well, she wasn't at the cottage when we called,' said Mary. 'We've waited all night but she hasn't joined us.'

Tom turned to his tired, dispirited men. 'Kate's missing,' he said. 'Who will come and help me search? She probably went out looking for me to warn me.'

Without hesitation, the men got to their feet and prepared to help a frantic Tom search the marsh for his beloved Kate.

17

A Cradle of Oak Leaves

Kate, in fact, had fallen not very far from the black barn. Exhausted and stunned she had lain there for a long while. She could not move, could not drag herself out from the wet mire.

'Please, God,' she prayed, 'give me the strength to get there in time to warn Tom.'

After a while, she tried to get up but a great pain gripped her. It felt like a tight girdle around her belly. 'Oh Lord, it's the baby,' she moaned. 'But I must go on.'

It was now very dark. Kate struggled on, crawling on her knees through the thick muddy ground. Every now and then, as the pains came, she screamed. But the fierce wind carried the sounds away into the night so no one heard.

She still had the widest dyke to cross. When she got there, it was flooded. She could not stop now. Forcing her legs to move, she clambered into the cold, brackish water. She tried to swim but the weight of her clothes dragged her down. Trying hard not to panic, she waved her arms about and managed to catch hold of a branch of an old oak tree which leaned low over the water. Clutching it in desperation, Kate tried to pull herself out of the water. The pains were getting stronger all the time. 'Oh, Tom, Tom, where are you?' she called many times on that stormy night.

With one last supreme effort she held on. The storm howled and the old tree bent over in protest. Slowly, at last Kate pulled herself out of the cold dark water. The pains were intolerable and she had no strength left. She lay gasping like a fish on the muddy bank.

Suddenly she felt a strange sensation between her legs and she let out a final scream of agony. Then she felt something slip from her. Lifting her head, she saw in the darkness the little body of her newborn child floating off with the outgoing tide.

'Oh, please, Lord, don't let me lose this baby as well,' she cried. 'Not this baby as well . . .'

Somehow, the child had fallen onto the branch Kate had been hanging on to. The branch was spread out like a fan, creating a cradle of oak leaves. The baby was alive. It wailed and kicked in the centre of this nest.

As she watched her baby floating away, Kate suddenly heard a terrible cracking sound as the old oak tree gave up, keeled over and crashed down towards her. Kate did not have a chance. Her spirit soared up over the marsh to join that of her ancestors.

Walking across the marsh in the cold dawn Tom was still calling for his wife. 'Katy, my love, where are you? Please answer me.' He had covered ten miles of marshland before he found her, though her body was a mere mile away from the black barn and the safety she had sought.

Many good strong men wept as Tom uncovered Kate's battered body. He tenderly picked her up and carried her back to the barn. There, the women who were tending to her body asked each other in whispers: 'Whatever had happened to the baby?'

'It could not possibly have lived. It must have been carried out on the tide.'

None of this was said to the distressed husband, nor did he ask. Their own husbands went back to the big dyke where they had found Kate and searched the area thoroughly but there was nothing to be seen. The baby had vanished for sure. Back at the barn, Tom just sat and wept.

Just off the Kent coast that same dark stormy night was anchored a long boat. It was the usual custom of these longboats to stay anchored until the Thames barge skippers collected the cargo and took them downriver. But this was such a very wild night and Skipper Herr Jaeger had anchored in at Clyve Shore to shelter from the storm. With him was his sturdy wife, who always sailed with him. As the tide turned and the storm abated, Frau Jaeger made her way to the wheelhouse with hot broth for her husband. 'Well, my dear,' said Herr Jaeger, 'the storm is over now. It looks like a clear day ahead of us.'

He looked towards the shore where clouds of smoke still drifted out to sea. 'Something bad happened out there last night. I could hear cries and screams above the storm.' He puffed at his pipe, his keen eye sweeping the shore. 'I think it's time we pulled anchor,' he continued. 'These are troubled times and we don't want to get involved.'

As he glanced at his wife, he saw that she was pointing at something across the water.

'What's that?' she asked. She had seen something small and white floating rapidly down on the shallow streams and rivulets of water emptying into the sea. As the object floated nearer, she saw to her astonishment that it was a baby laid on a fanshaped branch of an oak tree. 'My God,' she cried. 'It's a child!' With hardly any hesitation, she stripped off her skirts and petticoats and plunged over the side of the boat into the sea. Swimming with strong strokes, she reached the child within seconds. She grabbed the naked infant from its cradle of oak leaves, and turned back to the long boat. With her husband's assistance, she clambered back on board with the baby. Holding it upside down, she slapped the baby's back to drive the water from its lungs.

Within moments it spluttered and cried. The excited Jaegers soon had the child in the warmth of their cabin wrapped up in warm clothes.

Examining the child, Frau Jaeger had discovered that the umbilical cord was still attached. 'My God,' she said, staring back at the shore, 'what terrible tragedy has happened there?'

'We cannot take the child back,' replied her husband, pulling anchor. 'There's too much trouble there already. I can't risk losing the cargo.'

And so Kate's baby girl was taken to a foreign land and brought up on a little island off the coast of the

Netherlands. She grew up into a beautiful girl whom they called Nielte, a lovely raven-haired, blue-eyed child who was popular with a host of blond cousins.

Kate was buried in a small corner of Clyve church-yard. There was no priest available, for he had fled from the fire. Richard Little had ridden over with help for the stricken families, and it was he who read the burial service.

After the service, Tom sat for several hours leaning thoughtfully against the cracked wall of the church. As he sat and thought, he carved a bust of Katy. It was almost an exact replica of her with its wide full mouth, heart-shaped face and long mane of hair, tight under a little cap. When finished, he placed it gently on the newly turned earth. 'That's all I have to give you, Katy, but my heart is with it,' he murmured.

Then he got up and quickly left the churchyard to join his band of followers who waited for him down the road. They slowly made their way to the next village.

In the weeks to come, they built a small meeting house there, and in time Tom gained great fame as a preacher. Within a few years, the King had broken away from the Pope and the Church of Rome. This act, devastating though it was on the churches and the lives of the so-called men of the church, allowed Tom and his followers a few years of peace to worship as they pleased. Tom eventually married a niece of Richard Little and had many children. But he never forgot his little Kate and their child who was lost. He and his followers built a small community which sailed for the New World in the time of Mary Tudor, when their persecution began again. The ashes of the village of Clyve were blown across the marsh and all was silent.

One day Kate's brother Nicholas returned to Clyve as the priest. He enjoyed a meteoric rise in the church and finally became Bishop of Rochester. He exhumed his parents' bodies and had them buried again in front of the altar in Rochester, enclosing their graves with elaborate brasses. They are there to this day. But all that is left in the memory of Kate is the simple carved bust. It sits on a windowsill inside the cathedral and no one knows who placed it there.

And a few years later, a beautiful, elegant, white-haired lady, with a pearl brooch pinned on her gown, rode down from Scotland with her handsome and gallant son. His name was Robert Mortimer and he had come with pride to claim his right to be Lord of Clyve Castle.

TWO SWALLOWS

Two Swallows

I have always been fond of the Kent Marshes, where old Father Thames runs down to the sea. Around the river the land twists and bends, dwindling down to a narrow peninsula where the Thames and the River Medway run almost side by side, as if racing anxiously to reach the sea before the other.

Only a five-mile strip of marshland divides them. It is very desolate and windy down there, with nothing to encourage visitors, unless, of course, they are interested in the wildlife that is so abundant in the hedges, and the tall reeds and flowers that grow around the dykes.

In springtime, this whole area is alive with the noisy thin cries of the gulls and the low cackling of the Canada geese that migrate here from northern shores. These nest out in the shallows and the air is heavy with their mating calls.

But below the bird cries, there remains an atmosphere of tranquillity and peace. The little moorhen floats along water in the dykes, the bright blue kingfisher builds a nest and darts from bank to bank. And the young bullocks, happily unaware of their destiny, chase each other over the emerald-green marshland, and disturb the frogs croaking in the mud.

For many years I have spent my holidays

bird-watching, and roaming around on the green shores where nature continues to breed quite oblivious of the rapidly changing world.

There is a little village tucked away down there, old and picturesque. It has barely changed in two or three hundred years. It is more of a hamlet, really, made up of a pub and several thatched cottages built in the days when pirates and smugglers regularly used these quiet creeks and backwaters. Later, in relatively recent times, big convict ships used to lie out in the bay and wait for the high tide, before they set sail to take those poor devils out of sight of their native land across the world, to Australia.

On this particular summer evening I had just started on my usual walk after tea, when it began to rain. Having no raincoat, and remembering how wild a stormy night can be out there on the marsh, I decided to take shelter in the little village pub.

I knew it well, having enjoyed many a lunchtime pint in the public bar in between my bird-watching sessions. The landlord was new. Called the Red Dog, the pub was an old-fashioned place, situated at the end of the village, almost where the village meets the green marshland. It had old weather-beaten walls, a thatched roof and one extremely high brick chimney.

Just outside the door, in a cobbled courtyard, was an old oak bench, carved with the initials of many generations. Ah, there was so much history in that piece of furniture! It always fired my imagination whenever I passed it.

If you sat on this old bench and looked across the yard, you got a marvellous view of the village church with its square Norman tower and dog-tooth carving around the east door. The church was surrounded by an overgrown graveyard, and on the far side there was a low rambling brick wall which trailed down the hill towards the sea.

Inside the inn was also pleasant. The low ceilings and thick black beams made it very welcoming. The rain had now begun to teem down, so I was not sorry to sit in the bar nursing my drink.

The landlord was a chatty man, as country people often are with strangers or people they do not know well. I admired the brasses and horse harnesses hanging over the massive brick fireplace.

'That's quite a fireplace, too,' I added in a conversational sort of way.

'Been here a few years, that has,' said the landlord. 'You could roast a blooming ox on that, if you had a mind to.'

'It is very old,' I remarked. 'Is there a history to it, do you know?'

The landlord laughed and shrugged his shoulders as he wiped the counter clean. 'Well,' he replied, 'don't know about history, but we got a ghost in this pub.'

I smiled indulgently, causing the landlord to look very serious.

'No jokes, mate,' he said. 'This ghost ain't no trouble, though. You just see his face on the wall out there at full moon. And sometimes you hear him walking about outside, making a sort of tapping noise. I'm the fifth landlord they've had here in five years. Most folks don't like the idea at all, and run off at the first opportunity. But my missus, she believes in that sort of thing. She gets real chummy, she does, always saying she likes to see spirits and the like.'

I listened with interest. I am not a believer in the supernatural but there was a genuine sincerity about this man that made me ask if his wife would tell me more. And she did. A large, pretty woman, she came downstairs to tell me about her sightings of the ghost.

'He's an earth-bound spirit,' she said, 'and seems quite happy. Why should we disturb him? He's no bother.'

The woman's logic was impeccable. 'Quite, madam,' I said. There was indeed something about these accounts that fascinated me. I had a couple more glasses of that delicious strong Kentish cider and, since the rain had finally stopped, I decided to continue on my walk.

As I stepped out into the clear night air, I was feeling strangely excited. It could have been the potent cider or the effect of a fresh, salt breeze blowing in across the marshland. But I felt it was more. It was quite warm, and a cool mist was now rising, creeping slowly over the fields. It did seem quite eerie.

I stood breathing in the salty air, and all of a sudden the clouds parted, revealing a full silver moon hovering proudly above the horizon. Yes, the spirit of adventure was awake in me.

I walked down to the quiet shore to watch the moon as she floated over the sea. It was glorious down there. The white moonlight flooded the empty beach, while small white-crested waves lapped quietly on the sand. I could see the lights flickering on the big ships as they made their way silently out to sea on the high tide. Occasionally the stillness would be broken by the doleful ding-dong of a buoy ringing its bell out into the night.

I was in a thoughtful mood as I walked back towards

the pub and I began to wonder what sort of earth-bound spirit would want to haunt a place like this, and why. Was it a seaman, perhaps, or possibly a pirate? What was it the landlord's wife had said? That the ghost walks around the yard at full moon? On such a night as this, no doubt. Well, this seemed to be as appropriate a night as any for ghost-hunting.

I had not realised how quickly the time had passed. As I entered the courtyard of the pub, the church clock struck midnight, the witching hour, as they say. The lights were out in the pub and all was still. I sat on the old oak seat. The moonlight flooded the cobble stones in the courtyard. It was very quiet; all the locals had gone home to bed. Having nothing else to do, I just sat and stared at the church tower in the moonlight and tried to trace a pattern on the old grey stones. The tall chimney stack of the pub cast a long shadow across the yard. Well, I thought to myself, the moon is full and the atmosphere just right. So where is the ghost?

I must have dozed off for a while because I suddenly woke up feeling cold and stiff. The night was still, the moon high. Suddenly I realised that somebody was sitting on the bench next to me. Still half-asleep, I muttered, 'Good evening.'

My greeting was returned in a peculiar gruff voice. I sat up straight and turned to look at my companion. He was a young man in his early twenties. He was well built with strong forearms and thighs. As I noted his ruddy complexion, even in the moonlight, I instinctively knew that this was a seafaring man. In fact, it was fairly obvious, for he wore a dark blue coat with brass buttons over a striped shirt. His long reddish hair was tied back in a little plait and a flat black hat sat on the back of his head.

As my gaze travelled down, I saw in fact that below the thighs, he had only one leg.

I stared at him and I suddenly felt as though a cold wind was blowing at me. My heart had begun to beat very hard and I could feel it in my throat. This was the ghost …

I did not know whether to jump up and run, but any such decision would have been impossible, for something held me down on the seat. I just sat there staring at this figure and waiting for something to happen.

The man, ghost, what have you, seemed to sense my embarrassment. He looked at me with a wide grin, his white teeth shining in the dark. 'Pleased to make your acquaintance, mate.' He held out his hand for me to shake.

I gingerly held out mine and we shook hands. Well, it felt like flesh.

'I'm Bill Davies,' he said. 'Late of High Majesty's Navy, I died one hundred and sixty years ago.'

'You're out late,' I said inanely. I was desperate to make polite conversation while I gathered my wits together.

'Who, me out late? That's funny!' the man rocked backwards and forwards laughing so loudly that I thought he would wake up the landlord and his wife.

'I've been here all the time, mate, over a hundred and sixty years.'

Suddenly I was not afraid any more. I just felt a little bit astonished. After all, I had wished to see this ghost and what a marvellous story it would make! I smiled at him and he smiled back. I knew that he could guess what I was thinking.

'*Make yourself comfortable, mate,*' he said, '*and I'll tell thee how I got to be an earth-bound spirit.*'

So my ghost began.

I was born and grew up in this very village, in Star Cottages over there.

He pointed down the lane to four small cottages; I had noticed them earlier. They were now empty and derelict, their windows like eyes staring out at the moon. I shivered convulsively. It did feel a bit cold.

The man noticed me draw my jacket around myself. 'It'll get warmer in a minute,' he said, 'once the dust settles.'

Well, I was about ten years old. It was the year 1802. My parents were farm labourers. For a small wage and a free cottage, they worked on the farm from sunrise to sundown. There were nine of us living in that small cottage – seven children and my ma and pa. If they could afford threepence, one or two of us would go to school in the winter, but seeing as I was not studious, the privilege of school was not often mine. Instead I roamed the marshland with my pal Jim who lived next door. We were as free and happy as lads can be. Our job was to help bring in the cows for milking early morning and evening. But once we'd done that, the rest of the day we would run wild out there, Jim and I.

It was a boy's paradise out there. Huge bullfrogs croaked in the dykes, and at every low tide the rocks were swarming with all kinds of sea birds. If we could manage to borrow an old gun from the farm, we would bag plenty of wild game. The landlord of the tavern would give us ginger beer and sweetmeats in exchange for them, and then it would be a picnic on the wall out there. *He pointed to the wall running down to the sea.* We would sit inspecting the big sailing ships going down on the strong tide, their white sails billowed out ever so grandly. It was a great thrill. I loved it. I loved the water. I felt that I could not grow up quickly enough to go to sea. We sat there hour after hour, spotting the great schooners that came down the Thames bound for the Indies. We knew all the names of the famous ships of war, and many a fight we had up there arguing as to whose ship was best. I always won. Jim would inevitably give in, in the end. We were great pals, and it was a wonderful youth we spent out there on the green marshland. The shoreline was our gateway to the outside world, for up to that time we had never left the village.

Sometimes we would sit and watch the huge transport ships that anchored out there waiting for the high tide. They were packed tight with convicts destined for the penal colony on the shores of Port Jackson in Australia. We used to see the poor devils on board taking a farewell glance at their homeland. And every so often, one of them would take a chance and jump overboard.

Whenever that happened, there was the added excitement of watching the soldiers taking shots at them, and not stopping until the sea ran red with blood. If one of the convicts was lucky enough to get ashore, the soldiers moved in for the kill, and woe betide anyone who tried to protect a prisoner.

We were wading out in the shallows one day towards a line of rocks that only showed above the waterline at low tide. There, feeling happy, we had spotted a gaggle of wild geese, and were anxious to bag a few. We had the old shotgun with us, and we crept along very slowly, trying to avoid the deeper pools.

When we were halfway out, the geese suddenly rose and circled overhead. Something had evidently disturbed them.

'Hey,' whispered Jim, 'there's something on the rocks over there.'

Squinting into the sun, we could see, just ahead of us, the figure of a man clutching the edge of a jagged rock. His bedraggled shape seemed to be hanging grimly on for dear life.

As we got nearer, the heavy swell of the incoming tide surged over the rock with some force. We watched helplessly as the body dropped suddenly into the sea. The man's strength had gone. He could hold on no longer.

Throwing the gun out towards the dry sand, Jim and I both dived in. We were strong swimmers and we managed to grab hold of him at the same time and pull him back on a flat rock.

Looking down at him and seeing the blue serge outfit he wore, we knew he was one of the convicts.

'Shove him back,' said Jim callously. 'He's a goner, anyway.'

I bent over the body wondering what to do. He was a thin, scraggy-looking man, with brown hair and a thin beard. Suddenly he opened his eyes and stared at us. He placed his hand around his neck, gave a sort of funny gasp, and then shuddered. We both knew instantly that he was dead.

'What's that round his neck?' said Jim.

Peering down, I saw a little oilskin bag hanging outside the wet blue shirt. I reached out and took it. Just as I did so a huge wave surged up and hit us. Jim and I staggered backwards, as the man's body was washed off the rock and into the sea.

'Come on, Bill!' Jim yelled. 'I left the gun down there and the tide will get it.'

Both dripping wet, we turned and clambered back to save the gun.

Back on safe ground, clear of the tide, I eagerly opened the little oilskin bag. Well, you can imagine our disappointment to find that inside was just a shiny piece of rock.

'What's he want that for, I wonder?' said Jim, gloomily. 'No wonder he got drowned.'

'Perhaps it's a lucky charm?' I said hopefully.

'Chuck it in the sea,' said Jim dismissively.

But for some reason I did not do as Jim suggested. Instead, I tucked the rock into my pocket and went running after my friend who by that time had begun potting at some birds on the churchyard wall.

I had become so interested in Bill's story that I did not notice the grey pink dawn that was coming up over the sea. Then, without warning, he suddenly said: 'Got to go now, mate. I'll be back tomorrow.'

When I turned, the seat beside me was empty.

Feeling very peculiar, I got up and walked stiffly back to my lodgings. In the dawn light, I could scarcely believe all that had happened to me.

The following night at about ten o'clock, I set out again, complete with a notebook and pen. I wore a warm overcoat and tucked a flask of coffee in my pocket. I felt pretty silly, I must admit. It seemed ridiculous that I had a rendezvous with a ghost. For Bill was nothing like a ghost. He was not in the slightest bit creepy and I did not feel scared of him. At moments I thought it might even be an elaborate hoax organised by the landlord of the pub and his wife for my benefit. But still, ghost or not, I wanted to hear the end of the story.

I saw him as I approached. He was standing with his back to the wall, and a silver shaft of moonlight was shining down on him. I caught my breath for a moment. The same queer excited feeling I had felt the night before passed over me.

He stepped out of the silver shadows to greet me. 'Glad you came, mate, I gets a bit lonely some nights.'

So, with a Kentish burr to his voice, Bill Davies went on with his story.

It was a lovely, hot, dry summer. Jim and I had both reached the wonderful age of fourteen. We were lively lads, bursting with good health and filled with an excitement about life. Many a long, summer evening was spent on this seat, making plans.

I was all for going to Gravesend and hopping aboard a cargo ship but Jim was hard to convince about this. He was no longer quite so mad about the sea, and he kept talking about going up to London. Somehow he had got some daft idea of getting rich quick up there.

Yes, sir, in this very spot we used to argue and fight like two tomcats until we finally reached a decision. We would leave home in September but first we would build up a store of money earned during the apple-picking season.

For the next few weeks of that glorious summer, we worked like slaves. We would be in the fields in the morning and the orchards in the evening. Our little stash of money mounted up quickly and we hid it away in a tin with the rest of our treasures, which now included my piece of rock from the dead bloke out on the shore. I had been careful not to lose my lucky charm, and I had grown quite attached to it. I put it in our treasure tin so as to bring us luck on our travels.

Oh, those dreams! I still remember every detail of our wonderful plans. I would imagine myself coming back from my travels abroad and strolling through the village, very handsome and well-dressed. I would bring back a special present for Lizzie, with whom I was stepping out. I suppose I must have loved her. Even in those early days I had my eye on her.

Lizzie was about twelve years old then. She was fair-skinned with blue eyes and a real sunshine colour to her hair. She was very small and as sweet and as cuddly as a kitten. She lived in the same row of cottages as me and Jim, just two doors up, in fact. There was a bit of a story about her father – no one had ever seen him – but you saw and heard her ma, all right.

Lizzie's ma, Bess, was a proper dragon. When she shouted, the whole row of cottages shook. She was a massive woman – very tall, at least six feet tall. She had a long plait of coal-black hair wound around her head, deep-set black eyes, and high cheekbones. She had probably been very good-looking when she was younger but now her skin was dry and weatherbeaten and two deep frown-lines ran down between her eyes. Still, it was always a truly magnificent sight to see her stamping through the village on her way to church every Sunday, her petticoats flying in the breeze like a ship in full sail.

My little golden-haired Lizzie always trailed along behind her, looking very demure in her blue Sunday bonnet. It was more than anyone's life was worth to say hello to Lizzie or even to call out. If you did, old Bess would fetch you a clout across the ear that you'd feel for a long time after.

All through the week Bess worked on the land. All agreed that she was as good a worker as any man.

I clearly remember one time when I was a small boy, I was waiting in the lane for Jim. Suddenly I spied old Bess coming down the lane so I ducked into the ditch to hide. As she passed me in great stomping strides, I stared at her and saw on her feet she was wearing men's boots with the toe caps cut off, exposing a line of large mud-caked toes. I never forgot the sight of those dirty great toes sticking out of each boot – it seemed as though an elephant was going past. I used to have horrible nightmares in which I was being trampled by Bess's great feet.

The village gossips talked about Bess's lodgers, none of whom ever stayed for long. I remember one man who could not speak. He had slinky black hair and dark skin. He used silently to watch us playing in the lane.

One day we saw him crawling out of the pigsty, all smothered with muck. He looked so sorry for himself that we decided Bess had probably pitched the poor fellow out of the window and into the sty. He held out a coin to us and pointed to the field. We knew that he wanted us to watch out for Bess, while he made a quick getaway. Last we saw of him, he was scooting up the road as fast as his short legs would carry him.

Old Tom Abbott was the oldest inhabitant of the village. His favourite pastime was to sit on the wall and tell fantastic stories of the old days. We lapped them up with eager glee.

'Her be a bloody man-eater,' he said of Bess. 'Old Bess gobbles 'em up, she does.'

In my child's mind, I thought she was a cannibal and would run like hell whenever I saw her coming.

Anyway, I'm digressing. To get back to Jim and me, we had nearly saved enough money to leave the village and set out to see the world. There were too many mouths to feed in our homes anyway, so we would not be missed. But we did have a problem, and that was how we were going to get boots to wear for our long journey.

You see, this may seem funny to you, sir, but we were not allowed to wear our boots in the summer. Only when the real bad weather came was we allowed to wear them. These were very hard times, and boots were expensive items.

To tell the truth, I never realised how hard those

times were until I left the shelter of the village and went out into the cold, hard world. I could hardly believe my own eyes when I saw the misery of the children in the towns. I saw them being driven off to work in the factories – very young, dirty, and ragged, driven along like cattle to work. It was then I knew and appreciated how good my folks had been to me, struggling to bring up seven of us. But by then it was too late to recompense them, for when I returned to the village, everything had changed.

Anyway, Jim and I both had to get our boots but not raise any suspicion that we were pushing off. The villagers didn't like anyone to leave.

We were allowed to wear our boots for church on Sunday, but then we always had to go straight home and take them off before we were allowed out to play. There was always trouble in our house over the boots.

I had four brothers – two older and two younger than me. The eldest brother would always get the shiny new boots made by the village cobbler. These were then handed down from boy to boy as our feet grew over the years. Then I had shot up in height and overtaken both my older brothers in size, so it was my turn to get the brand new boots that year. This made me very unpopular with my eldest brother who clearly felt humiliated at having to wear old rather than new boots. These new boots were my pride and joy. They were the first new items of clothing I had ever had, and I had no intention of giving them up. Jim and I planned to leave the village the following Sunday immediately after church.

That Sunday was the first Sunday in September. The year was 1804. After the service, all the respectable churchgoing villagers had started on the walk home to lunch. It would be game pie, if they were lucky. Jim and I lingered and then sat on the churchyard wall. We looked very dandy in our best breeches and knitted sweaters, swinging our legs to show off our precious boots. We waited until everyone had disappeared into their homes and then jumped down. Clutching our few possessions we had hidden nearby before the church service, we set off as fast as we could into the forest.

It took us a long time to make our way through the forest. And it was hard work, with the path winding uphill all the way. But it was certainly worthwhile. Once we had reached the top of the hill, we saw before us a breath-taking view of the Thames Estuary where it joined the sea. We stood for a while looking in wonderment at the wide sweep of the river as it wound across the plain like a long silver ribbon amidst a patchwork of various greens from the fields and hedgerows. Away in the distance, the boats in the bay looked like tiny toys.

Suddenly excitement gripped us both. We whooped for joy at our freedom. 'The sea!' we yelled, throwing our caps in the air. We started running down the hill, kicking up our legs like young ponies.

After we had left the shade of the tall trees, the sun made us hotter. We trudged along paths and tracks and roads until we finally reached the town of Gravesend.

The air was stuffy and hot and claustrophobic. And to two country yokels like us, the town itself was strange and overwhelming too. We had never seen anything like it – the tall houses and narrow streets. And the crowds of people that thronged the pavements.

Gravesend was a very busy port. All kinds of ships docked there and seafaring people from all over the world could be seen near the waterside. Jim and I wandered about staring at all the shops. We were astonished by the lights. And we even saw a man from India, with dark skin and a turban on his head.

Later we sat on the dock watching the great ships out in the bay. Tall, white-sailed men-of-war were positioned out on the horizon.

Towards evening, we were getting tired and hungry. We made our way to a dim-looking alehouse. It was dark and smoky inside. The sour smell of beer hung in the air. As soon as we entered, the landlord called out: 'What do you two boys want? Hop it!'

'We would like some ale and bread and cheese, sir,' said Jim in his most respectful voice.

'I hope you got some money,' the landlord snapped back.

'Of course we have,' said Jim, taking out our tin box and rattling it.

The landlord and the other customers in the bar started laughing. A fat slovenly woman sat up, and stared at us. I felt very foolish.

The landlord brought us two flagons of ale, and a platter of cheese and bread. Counting out the coins with great care, Jim paid for the meal with pride. After we had eaten, we sat back and began to chat a bit.

Jim was still wanting to get on a barge and go up to London, but I was keen on the deep sea. It was hard trying to convince him.

The landlord was clearing the table and overheard our conversation: 'So you're running away to sea,' he said, raising his thick eyebrows quizzically.

I nodded and the landlord turned to call to a tall man standing near the bar. 'Davey, they want to go to sea, these lads do.'

Davey put down his tankard and walked over to us. 'Now, how are you going to do that?' he asked. He was heavily built with deep-set eyes, and a long black bushy beard. He stared straight at us with a piercing look. 'Want to be sailors, do you?'

'Yes, sir,' I said politely. 'We are hoping to get on a ship here.'

Davey's eyes smiled under his bushy brows. 'You're from the country,' he said in a matter-of-fact tone of voice. 'Strong boys like you won't find it hard to get a ship. Tell you what I'll do, you wait for me and I'll help you. I got a bit of business to do first. When I get back I'll take you on board my ship.' He held out a coin. 'Here's a nice new shilling each to spend while I'm gone. So long, me hearties!' he shouted and rolled out of the bar.

'That's a bit of luck,' said Jim. 'See his coat, he's a captain.'

'Don't be soft,' I said. 'He's a bosun; we have just joined the Navy, Jim. He gave us the King's shilling.'

Feeling very pleased with ourselves, we ordered some more ale and went on drinking.

Davey was away a long while. It was dark outside when he returned. By then we had drunk plenty of ale and had never a care in the world.

Davey whistled from the doorway. 'Avast, there, lads! Come on, we'll have you shipshape and seaworthy in no time.' He seemed drunk and very merry as he collected us up to join the Navy.

Soon we were being rowed out to our ship. Overwhelmed by the ale and exhaustion, Jim had passed out. I took a good look around me. We were in a large rowboat rowed by four hefty sailors. Davey, the bosun, was sitting bolt upright in the stern. All the men were a bit merry and they sang as they pulled rhythmically on the oars. Then my gaze met a most depressing sight at the other end of the boat. There were two men with their hands tied behind their backs, dressed only in shirts and blue pants. Both their miserable faces were bloodstained and one had a huge hump on the back of his head. They cursed in unison and the elder one wept, hanging down his head pathetically. He kept muttering. 'My poor wife,' he said, over and over again. 'My poor wife.'

'Crikey,' I thought. 'Pressed men, poor devils. Fancy being dragged off to sea like that.'

'Look at the blighters,' said our jovial bosun, Davey, noticing me staring at the men. 'Didn't want to go to sea, they didn't. Never wanted to join the glorious Navy, not like you likely lads. Volunteered, you did.'

He laughed loudly, and seemed to regard it all as a marvellous joke.

This was the first glimpse I had of the cruel life in the Navy. Davey's callousness suddenly made me feel afraid for the first time.

Well, I needn't have worried. I soon got used to the brutality, and I took to life on board ship, like a duck takes to water. But it was indeed a rough life.

Poor old Jim took a longer time to get his sea legs. He was always being sick and could not eat the food. I expect that that was because he was down in the galley most of the time, helping the dirty old cook. But from the beginning I was the bosun's bright boy. I was never so happy as when I was climbing high in the rigging, or holy-stoning the decks. We were on a supply ship that sailed up and down the lines of big war ships. It was a happy little ship, in its way. Davey was good to us and we soon settled down to life at sea.

When I replaced my old civvy breeches for a smart new navy uniform, I put my lucky piece of rock back into my pocket. I had great faith in that piece of shiny rock. I certainly seemed to have the luck of the devil; whatever I attempted seemed to go right. Now it never left my possession.

The first year aboard ship fled by, and then the war with France began. We had to leave our happy little ship, and were transferred to a much bigger man-of-war. It was called the *Billy Ruffan* by us. It had been a French ship captured by the English, so its French name – which none of us could pronounce anyway – was changed to *Billy Ruffan*.

It was a rough, tough ship, and we were no sooner aboard than we sailed to join the fleet of naval ships in the Mediterranean.

Jim and I both had jobs on deck as powder monkeys, which meant that we had to keep the gunners supplied all the time with ammunition. We rolled kegs of gunpowder over the wet, slippery deck and staggered about in the height of battle with great canon balls as we helped reload the guns. This was my first taste of war, of battle, even. No words can describe that bloodiest of blood baths. All I can say is that you never forget the noise of the guns and the screams of the wounded and dying men. We slithered over a deck awash with blood and salt water. It was every man for himself. There was no time to think about what was happening to the man next to you, so when I saw poor old Jim lying on the deck screaming in agony, there was nothing I could do. I just had to get on with the job and hope for the best, and hope that my own luck would hold out. Fortunately, it did. I was one of the lucky survivors from that great Battle of the Nile, a victorious one for the English, which has been well recorded in history.

When it was over, there was a great celebration on board. We all danced the hornpipe and got hopelessly drunk on rum, and wine taken from the French ships. I was treated like a minor hero. The older Jack Tars patted me on the back and said, 'Good lad,' when the news of how I had stuck to my post regardless, went around.

In spite of my elation at our victory, I kept thinking

of poor old Jim. Later I went below to try and find him. The sight down below decks that met my eyes was almost more than I could stand. I retched several times and was almost sick at the sight of some of those wounded.

All the wounded were waiting to receive attention from the overworked medical men, and there was Jim lying on the deck. His head was wrapped in a blood-stained bandage, his eyes were shut, his mouth was open, and his face was a ghastly white colour.

'Is he dead?' I nervously asked another man who was sitting nearby and holding his badly gashed leg.

'No, mate,' the man replied. 'He's just passed out. We will all bleed to bloody death if they don't get a move on up there.'

I looked up towards the far end, and there the scene was even worse. Men lay everywhere, all groaning and shouting and swearing in their pain. On the large table at the end, the medical men were working hard. By the light of a lantern they were chopping off damaged and useless arms and legs. The smell was quite terrible. I could stand no more. Holding back the bile rising in my throat, I rushed back up on deck to breathe the fresh air and drink more wine and rum until they carted me off to my bunk, dead drunk.

I never saw them take Jim away on the hospital ship. I felt bad about that the next day, as we had never been apart since we left home.

That was my first taste of battle, but not my last. We went into port for a refit, and I spent some time ashore. I am sorry to say that I was not very well-behaved. I slept with plenty of women and loved them and left them as I chose. I soon learnt to take care of myself. 'Pull up the ladder, Jack, I'm aboard,' as the Jack Tars used to say. We had a lot of fun, me and the other sailors, and I enjoyed every minute of my time on shore. But it was not long before we were off to the sea again. This time it was Trafalgar.

Bill Davies paused and looked sideways at me. 'I suppose you think that's where I lost me leg,' he said.

I stared at him, my pen poised. I had been very busy taking down Bill's story in my notebook.

Bill shook his head. 'No, mate,' he said, 'it wasn't in war that my luck ran out. On, no. It was only in love. Still, the day's nearly here.' He pointed to a pink strip in the sky and suddenly he was gone.

My landlady was beginning to look at me in an odd sort of way. I could tell that she thought me most odd for being out all night and asleep all day. In fact, I believe she was beginning to think that I was some kind of vampire. I tried to satisfy her growing curiosity by reminding her that I was a bird-watcher, and was at the present time concentrating on a very rare species that only came out at night. So, I was sorry I bothered when I heard her mutter to her husband: 'It's more than a blessed bird that keeps him out all night.'

Doing my best to avoid any more comments like that, I waited until they were in bed before I crept out again to meet Bill.

I arrived slightly late that night and was rather concerned when he wasn't there by the bench. But then I heard the tap of his leg. It made an eerie sound which rang out into the night.

'Hello, mate,' Bill grinned in greeting. 'I just thought I'd go on me rounds. I don't want these locals forgetting about me now, do I?'

Sitting down on the bench beside me, Bill continued with his story.

I missed old Jim. We had been together all our lives. We had been like brothers. But there was nothing I could do abut his situation. I didn't even know where my pal was any more. I left the *Billy Ruffan* and was transferred to a little frigate called the *Mars*, where we had a good captain. He was from the Highlands of Scotland, and his name was Mackenzie. He had his young son, Alastair, on board too, a lad of about twelve years old. He was a bright, fair-haired lad with a very happy disposition. He was also very keen to be a sailor.

Alastair took a fancy to me, as I was close to him in age, and we was always chatting. I used to tell him of how my pal Jim and I had run off to sea and had many adventures. I have to admit that some of the stories I told him were rather embellished but that made them all the more fascinating to the lad. There's no harm in that.

On that October morning in 1805 we all stood ready and waiting for the signal to go into action. The big ships were all lined up facing the enemy. As a spare gunner, I was ready to take over if the gunner was knocked out. Alastair stood close to me as we positioned ourselves silently beside the gun.

Captain Mackenzie was on the bridge, his three officers standing behind him. Suddenly he turned, saw his son on the deck, and ordered me to take him below and stay with him until I was recalled.

Just as soon as we left the deck, the French opened fire. An unlucky shot hit the *Mars* instantly and took the bridge away. Our poor captain's head was blown off and the two officers behind him were killed. The one who remained was too shocked and dazed to keep order.

With her mast shot away, our little ship sailed within range of the enemy guns which raked her fore and aft, till she drifted helplessly out to sea. Many of the crew were wounded and a fire now raged on board. There was a terrible panic on board, and I was crouched below deck cradling the shivering boy Alastair in my arms as I tried to calm him.

There were a few survivors on the *Mars*, but not many. So once again I seemed to have the luck of the devil.

Although we English won that battle against the French and Spanish, we lost our great Admiral Nelson that day. But his brilliant victory was decisive and it ended Napoleon's power on the sea. It certainly made a French invasion of England – perish the thought – impossible. After that battle, the fleet returned home from Trafalgar bringing our dead. All we battle-weary men were given two months' leave. So, feeling like a proper hero, I went back to my little village in Kent which I had left more than two years ago.

It was early in May when I arrived at the hamlet.

The countryside was full of blossom – the cherry orchards ablaze with colour, and the hedgerows thick with red and white hawthorn. You have no idea how lovely the village looked after my two years at sea. My family were pleased to see me and had all even forgiven me for disappearing with that precious pair of new boots.

There was my lovely Lizzie, too. Two years older, and better-looking than ever. She was bigger, more buxom, and her hair was glorious, still with its lovely shade of gold.

As I saw her coming towards me down the lane, my heart skipped a beat. She was wearing a pretty plum-coloured dress with white petticoats and a frilly collar. Without saying a word, she smiled sweetly, and I took her hand. I knew that this was my woman, and I have never wanted any other.

It was Saturday evening, and I wondered anxiously if old Bess was at home. But I said nothing. In fact, I need not have worried. My Lizzie had developed a mind of her own and, at her suggestion, we walked hand in hand to the woods.

That leave was exquisite and completely unforgettable. We spent the early mornings on the shore, collecting shellfish which Lizzie did each day for Bess to sell to the village. Then in the afternoon we made love in the woods on a bed of dry ferns.

We would lie under the cloudless blue sky while the birds sang their own mating songs. The air seemed as sweet as wine. And I can tell you, there was nothing half-hearted about our lovemaking. We seemed to belong to each other from the beginning. She was warm and womanly, Lizzie. She was not much of a talker but she was a good listener. I often stared down into her blue eyes and wondered what she was really thinking. One day I said to her: 'Lizzie, my darling, what about your ma? Don't you think we ought to tell her about us? Then we can be married before I have to go back to sea.'

This suggestion seemed to throw Lizzie into a wild panic. She just stared back at me, wide-eyed with fright. 'Please don't tell her,' she whispered. 'Ma will spoil it all, Bill, and we've been so happy.'

I suppose I should have been firmer with her but I loved her so much and could not bear to see her unhappy. So I gave in. 'All right, my love,' I said, 'if you don't want your ma to know, we won't tell her.'

It was quite easy to dodge old Bess, for she spent all day working out on the land. In those days there were farm gangs, made up of women and children who worked for very little money from daybreak to sunset. To give old Bess some credit where it's due, she never let Lizzie rough it out in the fields. Instead, she arranged for Lizzie to help in the house at the Red Dog – it's funny how this pub has dominated my life. So it was easy to hang around the bar at the pub until Lizzie had finished work.

I forgot to mention that Jim was also back in the village, dressed up in a civvy suit and a black patch over his eye. I was pleased to see him but after a while my feelings of friendship wore off. For one thing, I was too busy chasing Lizzie, so I did not have much time for him. But the other thing was that Jim fancied Lizzie himself, and he seemed to have become quite jealous of my success with her.

I remember one afternoon when I was hanging around and waiting for Lizzie to finish work, old Bess suddenly came charging down off the open fields towards the pub. She was roaring like a lion, her skirt was hitched up to her knees, and an old sack was tied around her waist. She came at me with great strides, shouting: 'Hi! You sling yer bloody hook! My gel's not for the likes of you. Hop it!'

I just knew then that Jim had informed Bess of my interest in her daughter.

I did not waste a moment. I indeed hopped it: the gallant sailor home from the sea ran from a woman. But then, Bess was no ordinary woman.

Bill chuckled. Then he nudged me in the ribs. 'I'd better be going, mate. Dawn's coming up again,' he said. Once more he left me.

The story was becoming quite gripping. In my mind's eye I could see the lovely blonde Lizzie and I could hardly wait until the next evening to hear the rest.

The following evening I did not arrive until midnight. You can imagine my disappointment when I saw the seat empty. Bill was nowhere to be seen. I felt quite desolate. Surely he was not abandoning me at this point. I decided to wait a little longer. Soon I wandered over to the church-yard and there, to my delight, was Bill, his sturdy figure standing beside an old gravestone.

As I walked towards him I was thinking what a

*good-looking chap he must have been. A pale moon sailed
from behind a cloud, and for the first time he did not look
like the ordinary being he had seemed on the nights before.
Words froze on my lips, I could not utter a sound. I just
stood there looking at the halo of moonlight that surrounded
Bill's red-brown curls. The light revealed the perfect
straight line of his features.*

*Bill turned towards me with his usual friendly grin:
'Hello, mate. Found me out, did you?'*

*I cleared my throat and found that my speech had
returned. 'Good evening, Bill. You've changed your habits,'
I said.*

*He shook his head. 'No, sir, I was just looking at where
my Lizzie is buried. Smallpox took her when she was only
twenty-five. She died in 1818. That's where I'd like to be,'
he said sadly, staring down at the lichen-covered gravestone, 'with a good decent burial – church and all. Then
maybe I'd see my Lizzie again.'*

*'Finish your story, Bill,' I said, 'and I'll see that you get
all that is due to you.' I don't know why I said that but I
hoped that I could indeed help the poor fellow.*

*'I believe you will, mate,' said Bill with a grin. And with
him in a more cheerful frame of mind, we walked back to
our seat in the pub courtyard.*

After my first leave when I had fallen head over heels
in love with Lizzie, I returned to Portsmouth with my
head in the clouds. In spite of Bess's objection to our
match, all I could think of was my lovely girl. Now I
found that I was planning on how to get out of the
Navy, settle down and get married to her. I was

confident that my inevitable success at sea would change Bess's view of me as a future son-in-law.

Our last meeting before I left was very sweet. We said goodbye under the great oak tree up there on the hill. I was full of plans for the future, of buying a farm and raising a brood of children. It was typical of Lizzie to say very little, even on such a special occasion as this. She just snuggled close to me and shyly hung her head.

'You will wait for me, darling?' I pleaded.

Lizzie smiled coyly. 'Don't go on so, of course I will,' she said.

'No more drinking for me,' I said, 'and no more gambling. I am going to save all the money I make on my next trip. Here you are, Lizzie, this is my lucky charm. It's never been out of my pocket since I found it. I'll give it to you to take care of for me. That will bring you close to me, my darling.' I pressed my lucky stone into her hand.

Lizzie stared down at the dull stone with a bemused look on her pretty face. 'Oh, Bill,' she giggled. 'It's nought but a pebble.'

I shook my head. 'Don't matter. It's taken care of me in danger, and now I want it to take care of you.'

'All right, then,' said Lizzie, but she did not sound very convinced. She dropped the stone into the pocket of her dress, and threw her arms around my neck. We made love again for the last time before I left.

I was soon back in the old routine on another ship and a voyage to the West, and it was not long before I had begun to think that I should never have parted with my lucky stone. This was a bad voyage right from the start. Terrific gales in the Atlantic blew us off our course. We had frequent trouble from the Dutch and the Spaniards, so it was the next spring before we reached our final destination – Jamaica.

I had managed to send Lizzie a letter. I am ashamed to admit to you, sir, that it was not easy for me to write a letter. I could read fairly well, but not having had much schooling, I found it difficult to put my thoughts on paper. But now I was waiting anxiously for a letter from her.

Our first call was in the port of Jamaica. This place was one of the worst areas for vice I had ever seen. Once the fleet arrived, the crew were eager to get on dry land. I was now on my best behaviour, and volunteered for watch while everyone else went ashore.

I was feeling proper fed-up. I hated this ship. I had lost the best skipper I ever had at Trafalgar, and the present one was a bastard, if you will pardon the expression, sir. We had a fever in the ship and the poor fellows who had been pressed into the service dropped like flies. The captain showed no concern for anyone.

I was sorely tempted to go ashore and have a good time but the thought of my lovely Lizzie back at home made me control myself and reminded me of the need to save all my money.

For a while I watched a big ship unloading its cargo of slaves. My God, that was a depressing sight! These men and women from Africa, with the blackest of skins, were chained together like a lot of cattle. It was a terrible scene. They looked broken, all weeping and wailing as they dragged their sore and weary limbs down the gangplank.

Towards evening, the crew began to drift back to our ship, bringing their doxies with them. For the next few days the ship was a hell-hole. The women had all brought strong rum on board with them and the men were drunk the entire time. And some of the women were very attractive. I can tell you, it was not easy to keep away from them, but I kept my mind on Lizzie and made plans in my head for our wedding.

The news came at last that our long-delayed mail had finally arrived from England. There was one letter from Lizzie but it was dated August. Yet it was now April, eight months later. After such a lousy voyage, this was the final blow. And the contents of her letter made me feel quite sick.

In her neat handwriting it read:

> *Dear, dear Bill,*
>
> *I do hope you got on board all right, and never got in trouble. I am sorry, darling, to have to tell you, but I am in trouble.*
>
> *I am almost sure now that I am with child, so please hurry home and marry me. My ma will kill me if she finds out. She says she wants me to go and work for that posh family in London she used to work for. I am glad I am going to be married so that I won't have to go now.*
>
> *Lots of love,*
> *Lizzie*

Bill's eyes had filled with tears and his lip quivered as he stared at the distant shore.

It was like a bloody cannonball had hit me. This situation was one that I had never anticipated. I cursed myself for being such a fool! There was my poor little Lizzie having to face it all alone. It was a year since we said goodbye. I can tell you, I was sunk.

Well, I did what the average ignorant sailor would do. I went ashore and got drunk. I went on a real rampage. I did not remember any of it until I woke up in hospital minus one leg. Seems I got so drunk that I fell in the harbour. I was fished out before I drowned, but not before a shark had had a good chew at my leg. *'That's how I ended up like this,' he muttered, banging his wooden stump on the cobbles in the yard.*

I did not hear another word from Lizzie. While I was in the hospital, the padre wrote to her for me, and then I sent a letter myself but no reply came back. There was nothing I could do except wait for a boat home.

It was another six months before I got my discharge at Portsmouth, and I still had heard no news from home. As we sailed up the Solent, it was a lovely spring day. When I saw the coast of Southern England, I began to think of my lovely Lizzie with her pale-gold hair and her little tip-tilted nose. I wondered what reception I'd get from her now. Here I was, only twenty years old and a cripple. And she had every reason to think that I had abandoned her. The Navy was finished with me, too. What should I do now? The more I added up my misfortunes, the more I thought about how my luck had changed in the last two years. They had called me lucky boy aboard the *Mars* but all that luck had run out a long time ago. Perhaps I should not have given Lizzie my lucky charm. Perhaps I should take it back from her. I had no job, just my pay and a bit of prize money. I did not lose my leg on active service, so there was no pension for me, not that they gave those poor devils much anyway. A feeling of horror crept over me as I recalled the sight of all those disabled sailors who hang around the ports begging. But I shook it off. I knew it was no good getting despondent, not yet anyway . . .

I got as far as Gravesend and waited a few days in the hope of bumping into someone who knew Lizzie and could tell me what she was up to. In one moment of madness I even considered going to sea again. There were plenty of ships in the port – slavers and privateers – who would take a seafaring man with only one leg. But it was a crazy idea. And all the time inside me I had a gnawing hunger for my Lizzie. So I made my decision, and started towards home.

It was an early summer morning when I slung my bag over my shoulder and set off finally for the last stretch towards home. I decided to take the footpath beside the river. Dear old Thames, I thought, it suddenly seemed to mean much more to me than it used to. I felt great affection for it.

The river seemed busier these days. There were hundreds of different kinds of craft, some going up to London, others out to the deep sea.

I passed the fish market just as the early morning

catch was coming in. The noise was terrific with the buyers all yelling and the supply carts rattling past with their cargoes. I was glad to leave this noisy scene for the peace of the riverside.

I had begun to relax as I strolled along until I came to the marshland. The hedges were full of wildflowers and every orchard was in bloom. There is no place like Kent for the scent of apple blossom! I drew great breaths of the clear morning air. Now I began to feel that I was really coming home again. The dykes were full of life. Water voles swam across the water, bull-frogs croaked their welcome to me, and huge brightly coloured dragonflies hovered between the reeds. Yes, this was where I belonged, I thought, and a great happiness possessed me, I had not felt so good for a long time.

As I left the marsh behind and approached the village, I spotted the women working in the fields, their young children beside them. Some of them waved gaily to me, and my mind began to drift back to the time, years before, when Lizzie and I had sat down under the hedge together, and old Bess had caught us and fetched me a clout with a heavy bucket. My head was full of thoughts about the girl I had left behind until the square tower of the church came into sight and I was back in the familiar playground of my youth.

The hot afternoon sun was scorching the road as I reached the row of little cottages. It was very quiet in the main road because every able person was out working on the land, and the old folk and even the dogs were indoors in the shade.

I looked in at my own old home first. I knew it would be empty because my older brother had taken my mother to live on his farm with his family after our father died four years before. And my other brothers and sisters had flown the nest. The cottage had a forlorn air about it, neglected and unloved.

I quickly moved on to Lizzie's house. It looked rather different from how I remembered it. It was not as spick and span as it used to be. The gate was missing, and chickens were scattered over the garden. A brown swift darted from under the eaves like a bat; its narrow wings fairly twinkled as it flew off, making a rapid ticking noise, just like my father when he was telling us off. Perhaps it was the spirit of my father, I thought. But I didn't believe in ghosts or such things then.

My heart was racing as I had no idea what kind of reception I would get. Going round to the back door, I knocked gently. To my surprise, an unfamiliar young girl answered the door. She was about thirteen years old and she wore a red, ragged dress. Her feet were bare and she had a lovely pert little face topped by a mop of black curls.

'Hello!' she said in a very friendly manner.

'Is Lizzie at home?' I asked. I was feeling almost faint, my heart in my mouth.

The girl put her hands on her hips. 'Who's she?' she asked. 'Never heard of her.'

'But she lived here,' I replied in much confusion. I had not expected this.

'No, she don't, I live here,' the girl replied with a cheeky grin. 'I'm Rachel Wells. Who are you?'

I was getting nowhere. I tried again. 'Is your mother home, dear?'

'Got no ma,' returned Rachel, 'she's dead.' Then, as if to warn me not to start anything, she added quickly, 'Me pa and me brothers will be home soon. They only work down the brickfield.'

'Have you lived here long?' I asked.

'Since last year,' she said. 'But I don't like it,' she added, tossing her curls. 'It's too quiet for me.'

Well, well, I thought, here's a harlot in the making, if ever I saw one. But I felt I had to soften her up. I gave her my most charming smile. 'So you did not know Elizabeth, then?' I queried. 'Her ma was a big woman, very dark.'

My description prompted an immediate look of recognition. 'Oh, you mean old Bess!' Rachel said.

'That's right,' I answered eagerly.

'She's down the Red Dog. Her daughter married Jim White, whose mother lives next door.'

Well, at last I had got what I came for. But what I heard was a bit of a shock, too. I stood silent for a moment or two, taken aback by the news. Rachel was looking at me with a funny expression on her face. She looked almost adult. 'You're a sailor, aren't you?' She stared down at my wooden stump of a leg. 'Oh, you're wounded,' she said with much concern. 'Come and sit down and I'll get you some cider.'

Rachel's manner had changed completely to that of the little mother. I don't think I had ever met such a character as Rachel. She was as changeable as the wind.

A wobbly wooden chair was produced from the dark interior of the cottage, and a cool jug of cider was placed in front of me. I was feeling hot and a bit bewildered. But that cider tasted fine.

'You ought not to have walked all the way up here,' said Rachel, clucking like a mother hen. Her manner was touching and amusing. I had to laugh.

'Now, you feel better?' Rachel enquired. 'You can stay until me dad comes home.'

But I had no desire to stay here until her father returned. In spite of the hospitality I was getting, I wanted to go fairly soon.

'They won't be long,' continued Rachel. 'The fields are only down the road.'

I knew what a rough lot those brickies were. They had only recently started to drift into our village from northern areas. They brought their women and a string of children with them. It was very hard work for them in the brick factory. The women and children were worked as hard as the men. It had always disturbed me to see the little slaves covered in clay, and the dreadful sores on them where they got burned. They started to work from the age of five and then they grew old before their time. Although these people came in droves, they did not stay long. They always became unpopular with the local people who often reacted against these ragged families and drove them out again.

Rachel held out her hands to show me the scars she had got from humping the hot bricks in the brickfields.

As I stroked the rough little hands Rachel held out,

she said cheerfully, 'I don't work there now. Me brother won't let me.'

'Want some perfume?' I asked. Reaching for my shoulder bag, I pulled out the present I had brought for Lizzie. She grabbed the little parcel. From her expression, I could tell that I had made a friend for life.

It was time for me to move on. I got up and made to leave. 'Now, you say Lizzie lives up the Red Dog,' I said.

'Yes, of course, she does,' repeated Rachel. 'Jim, he bought that pub. They've poshed it up, they have.'

'And old Bess lives there too?' I asked.

Rachel nodded. 'Yes, that's what I said, and that's the truth.' She was getting a bit cheeky again. 'You wouldn't be asking me to take a message for ye, would ye?' she asked, taking the stopper out of the perfume bottle, and sniffing the contents. 'Because I won't, not to her. I don't like that Lizzie, she's too stuck-up.'

Well, that was that. I said goodbye to Rachel and drifted off.

Bill Davies sighed wearily and turned to me. 'Better turn in for the night, mate,' he said. 'Dawn's coming up. I'll see you tomorrow.'

Once again I was left alone on the seat.

The next night I found that I was quite upset when I met up with Bill and he reminded me of his transitory bodily state. 'Better get on with it tonight, moon's on the wane. I won't be here long now.' I had become very fond of my companion.

★ ★ ★

After I left Rachel, I drifted down to the shore to my favourite spot on the seawall. I was very very confused. There were so many questions I had wanted to ask. Why did Lizzie marry Jim, why him? But thinking it over now, I could remember how he was always hanging around Lizzie in the past. Perhaps she had fancied him too, and had forgotten me? I was a fool! And, why had I not asked Rachel if Lizzie had a baby?

These questions churned over and over in my mind as I sat there. I was quite puzzled as to how Jim had got enough money to buy an inn. Perhaps he did a bit of smuggling. Perhaps it would be better if I just went on my way, left the village, and forgot Lizzie.

It was now eight o'clock and the sun was beginning to go down in a blaze of glory. If you have never seen the sunset over the marshes, then you have missed one of the world's greatest sights. The sun was like a huge orange ball suspended over the sea. Blue, pinks and greens intermingled in the sky. There would be a breathless hush in the air as the birds settled in their nests for the night, and then suddenly, it would be dark.

A cool mist was creeping towards me. Having seen the sunset again, I knew I had to stay. I would take lodgings in the village. I would stay a while, anyway, and see what the situation was like.

Bill Davies pointed to a newsagents' shop across the road. 'I got lodgings in that house there. After the pub, it's about the oldest place around here.'

The old gal, Nell, who lived there, was right pleased to see me. 'You're more than welcome here, Bill, lad,' she said kindly. 'I saw ye grow up and I was a friend of your dear mother.' Nell was like a mother to me. She gave me a good supper and a nice bed.

By the next morning, my courage had returned. At breakfast Nell was full of gossip about the village. Her wrinkled face moved in all directions, her long chin wagged up and down, and the little lace cap on her head was all to one side as she talked and talked, bursting with the last two years' news that she was determined to tell me.

'Her,' she said, 'over there.' She pointed towards the inn. 'She's up to no good, that Bess, I can tell you. I don't know what it is exactly but she's not a good person . . .'

'Who?' I asked. 'You mean her at the Red Dog?' I was intrigued.

Nell nodded. 'Funny that she thinks I don't know. Never no good, she wasn't, so far as I could make out.'

I was afraid to quiz old Nell about her feelings for my Lizzie too, so I thanked her for the breakfast and prepared to go out. I spruced myself up a bit and went over to the Red Dog to find out for myself what was going on.

As I entered, I noticed that the long wooden benches had been replaced by shiny polished chairs. There was a fancy oil lamp hanging over the bar, and there was my old pal Jim serving pints of porter. He was wearing a white starched apron up to his chin. His hair was parted and plastered down over his scalp, and he still wore that black patch over his damaged eye.

Jim saw me immediately and looked astonished. 'Gor blimey, I thought you'd copped it.'

'No, I'm still alive and kicking,' I said. 'Give us a pint.'

Jim poured me some ale into a pewter tankard. I watched him silently and drank half of the brew before I spoke again. Jim watched me cautiously.

'How's Lizzie?' I asked.

Jim dropped his head. His one eye avoided my gaze.

'She's fine,' he answered flatly.

'Any family?' I enquired as casually as I could.

'One boy,' he said snappily and moved away to busy himself at the other end of the bar.

Well, I thought, this is getting me nowhere, I'll have a look round. Picking up my tankard, I went out the back way and there in the garden was my lovely Lizzie. I held my breath as I looked at her. She looked as glowing and golden as ever. And beside her, in a little swing that hung from the branch of a shady tree, was, quite undisputably, my son. His red curls shone in the sunlight, and his legs swung to and fro as Lizzie pushed him gently in the swing. She had not seen me and I wondered what to do. Then I called softly: 'Lizzie, darling.'

She did not hear me so I began to whistle our favourite tune softly, ever so softly: 'A-roving, a-roving, since roving's been my ruin.'

Suddenly Lizzie's body seemed to stiffen. She did not turn around but instead, she grabbed the boy from the swing and, clutching him in her arms, she ran away, around the side of the house.

I was very puzzled, and in a most unhappy frame of mind. I walked out to the shore. Reaching my usual spot on the sea wall I sat and tried to sort out the terrible confusion in my mind. Having seen my Lizzie again, I knew I loved her desperately, more than ever, in fact. And now I also knew that she had borne my son.

Out on the sands I could see Rachel. Her skirt was rolled up showing her slim tanned legs. She carried a basket on her arm as she wandered through the rock pools collecting shellfish. I watched her sadly, reminded of the summer I had spent with Lizzie doing just that.

Rachel came in as soon as she spotted me. Her basket was almost bursting with fresh cockles, mussels and whelks. 'You don't 'arf look miserable,' she commented flatly. She sat down on the sands beside me, drying her legs with her headscarf. She was looking a bit cleaner today. She was still wearing the same old red dress I had seen her in before and she had a row of seashells threaded on a string around her neck. Her black curls blew in the strong salt breeze. Suddenly, she looked more desirable to me and as she leaned towards me, the smell of the heady French perfume I had given her drifted out on the breeze.

'Don't I smell nice?' she asked.

I agreed, though I actually thought she had overdone it a bit.

'What have you got the miseries for?' she asked, staring straight into my face.

I could not help smiling, she was so charming, this half-woman, half-child.

'You fancy Lizzie up at the Red Dog, don't you,' she said teasingly.

I sat back somewhat stiffly. 'Suppose I do?' I said. I wasn't ashamed, so I continued: 'As a matter of fact, Rachel, I am very much in love with her.'

Rachel tossed her curls carelessly. 'You're daft,' she said. 'She's married.'

'Lizzie was mine,' I said. 'Jim stole her from me.' I said this hoping that Rachel's obvious interest would make her sympathise with my plight.

My ploy seemed to work immediately. Rachel looked outraged.

'Why, the dirty dog!' she exclaimed. 'You mean, while you was away at the war, he did that? You ought to go and beat him up!'

I smiled grimly. Well, I could see I had a staunch ally in Rachel. I stared forlornly down at my wooden stump.

'I'm sorry,' she said. 'You're wounded.' Leaning sideways she cuddled up to me like a puppy. 'I'll be your lass if you like.'

I smiled indulgently at her and patted her knee. 'No, my dear, you're still a bit young, but thanks for the offer.'

Rachel frowned and turned away sulkily.

I did not want to offend the girl and I could see that she could be useful. I picked up her basket of shellfish and shook it. 'Tell me,' I said. 'Where do you take your mussels and the like?'

'Up the Red Dog,' replied Rachel. 'Bess sends them on to the market.'

'I'll write a note for you to take to the inn. Now you see that Lizzie gets it, and I'll give you a shilling.'

Rachel's pretty little face beamed. 'A shilling? I'll go. I've not had a shilling to spend before.'

I quickly wrote a note to Lizzie asking her to meet me in the old spot beneath the big oak tree in the wood. Lizzie would know it. We had often made love up there under the huge tree right at the top of the hill. They call it the View there, because from it you can see the whole of Gravesend Reach.

Thus, with the help of my little friend, Lizzie rekindled our clandestine love affair.

It was wonderful, quite unforgettable! Although it ended in tragedy, I still believe it was worth it. We used to meet at three o'clock on Fridays and stay up in the woods until six. Rachel was a good little pal. As long as I parted up with a shilling, she hung around until we came down from the woods ready to give warning if anyone was in danger of disturbing us.

On our first meeting, Lizzie was shy and very scared. But as soon as I held her in my arms again, I knew we could not be parted. It had always been that way with her.

'Darling,' I pleaded with her as we lay under the trees. With my eyes I drank in the delicious sight of the golden freckles on her nose and the charming petulant droop to her mouth.

'I wrote to you, Bill,' she said, looking at me with mournful eyes. 'I wrote to you to ask you to come back quickly but you never replied . . .' Her voice trailed off and was whipped away by the wind.

'But I didn't get your letter until it was too late, my darling,' I explained. 'There was nothing I could do. I am back here now, and I have come as quickly as was humanely possible.'

Lizzie nodded her head gently and placed a finger on my lips. 'I know,' she said quickly. 'I understand that there was nothing to be done.' Her voice was flat and toneless.

I took a deep breath. 'But why, Lizzie, if you loved me and had faith in me, why didn't you wait? Surely you knew I'd return. And why did you marry Jim, my best friend, of all people! Why couldn't you have waited?'

'It was ma,' she replied. 'Ma made me.'

'Does Jim know that your child is my son?'

'Yes. We thought you were dead, and Jim knew that I was afraid of me ma. Besides, he was always asking me to go courting with him.'

I swore and cursed. 'That bastard stole my lass and my son. What sort of a chum is that?'

'He's good to me,' said Liz, 'or he means to be, at least,' she added enigmatically.

'That's not enough,' I shouted. 'You're *my* lass.' I was getting quite worked up. 'We will go and face him, see what he does.'

This proposal terrified poor Lizzie. She clung to me and begged me not to say anything. 'It's me ma,' she said. 'She won't let me, I know she won't.'

I sighed. 'It's always bloody old Bess,' I said. 'What's it to do with her? You're a big girl now, Lizzie.'

But my sneering did no good at all. Lizzie continued to beg me not to do anything until, like a fool, I gave in to her, as I usually did. I was not able to winkle out her fear of Bess, and because I loved her so, I accepted my role as her lover.

We met regularly once a week. Sometimes she brought our son with her. The boy was two years old and very bonny. He was called David. I was quietly pleased at this, what with my surname being Davies. It was strange how content I came to be with these crumbs from the table. It was a peculiar situation indeed. Here was I, single and free to go where I wished, but nothing would keep me away from Lizzie. I was hooked good and proper.

Each time we met I begged her to run away with me. But her answer was always the same: 'I am afraid,' she would say, but she would give no detailed reason. And after a while the question was asked and the answer given as nothing more than formalities.

We were so much in love that my disablement was hardly noticed by either of us. We made love in the woods all that long, dry summer. God, how jealous I was when she went back home to Jim! From my little window of my lodgings I could see the light in their bedroom over the road at the inn. Hell knows no torture like what I went through. It was agonising to imagine them in the same bed, or Jim touching Lizzie's sweet firm body. I could not bear it!

I began to drink heavily, finishing off a bottle of rum in my room each night. As I got drunk I would sit making plans to knock old Jim off. 'How did I get so bloody unlucky?' I asked myself morosely. What did I possess now? Nothing, not even employment. And the woman I loved, who loved me, was unable to be wholly mine. I was living in a nightmare.

I decided that I had to get back my lucky stone and one day I asked Lizzie if she would return it to me. Her reaction was astonishing. Even now I can see her. She started to tremble and shake, her cheeks paled and her eyes darted from side to side like those of a terrified animal.

'Don't ask me that,' she whispered urgently. 'You gave it to me, you cannot take it back now.'

I was amazed by this response and hugged her tightly, smoothing down her silky hair with my hand. 'Never mind, my darling,' I said quietly. 'You keep it, I hadn't realised how much it meant to you. I can manage without it. It's all nonsense anyway.'

Lizzie seemed relieved by my words. And so she should have been. Knowing what I know now, I can understand why she was so terrified. She was terrified for her life. It soon became clear that Lizzie was as distressed as I was by this arrangement. One day when we met, she suddenly burst into tears.

'Don't cry, my love,' I said gently. 'There's nothing to cry over.' But I did not sound very convincing.

As Lizzie sobbed she seemed terribly distressed. At last she said, 'I am sorry, Bill, but how long can we stand this, you and I?'

'As long as you need me,' I thought gallantly. But I had no answer.

For a while we were silent, both staring at the leaves on the trees. Summer was disappearing fast. The leaves were turning and beginning to drop to the ground to create a colourful carpet.

'Where will we meet in the winter?' Lizzie asked. She was looking quite forlorn. It broke my heart. I wanted so much to take care of her.

I was quite puzzled by our situation actually. I knew that Jim was aware of the trysts in the wood, yet he did nothing about it. Instead, he walked around the place looking unbearably smug all the time. And why was Lizzie so afraid to do what she knew would make her truly happy? There was a strange mystery to it all.

One day I decided to provoke Jim, to draw him out. I hung about near the Red Dog, but with my usual luck, instead of Jim, I soon encountered old Bess. Being so full of my misery, and troubles, I had not noticed her, but there she was, standing with her arms folded, right in front of me. I got quite a shock when I saw her. She had instilled such fear into me at such a young age, I must have known she would do for me in the end.

Bess was dressed in a smart black frock and her greying hair was piled high on the top of her head. She made a powerful, awe-inspiring sight. Certainly I was filled with fear. My legs refused to move.

Bess glared at me and then opened her mouth and yelled: 'Sling your bloody hook, Bill Davies. I don't want your kind round here!'

The whole village could hear. I wished the earth would open and swallow me up. I crept away as she continued to yell at me: 'My Lizzie has done well for herself, and so don't think I'm going to let the likes of you spoil it, because I ain't.'

I didn't argue. I just crept back to my lodgings

clutching a bottle of rum. I cursed and chastised myself as a coward, but I never had been able to face old Bess. I just never had it in me. What with the liquor, and the agonies in my head, I must have begun to look as bad as I felt. Old Nell was very motherly and started to have a go at me. 'Look here, Bill, you should get a job and go back to sea. If you get mixed up with that lot, you'll be sorry. No good, they ain't.'

She kept nagging on at me until I had to go down the shore to get away from her.

That morning there was a nip of autumn, even early winter, in the air when I escaped Nell's criticism and walked down to the shore. Rachel was out on the sand, her feet blue with the cold. She had matured over the last few months. Thanks to her regular shilling a week, she was better dressed, and she had recently been employed by Lizzie as nursemaid to my little boy as well.

'Listen, Bill,' she said, sitting down, and snuggling up to me. 'Why don't you pack it in with her? Lizzie don't love you. If she did, she would not let you be so miserable. I know I wouldn't,' she added with a sweet smile.

Her little face was close to mine, and I gave her a friendly kiss. I was fond of her, and extremely touched by her loyalty.

Rachel giggled and pulled away. 'Aah, you're all prickly, you ain't shaved,' she said with a laugh.

'What am I to do?' I asked the child hopelessly.

Rachel answered straight away. 'Run away with me,' she said. 'Lizzie is never going to go with you.'

I stared at her with a frown. Of course, she

probably knew more than I did about what went on at the Red Dog.

'Why?' I queried. 'How can you be so sure?'

'Well, there's always a lot of trouble going on there,' she replied, eager to tell all she knew. 'Lizzie is always crying and old Bess is always hollering. As for Jim, well he is nearly always drunk. Fancies me, he does,' she said, glancing sideways at me. 'But I love you.'

I sighed. 'Oh, Rachel, darling,' I said wearily, 'you only confuse me more. What's it all about?'

'Money,' she replied quickly. 'That's what it's all about. And believe me, Bill, they're all really afraid of you. They think you'll spoil it all for them. That's why they won't let Lizzie go.'

I did not know what she was talking about. I could not work it out. My brain felt confused, probably somewhat addled by the drink I had been consuming. What I did know was that I had come to the end of my tether and that I had to leave for a while. But I had to see Lizzie again first.

Next time Lizzie and I met she looked very pale. The evening was cold and windy, so we walked deep into the woods. She was wearing a blue cloak with a fur hood, and she looked quite serene and beautiful. But I had determined to end these meetings forever. One way or another, they had to stop.

Eventually Lizzie agreed to my plan, to a degree. I managed to convince her that I would take her away and her mother and Jim would never ever know where we were. This seemed very important to her. She also wanted to wait a while.

'The winter will be here soon,' she said. 'I cannot risk my child's life travelling the roads in the bad weather.'

While I was not delighted to hear this, I could see the sense in her words. She was a good mother, Lizzie, and would not have done anything that would harm the baby.

'All right,' I agreed. 'Swear to me that you will come in the spring, and I will be satisfied.'

'I swear,' Lizzie replied solemnly. 'I would swear on the Bible if we had one here. Now, why don't you try to get a job, Bill?' she suddenly pleaded. 'That would make the waiting time pass more quickly.'

Again, I could not disagree with her logic. We agreed to wait until the spring, and to part for a while – Lizzie to her home, and I to the town to find work.

I soon found employment in the port. It was very hard work, humping fish and sacks of potatoes off the cargo ships. I found it hard going, because of this damned stump, but I was happier than I had been for a long time. The break from Lizzie came as a relief. With a goal ahead I saved what I earned and drank much less. I even had a bit of luck at last!

I found a derelict old barge down in the creek at Hoo, and bought it very cheap. It was moored on the mud flats so I lived on board all the winter and brightened it up by stripping her down and polishing every bit I could. I had not possessed many things of my own during my life but this old barge became my most cherished possession. I spent all my spare time doing her up, and she began to look quite beautiful. I made the cabin cosy with a stove and even put curtains at the portholes. This last was a nice touch that Lizzie would appreciate, I thought. I bought new cooking utensils and made a bunk for my little son. I named my barge *Elizabeth* and was well pleased when she was all complete. I only wished that Lizzie was there with me then to see her.

It is not easy to travel to the town in the winter; the roads are dark and muddy with a tendency to get bogged up. Most people stayed at home until the spring and did not travel unless they absolutely had to. In spite of my loneliness, the winter passed quickly for me, busy as I was with my love-nest.

Bill Davies turned towards the shore. 'Looks like day over there again, I'd better leave the rest till tomorrow.' He paused and then said: 'It will be the last time tomorrow, for the moon will be gone soon.'

I was deeply involved in this story. I felt as never before. So gripped was I that I shared Bill's unhappiness with him. I went off home to bed and prayed for his peace, anxiously anticipating the end of this incredible love story.

The next night, Bill was already sitting on the oak bench when I arrived. He pointed to the window of the inn. 'The last look I had at Lizzie in this world was from up there,' he said. 'But I won't jump the gun. We will continue from where we left off.'

The March gales had subsided and there I was now well settled in the little home I had built for Lizzie. The wind blows hard down there on those mud flats and I was glad when the smell of spring was finally in the air again. I had always loved it when the buds began to swell and the sap ran in the tall trees again.

Anyway, I came home one evening after my day's work down at the dock to find Rachel installed in my cabin. She was looking very pretty and well-dressed in a blue dress and a dark cloak and, of all things, a bonnet trimmed with red ribbons. I was more surprised that she looked so grown up than I was to see her at all. It astounded me that the little Rachel of the bare feet and ragged dress was suddenly a young lady.

'Well, well,' I said with a smile. I was, of course, delighted to see a familiar face after all this time. 'We do look smart.'

Rachel flashed me a smile. 'I came up to town to do some shopping. So I thought I would find you. They told me where you were at the dock. I bought these,' she said, cocking her leg up to the bunk to show me the little brown lace-up boots she wore.

'Pull your dress down!' I chaffed. 'You're a big girl now.'

'Oh, don't be so prudish, Bill Davies,' she jeered. A mischievous smile played on her red lips.

She amused me, as always. 'I've got some kippers,' I said. 'Want some?'

'Oh, yes, please.'

'Well, get that bonnet off, and help cook them. Or is it stuck on?' said I.

We always chaffed each other, Rachel and I.

We cooked and ate a humble meal of kippers and bread. After Rachel had filled me in on the gossip from the village she suddenly seemed very wistful. 'Bill,' she said quietly. 'Let me come with you when you go.'

I shook my head ruefully. 'I am sorry, love, how can I? With Lizzie and the baby, there won't be room for you too.'

'Well, I won't go back,' she announced defiantly. 'I'll stay in Gravesend and get meself a fellow.'

I smiled, but I was concerned. Her statement needed thinking about. How could I, with any conscience, leave a young girl like Rachel alone in a seafaring town? 'I'll talk to Lizzie about it,' I said non-committally.

But little Rachel threw herself at me, almost knocking me backwards. 'I love you so much, Bill! *She* don't love you. Take me who does.'

'Hush, Rachel,' I said, as I cuddled her.

'That old Bess, she scares the wits out of me,' said Rachel.

I laughed. 'She scares me, too,' I said. 'She always has.'

'No, don't laugh, Bill,' Rachel pleaded. 'She knows something's going on. And Lizzie's all white and sad. She won't be a wife to Jim, and he chases me, he does.'

I know that she had mentioned this to me before but this time the information struck home. 'He does what?' I said, looking shocked.

Rachel smiled roguishly. 'Oh, don't worry, he only gets a clout off me. But old Bess, she keeps on at me. She knows you and I was friends. She gave me this hat,' Rachel added, prodding the gay bonnet.

'Well, she likes you, then,' I said.

Rachel shook her head. 'She's just trying to make me talk,' she said wisely.

I decided there and then that I did have to take responsibility for this child. 'Well, perhaps you had better come and take care of the boy. I can fix you up a little cabin in the stern. Lizzie won't mind.'

'Thank you, Bill,' Rachel exclaimed as she kissed me gratefully. She was all affection, my little Rachel.

Soon our plans were set. It was all arranged for a date in April on a day when the town held a big fair. Lizzie and Rachel would both come to the fair, bringing the baby. I would have the barge all ready to sail on the evening tide.

I'll never forget that morning as I waited down on the road for them. It was a lovely day. The sun had dried the road and the long line of carts went by full of farm workers and their families, all out for a day's sport. A band marched behind them and crowds of ragged children marched with the band, followed by the Morris dancers. Gypsies in bright shawls were selling lavender and telling fortunes. I didn't ask for mine. I knew mine, or at least I thought I did.

It was mid-afternoon and it had become cooler. The crowd was smaller now but there was still no sign of Lizzie. I went back to the barge and messed around with the sail, making sure that the vessel was truly shipshape and seaworthy. By this time there were snatches of song in the air, as the revellers were returning home. By six the sun had begun to go down over the sea, and black clouds tinged with red told of forthcoming bad weather. The river tide was running high. But where was Lizzie?

By now, of course, I had begun to get very apprehensive. What could have happened? A sick feeling gripped my stomach. Then suddenly, down the road came Rachel. She ran like the wind and was careless of her appearance. She wore no hat or cloak, and her black hair streamed out behind in the wind. It was most unlike her. She looked as though the devil was after her. I ran towards her.

'Oh, Bill,' she sobbed as she came up. 'They won't let her come. They found out. Look, Bess beat me!' She held out her thin arms to show me several great red weals and bruises. 'They took the baby away, and Lizzie is locked up. She told me to tell you to come.'

I took Rachel inside and tucked her up by the fire. Telling her not to move, I collected what I needed and with murder in my heart I set out for the village.

I hitched a ride to the village on a wagon loaded with lads and lasses who were making love. I ignored them and their happiness. I sat on the ledge at the back, my legs out stiff, and brooded.

Tonight, I would come back with Lizzie, or it would never happen. My hand fingered the sharp sailor's knife in my pocket as I plotted. It was dark, and the moon was full. The moonlight shone brightly on to the road as I came quietly into the yard. Looking up at the window next to the tall chimney stack, I suddenly saw my beloved Lizzie. There she was! I called and she came to the window.

At first I barely recognised her. Her face looked odd, twisted in pain. But there was no mistaking that golden hair. To avoid making too much noise, I unscrewed my wooden leg and placed it against the wall. I then climbed up on the roof, and nipped in through the window.

My lovely girl was hiding her face from me. She had thrown herself on the bed where she was sobbing piti-fully, her head in her hands. I went to her, dear God, and then I saw her face. The sight of it lit the fires of hell within me! Her beautiful face had been beaten till it was a mass of bruises. Her eyes were swollen and blood still dribbled from her mouth where teeth had been knocked out. Her lovely hair was torn and dishevelled.

'Who did this?' I asked, white and tense, my voice trembling.

'Bess,' sobbed Lizzie. 'She lost her temper. She's ready to kill when she's in a temper, that's why I'm so afraid of her. She loses all control and is quite mad.'

I looked around the room. 'And the boy, where's my boy, Lizzie?'

Lizzie shook her head miserably. 'I don't know,' she sobbed. 'That's why I can't go with you, Bill. They won't let me take the baby. But I'll tell, I said I would,' she said, vehemently. There was a flash of defiance in her eyes.

'Tell me what?'

'About your lucky stone, Bill ... it was an uncut diamond.'

Well, you could have knocked me sideways. 'A diamond?' I muttered. 'That old bit of rock? What nonsense!'

Lizzie wailed. 'No, it's not nonsense, you have to

believe me. They took it from me, they stole it and they sold it,' she sobbed. 'That's how they bought the pub.' She wailed pathetically. 'I just never dared tell you what had happened.'

I could feel the veins bulging at my temples. Now I was more ready than ever to murder Jim. He had taken my girl *and* got rich at my expense.

'Lie still, darling,' I whispered through gritted teeth. 'I'll get that swine, and I'll be back for you.' I climbed back out of the window and slid down into the yard.

I must have made a lot of noise because as I reached the ground, I heard the door open and a drunken Jim came roaring out of the inn. Spotting me, he let out a great howl and rushed at me, his arms flailing. I was taken by surprise but I lurched at him with my knife. But without my wooden stump, I could not balance at all. I fell to the ground and Jim went hurtling across the yard.

As I struggled to get my stump back on, suddenly old Bess appeared dressed in a long white night-gown, her grey hair streaming loose behind her. The last sound I heard in this world was of my Lizzie screaming my name. Then something hit me, and I knew no more.

That was the end. Now, this is the funniest part. I came to later on, while I was being buried. My spirit sat on the church wall watching the burial. They did not want the sheriff to know that they had committed a murder so they had to get rid of the evidence – my body – as quickly as possible. Jim was sobbing and shaking as he dug a hole behind the churchyard wall.

His face was almost as white as mine, so frightened was he. Old Bess was scooping up the earth with her hands. 'Keep digging, you fool,' she ordered the snivelling Jim.

Jim was moaning. 'He was my best mate. Who would have thought it would all end like this?' Tears poured down his face. 'If only we hadn't taken that diamond . . .'

Bess gave Jim a great clout with her forearm. 'Shut your silly mouth!' Shoving him aside, she grabbed the spade and then picked up my body. She dragged me into the shallow grave and rolled me in. Then she started shovelling the damp earth on top of me, stamping it down firm with her huge feet, those huge ugly feet I had been so scared of as a child.

I smiled as I watched the panic in their faces. Now I knew that nothing or nobody could hurt me anymore.

And this was true. I had become an earth-bound spirit, and now I could be here all the time to protect my lovely Lizzie and my son.

The funny part of this story is that old Bess killed me with my own wooden leg. She had hit me on the side of the head, on the temple. It knocked me off immediately.

For a while I had the best of both worlds. I watched my son grow big and sturdy. He always knew I was here. We played games together and he would tell people that he could see a funny old ghost. Of course, people just thought it was the child's vivid imagination, as most would. Or at least they liked to believe that that was the case.

And Lizzie I lay with every night. I made love to her, and I know she knew it was me. She didn't tell anyone for fear of being labelled mad, but those were happy days for us.

Jim died first. He fell down the altar steps dead drunk one day after he had seen me and run to the church for safety. Cracked his skull open, he did. Bess scarpered after I gave her a fright one night. Only Lizzie remained then, with my son David, looking after the inn and living for no purpose, really. It was very sad; for I could do little to comfort her then.

People stayed away from the inn after a rumour went around that it was haunted. It was ridiculous, of course. And then my darling Lizzie got ill with small-pox. She died very quickly and there was nothing I could do. I sat by her side and held her hand but she was no longer aware of me. That was the saddest time of my life. It was hard for me once Lizzie had gone, what with her up there in heaven and me stuck on earth. I was miserable. But then a little ray of sunshine came in the form of Rachel, who had taken on my little boy and now took on the pub too. She attracted customers, ghost or no ghost. Whenever I walked about, she would know immediately and say: 'Don't you wake the child now, Bill Davies.' I knew she still loved me even though I had never been able to give her what she had yearned for.

Yes, Rachel was quite a woman. She never married but she had countless lovers. She brought up my son and grandson to be fine, steady men. I missed her when she finally died, at the grand old age of ninety.

Bill pointed to the sky. 'Ah, there's the dawn again. That's it now, mate. That's the end of my tale. If you are moved by it then go have a word with the parson for me. Get him to give me a Christian burial ceremony and then I'll be able to join my Lizzie. She's still waiting for me and I'm sure I'll be joining her there – in spite of the misdeeds I committed in my life. I certainly won't be going where Jim and Bess found their final resting places.'

Bill Davies leaned over and nudged me. 'I'll be grateful to you for that, mate. And I'll tell you another thing . . . if you ever have a lucky charm, don't give it away, however strong the impulse might be. If it's lucky for you, there's a reason. Sometimes it's right to be selfish, and disastrous to be otherwise. I'll be leaving you now, mate.'

I took Bill's words to heart. The vicar of the village was a good man and, although I don't think he believed a word of what I told him, he was happy enough to say the necessary prayers over Bill's grave.

As he did so, I watched two swallows sitting on the telegraph wires suddenly rise on the wing and disappear into the clouds. My heart lifted. Who knows if they were really the two souls I thought they were but I went to bed that night knowing that Bill and his Lizzie had been reunited at last.

THE LONG SPOON

The Long Spoon

'To sup with the Devil, you need a long spoon.' How often have we said these words to one another, with a laugh, or perhaps fingers crossed behind our backs? Like many other superstitions, it is one we dismiss as nonsense but are never quite sure about. Are we?

Old Clara Buckley possessed a long spoon. It was very old and made of wood which had been originally carved in a medieval design – figures with ugly gargoyle faces and strangely contorted bodies and limbs. It was made from the wood of the yew tree, very hard and full of the mysteries of life.

The spoon was hanging by the fireplace when Clara had come to Marsh Cottage thirty years ago. It had been left by the previous owners who showed no inter-est in taking it with them when they left their three-hundred-year-old home for the last time. Clara was happy to have it. It looked decorative and seemed to fit there perfectly, as though it had been specially made to hang in that particular spot on the wall.

But the spoon was not just a piece of decoration. It was very useful. Clara took it down from the wall and used it whenever necessary.

At this precise moment, Clara held that long

wooden spoon and viciously stirred the gooseberry jam that hubbled and bubbled on her open range fire. Her wrinkled face worked up and down as her loose mouth sucked at the one remaining tooth projecting out in front.

'Darn the whole darn lot of them,' she muttered, giving the jam another vigorous stir. Her wispy hair stood out untidily from her head, and her blue cotton dress was faded and soiled.

Behind her, the back door was open. Beyond the garden lay the vast expanse of marshland that lined the furthermost banks of the Thames. Flat and rolling they were, a bright emerald-green, inhabited only by wild birds, white woolly sheep and herds of black and white cattle. It was always misty there, summer and winter, and a cold fresh wind blew in from the sea. In the evening, when the marsh gases rose, blue 'will o' the wisp' danced like fairies, almost up to Clara's back door. Not that it bothered her. Nothing much did. At the age of seventy-five, Clara was untroubled by ghosties or ghoulies or anything else, just as she no longer had an eye for the natural beauty that surrounded her, either. No, it wasn't nature that bothered her, it was her fellow humans that did.

She was in a temper now as she thought about the villagers sitting in groups in the local pub. 'Unfriendly lot,' she murmured. 'Been living in Bel Uncle Halt too long, I have. Knows too much about them. Don't ask yer to have a drink, or even give you the time of day. They forget I had money once and spent it with them, don't they?' Her beady eyes shot a glance at the black cat whose green unwinking eyes surveyed her from his seat on the table.

As Clara looked at the cat, her eyes fell on the box beside him. She drew up the spoon and wiped it along the rim of the jam kettle, banging it several times to knock off the last blobs of green jam. 'Well, now is the time to have a look, Jet,' she said to the cat. 'I've put it off for as long as I can, and now's the time to find out whether we have discovered treasure or not.'

The cat chirruped at her in response and got to his feet. He arched his back and curled himself around the dirty box which rested beside him on a red tapestry tablecloth. The box was very old. Its metal clasps were rusty brown with age.

Forgetting her annoyance at her neighbours, spoon in hand, Clara went over to the table and eyed the old box warily. 'Findings keepings, Jet. Well, it might be full of gold,' she pondered. 'Or it might be old bones!' She cackled softly.

The box had turned up in her garden that afternoon having been dug up by the bulldozers that were demolishing part of the old rectory next door. The rectory and its grounds were even older than Clara's cottage. Rumour had it that there was a ghost and that the bishops had held a sort of Last Supper there before going to Runnymede to witness the signing of the Magna Carta. And that was as far back as the reign of King John. Now it was all going to make way for an oil refinery.

When the demolition men had first moved in with their bulldozers and sledgehammers, Clara had been furious. She complained incessantly about the noise and the dust caused by the operation and she cursed the men who trampled about in her garden without permission. She only stopped moaning when the builders presented her with the box they had dug up at the very edge of her property.

'It's yours by right, ma'am,' the foreman said politely as he handed it to her by the back door.

'That should shut the old bag up,' he said to his men later. 'I can't see that there's much importance in it. It felt empty, to me.'

Now Clara circled the table cautiously. Well, now was the time to open it. Then with a surprisingly deft movement, she struck the box with the long, jammy spoon. The rusted clasps fell off, the lid popped open. Inside were old papers, yellow with age.

'Papers, only old papers!' Clara sniffed dolefully. She sniffed again at the strange smell that suddenly curled around her nostrils. 'Odd smell,' she muttered and hobbled across the room to get a heavy magnifying glass from the shelf. Then she unrolled the musty manuscripts and peered at them through the glass.

She saw strange uneven writing, some in red ink, some in dark brown ink. There were lots of little pictures. Staring closer, she could see they were human figures, all naked, some lying on top of others. She moved the spy glass up and down.

'Well, my goodness,' she cackled. 'They're having a bit of the other!' With a bony index finger moving along the paper, Clara tried to read the words, laboriously spelling out each letter, once, twice, then thrice.

The room suddenly became very cold, though the fire roared and spluttered. Jet ached his back and began spitting furiously.

'What's up with you, Jet?' Clara gave the cat a whack with the long spoon, causing the poor animal to shoot out of the back door, his tail bushy with fright.

'Drat the bloody cat! Now I feel as cold as Hades,' grumbled Clara. 'Well, no gold for us, after all,' she sniffed. 'It was ridiculous to think there might have been something precious. And who wants a load of smelly yellow papers? Might as well go and have a drink,' she muttered, looking in her purse. 'There's just enough for a glass of ale.'

Leaving the papers spread about the table, Clara took her old tweed coat from behind the door, and slipped her arms into the sleeves with a little shiver.

She set off down the lane to the village pub on her thin legs. Her wrinkled stockings fell about her ankles and her much-cobbled shoes looked too big for her feet.

The lane to the pub was long, dark and very winding, but it held no terrors for her.

Puffing and grunting like an old nag on a hill, Clara finally reached the pub and pushed open the heavy bar door. For a moment she stood in the doorway squinting at the sudden brightness of the lights. Her old face was pale and her wispy grey hair blew about in the wind.

A huge mountain of flesh surveyed her from behind the bar. Encased in fat, Jed's small, mean eyes gazed with hostility in her direction. The proprietor's fat arms rested on the old brass beer pump, and behind him was a shelf of fly-blown bottles. By the corner three men played cards. As Clara came in, one looked up. He grinned, revealing a row of very white teeth. 'Watch it, Jed!' he called. 'The old gel's out on her broomstick. It must be Hallowe'en.'

Not a flicker of a smile came from the large landlord as he served Clara her drink. She sniffed and took her glass of strong ale to a seat by the fire.

'It's turned darned cold,' she muttered to herself loudly.

'Old Jed will warm you up,' jeered the wit, his healthy red face shining as brightly as his magnificent teeth.

'Bah!' snarled Clara. 'Like a lot of damned bulls, you are, with nothing to think about except the mating season.'

Roars of laughter filled the bar.

Jed had now been joined by his daughter, Violet. She was dressed in navy overalls, a black beret and Wellington boots. She had a long bovine face. Violet always dressed in this manner, and she was much more at home in the stable or barn than in a bar. She was known by the Young Bulls (as Clara called the inhabitants of Jed's bar) as Sweet Violet, sweeter than all the roses, because of the stable smell that she always carried around with her.

'Good evening,' Violet greeted Clara.

Clara nodded briefly in response.

At ten o'clock Clara rose to her feet rather unsteadily. She had consumed four strong ales, three of which had been paid for by the Young Bulls. The beer Clara drank was called a BF, or Bishop's Finger. As she had drunk four Bishop's Fingers, the handsome wit in the bar could not resist a final quip. 'Why not stay and have a Bishop's Thumb?' he called to Clara as she fumbled with her coat.

This, of course, just set the old woman grumbling again, and she said nothing in return.

Clara left the pub and made her way down that dark lane towards her cottage once more. As she walked she thought about the inhabitants of the bar again. 'Miserable hole,' she complained. 'Fat old pig,' she declared of Jed. 'And that half-witted daughter looks more like a cow every day.'

The lane was now completely black. Mud squelched underfoot. Feeling breathless, Clara paused to rest a while. As she stood in the middle of the muddy lane, she heard a sound ahead of her. She narrowed her eyes and peered out into the blackness. 'Who's there?' she called. At first there was nothing. But then, from the deep night, a pale slim figure came towards her. A faint shaft of moonlight seemed to pierce the clouded sky.

The first thing Clara noticed was the bare feet walking in the muddy lane. There were two small white feet. Then the moon was suddenly shining down on the slim figure of a young girl. Clara was momentarily startled. But not much could frighten Clara. Within seconds, she had recovered sufficiently to shout: 'What the hell are you doing lurking about in the dark and frightening people?'

A sweet voice that tinkled like a bell came back through the dark, 'I came to meet you.'

'Meet me?' snorted Clara. 'And *who* are you?'

'Don't you know? I am related to you, Clara.' The voice went on, sweet and cajoling.

Clara moved in closer to stare at this lovely apparition of a young girl with long golden hair. She was dressed in a full-length printed frock but had no shoes or stockings on her feet. It was most odd.

'Who are you? I don't know you,' Clara quizzed her repeatedly. 'You ain't Elsie's girl, that's for sure. She's very dark.'

'No, I am Theodora. You sent for me,' the girl replied.

As Clara started walking again, the girl began to walk along beside her.

'No good coming with me,' grumbled Clara. 'I can't be bothered with kids any more. What's the point? Never worry over me, do they? Nine, I brought up, and not one cares now if I live or die.' Clara marched on still complaining.

A soft giggle came from Theodora's mouth as the girl walked alongside. On the doorstep of the cottage, Clara fumbled for her latch key. 'Don't think you are coming in here,' she warned. 'I can't keep meself. Besides,' she added, 'what are you doing without shoes and stockings on? One of those hippy drop-outs, I suppose.'

But the girl ignored her. She slipped in beside the old woman and squatted by the fire. 'You go off to bed, Gran,' she said. 'I'll stay here beside the fire.'

Clara noticed that she had a strange heart-shaped face and a halo of golden hair. Her almond-shaped eyes glowed darkly, veiled by heavy lashes. Her eyes were a strange opaque yellow, almost like those of a cat.

'I ain't going up yet,' said Clara. 'I like a good warm drink before I go up to bed. Besides,' she peered suspiciously at her guest, 'how do I know who you might be? You might murder me in my sleep. You look just like one of them hippies, you do.'

But Theodora was not listening. She was staring with a strange expression at the yellowed papers on the table. She got up and went forward towards the table. Two slim hands reached out towards the papers. Strange foreign words poured from her lips.

'Ere,' cried Clara. 'Leave them be, they ain't yours!'

But the girl had gathered them up and held them tight to her breast, her eyes gleaming with a strange sort of yellow fire. 'These are mine, all mine,' she cried. 'These are my master's papers.'

Old Clara tried to rise but an invisible force held her down in the chair. Speechless and paralysed, her mouth worked and her eyes rolled helplessly as the fair young maiden came and sat cross-legged in front of her.

'You are going to die, old woman,' tinkled the bell-like voice. 'You are having a fit. In two minutes you will have left this world of mortals.' The beautiful almond eyes stared at her hypnotically.

Clara gasped. She spat and dribbled but she could not move a limb.

'I can save you,' continued Theodora. 'I know the

dark secret of the ages. You need not die. Give yourself to me. Come, Clara, be mine.' The slim hands caressed Clara's wrinkled face. 'Come on, my dear, it's easy,' the cajoling voice went on.

'Help me,' groaned Clara. She reached out to grasp the slim white hand that was held out to her. Then she passed into oblivion.

The morning sun rose like a ball of red fire. Jack the shepherd was tired and hungry. He had been out on the marsh all night trying to rescue an old ram that had got stuck in a dyke. He was now on his way home to his breakfast and his black and white sheepdog trotted beside him.

To his left was Marsh Cottage, standing dark and gloomy on the frosty skyline. As he came level with the cottage and was about to turn into the lane, the dog went down on its haunches and set up a terrific howling, letting out long mournful sounds that echoed out uncannily into the silent morn.

'Quiet,' ordered Jack. 'What the hell's wrong? Come on, old boy.' He called but the dog refused to move. It continued to howl, nose in the air.

'Something's upsetting him. It might be a fox in old Clara's hen house.' He went forward, his eyes scouting the yard. Then he peered through the window. Through the dirty glass he could see old Clara, lying back in her chair, her mouth wide open. On her face lay the pallor of death.

'Oh my God! The old gal's snuffed it,' he cried and went hurrying off to get help.

By mid-day the cottage was full of people bustling around – Clara's relatives. There were Doris and Joe from Hadlow, Mary and John from the town, Bet and Peter from the village. All were anxious and eager to share in the spoils of Clara's death.

Downstairs Mary and Bet were rummaging around in the china cabinet. Little figures stared out at them, real Dresden shepherds and shepherdesses, a pair of porcelain horses and a complete bone china tea-set.

Red-faced and breathless, Bet goggled at the sight. Her mother-in-law had never allowed her even to look at it before.

Mary was slightly superior to the rest, with her smart hair-do and her horn-rimmed spectacles. She was holding a small jug up to the light and gazing with professional interest at the anchor mark on the base. It was genuine all right. It must be worth a great deal. 'It's all this that old Pete left her,' she said. 'Fancy her being so hard-up, yet hanging on to all this precious china for all those years.'

'Wouldn't give nothing away, she wouldn't,' complained Bet. 'Old Clara was a mean old cow. Anyway, my Peter is entitled to this lot, what with him being old Peter's son. You know, being the youngest, who else could have been his father?'

Mary's thin lips tightened. 'Well, never mind all that now. It's fair shares all round. It has to be because you can bet your life Clara never willed any of it to anyone.'

Bet's bulbous nose and her loose mouth worked in agitation. 'Worth a bomb, all this china is, let's get in before Elsie comes,' she suggested. 'She don't know what's here. And she need never know, either!'

'It's an idea,' agreed Mary, possessively holding a perfectly formed white china horse.

Upstairs Peter and Joe, two of Clara's sons, were staring down at their mother, not so much in affection as in awe. They had never seen her down and silent before. In their memory she was always up and fighting fit, was Ma. Now she lay neat and still in her white bed while they waited for the undertaker to arrive.

'Let's go down and have a drink,' suggested Joe. 'It feels creepy up here.'

'Yes, there might be some old whisky down there. She hoarded a lot of stuff.'

'Wonder what this cottage is worth now,' said Peter. 'It belonged to my father, it did.'

Joe frowned at this remark. 'That's only hearsay. Don't forget there are nine of us to share in everything Ma left.'

Nothing more was said but as they climbed down the narrow stairs, the atmosphere between them was rather strained.

The cows lowed out on the marshland and lunchtime workers were going back to the fields, when a strange thing happened in Marsh Cottage. Soon after two o'clock, Elsie had arrived from London, having jumped on a train the moment she heard of her mother's death. Now a heated argument was in progress, Elsie's arrival having sparked off the brewing argument between the siblings and their spouses. Now all restraints had been lifted and they squabbled like a lot of vultures over the spoils of death.

Far away, from upstairs, a strange sound was suddenly heard. The family stopped shouting at each other to listen. It was like an angry yell. They all looked up at the ceiling.

Their hearts were thumping in their throats as they listened to the tapping noise and heard a kind of rumbling. Then they heard someone coming down the stairs. They stood motionless, their faces white with shock as they watched old Clara walk down the narrow stairs wearing her long white calico nightie. The tapping came from the umbrella which she used to steady herself as she walked.

Jaws dropped, faces paled and silence reigned. Suddenly there appeared on the windowsill outside a strange yellow cat which stared with obvious amusement at them with its opaque yellow eyes.

Mary was still possessively clasping the white porcelain horse. She fingered it nervously as Clara's beady eyes settled on it first.

'Hi,' Clara yelled. 'What are you doing in the cabinet? Put that back!'

Mary let go of the horse and it slipped between her fingers and splintered on the hard oak floor. Letting out a terrific scream, Mary rushed for the door.

Clara gave her a hard whack with the umbrella as she passed. 'Careless bitch!' she yelled. 'Nosy lot of buggers! What do you all want? Why is me best sheets on the bed, and who put this bloody tent on me?' She pointed at the long white gown she was draped in.

Their initial terror had worn off once they realised that Clara was not a ghost at all but her old self in the flesh. Her children all began to make their excuses and left.

Half an hour later, dressed now in her old blue cotton dress and ragged cardigan, Clara made herself a cup of tea. On the sill sat the yellow cat.

'Shoo, go away!' roared Clara, rattling the window. 'Whose bloody cat is that? And where is me poor old Jet?' She walked about the cottage muttering and mumbling. She was feeling rather bewildered as though there were something she had forgotten.

'Funny waking up and finding myself dead,' she pondered. 'Must have slept heavy. Could have been the beer!' Then she brought in the logs from the garden to make up the fire; there, sitting in a chair and toasting her bare toes, was the young girl from the previous evening. She had the same inscrutable smile on those fair features.

Clara goggled at her. 'Here,' she said fiercely. 'Hop it! You go with the rest of them and bloody good riddance, too.'

Theodora only giggled. 'You chose me, Clara. You asked me to stay.'

'Don't tell bloody lies,' stormed Clara. 'Worse fibber than Elsie, you are, and that's saying something.'

But those strange penetrating eyes glared balefully at her for a second. 'Sit down, you bad-tempered old woman!' Theodora ordered.

Clara didn't know why but she sat down facing her, aware of a warm kind of radiance that seemed to exude from the girl.

'You died last night,' whispered Theodora. 'But I saved you, so for a short while you will belong to me, to do as I wish.' In these honeyed tones she went on. 'I have lived in this cottage before. My name was Dora Buckley. At the Hallowe'en of sixteen hundred and six, they burned me as a witch. Look!' She pushed back her golden hair to expose a deep scar that ran along the side of her neck almost up to her ear. 'That's what they did to me – the innkeeper, the farmer and his sons. They killed my betrothed who tried to rescue me. I fled to the pond but they caught me and tied me to a stake and built a fire around me. They poked me with pitchforks and shouted curses at me. I did not burn. I still live on and *you* called me, Clara. You found the master's papers and evoked the spell that gave me back my body. Now you can never be rid of me until I've had my revenge on this accursed hamlet.'

'I know, you're the ghost that old Pete said haunted the rectory.'

'Yes, your lover knew me,' agreed Theodora.

'He was an odd one, old Pete – always looking for spirits,' said Clara. 'Some said he was barmy but I loved him,' she continued. 'Had a son by him, and I was turned forty!' She cackled. 'It didn't half upset that lot in the village, it did.' Clara cackled again loudly.

'So you do now believe?' asked Theodora.

'If you say you're a ghost, it's up to you,' replied Clara irritably. 'Got enough to keep bloody going, as it is.'

Dora came towards her, her eyes softening as she

stroked the wrinkled cheek. 'Don't worry, old woman, your aches and pains will go. I can give you youth.'

'Money would be more handy,' snorted Clara.

'If that is your desire, I've gold and silver at your command.'

And a pile of coins dripped from those slim white hands into Clara's lap.

A deep dark cold mist floated up the Thames and over the marshland encircling Gallows End and rising in between the red brick chimneys. It skimmed the village pond and completely obscured the tall reeds and the green slimy water.

For years the locals had complained about this pond. What a place for a deep pond they said, just outside the door of the one and only pub. It was five or six steps down and there were slippery banks underfoot. The number of folk who had disappeared into this pond after a good night's boozing could not be counted.

The pond was extremely deep and seemed almost bottomless. And it was dangerous. Had not old Bill Taylor, recently deceased, caught pneumonia after being pulled out blind drunk one Saturday night? And he was only the last of many. So the villagers groused and protested to old Jed, the landlord, but still he had done nothing about it.

'Fill in the bloody pond? And who's going to pay for that?' he would argue. No one had an answer, so the pond remained, and so did the customers as there was nowhere else to drink.

Tonight the green water lay still and silent under the mist. Inside the dimly lit bar the locals gathered. Saturday night was gala night when the women joined their men for a drink and sat in little groups gossiping. Then the men played darts or hung about the bar.

Jed the landlord was as big and as aggressive as always and his sweet daughter, Violet, had her bobbed hair brushed flat and was wearing a plain jumper and skirt which made her look a little less masculine than usual.

Amidst all the gossipers was Clara's daughter-in-law, Bet. Her face was wet and shiny after several gins. Her chin wagged up and down and she eyed the door nervously. The other women gazed at her with avid interest as she told of her mother-in-law's rise from the dead.

'Honestly,' she quivered, 'dead as a doornail, she was. It upsets me so, I can't hardly bear to think of it.'

'How awful, shocking!' muttered her cronies. 'Never have forgiven yourself if you had buried her alive.'

Suddenly there was a cold draught as the door opened with a bang. Then all eyes turned towards the door, all with the same expression of astonishment as Clara walked in wearing a new fur coat and a smart hat. The most astonishing thing about her was that her face looked ten years younger.

Behind her walked a young girl, a beautiful girl with long blonde hair and a low-necked print dress that had a very unusual paisley pattern. From beneath the long swinging skirt peeped two bare feet.

As the Young Bulls moved over to make room at the bar, they goggled like barn owls at this beautiful hippy and at Clara who looked like a duchess. Just two high stools stood near the bar. Theodora wriggled daintily up on to one, crossing her legs and revealing a long bare expanse of well-shaped flesh. Clara, as agile as a teenager, climbed up on to the other stool and took out a five pound note from her bag. 'Two double brandies, please,' she said loudly.

Violet just stood and gawked at the newcomers, but surly Jed poured the drinks and handed over the change. The quizzical look in his crafty deep-set eyes was obvious when he saw the young girl pursing her lips and leaning forward so that he could get a good view down that low neckline. Jed's thick neck quivered, and his rolls of fat wobbled like jelly as he stared back at her. The Young Bulls licked their lips and the gossips brought their heads closer. Not for a long time had there been such excitement and tension at Gallows End.

Clara consumed many brandies, smoked endless fags, and sang 'April Showers', in a loud untuneful voice. Then finding her audience unappreciative, she became very insulting to the knot of females seated about a small table. One of them being, of course, her own daughter-in-law, Bet.

'Thought I'd snuffed it, didn't yer,' she yelled. 'After me bits and pieces, wasn't yer!' But Bet made a quick exit.

Bill was the eldest of all the Young Bulls. He was in his late thirties and a bit thin on top. He had intelligent green-grey eyes and a little barrel belly rested on the top of his trousers. He was cautious of women, his sweetheart having done the dirty on him years ago, so

Bill stayed at home in the cottage with his mum. He worked on the farm all day and drank in Gallows End all the rest of the time.

After a while, Theodora seemed to lose interest in Jed, and instead, with her bare feet, wriggled her toes against Bill's trouser leg. But Bill was not going to be taken on by some doped-up hippy. Not Bill. 'What's your game?' he said, as a hot tingle coursed right up his leg. 'Go and put some bloody shoes on!' he snarled.

But Theodora only shook her blonde hair and leaned nearer.

'Get your tits out of me beer,' he yelled coarsely.

But now Theodora only flicked her dark lashes and looked at him provocatively with those opaque yellow eyes. Now this was the language that Bill understood. He knew when a woman fancied him. He pricked up immediately and his posture became that of an aggressive young rooster. 'Get the lady a drink,' he called to Jed, who filled Theodora's glass with brandy but banged Bill's empty pewter pot loudly upon the counter. The two men then glared at each other like two fighting cocks preparing for battle.

Old Clara laughed and cackled. 'Got them both on a bit of string,' she whispered to Theodora. 'Serves them bloody right.'

The evening's entertainment ended with Clara staggering out holding on to Bill's arm. They made slow progress down the lane. Beads of perspiration appeared on Bill's brow in spite of the cold mist.

Theodora brushed close to him, her eyes giving out suggestive glances.

Bill thought he had the situation in hand. 'Let's get Granny home and then you and me will go for a little walk, darling,' he said.

Theodora gave him a demure smile in response.

Ten minutes later, Clara was pushed unceremoniously into her cottage where she collapsed in her chair, singing snatches of old songs and then breaking off into long arguments with herself.

Bill closed the door quietly and then made a grab at Theodora. The girl came willingly and floated like thistle-down into his clumsy bearlike embrace. A strange excitement shot through him as she kissed him full on the lips. He felt helpless and hopeless. No woman had ever done that to him before. 'Come on, let's go into the old barn,' he whispered hoarsely.

'No, let's go to the woods,' said Theodora very sweetly.

'But it's cold up there, and misty,' protested the frustrated lover.

But Theodora had drifted from him. 'To the woods or not at all,' she said firmly. She walked ahead, her finger beckoning to him.

Bill crashed after her, 'Wait for me, my love. It's misty. I might lose you.'

First the girl's fair slim shape was there calling him. Then she was way ahead, behind a tree.

Bill panicked. 'Wait for me!' His huge body crashed through the undergrowth as he called louder and louder. All he heard was the slight tinkle of silvery laughter from his elusive love. He stood motionless on the woodland path, the deep dark night all around, then he held his head in bewilderment. She was playing up. Now he was getting annoyed, even angry. Wait till he got hold of the bitch! He'd make her pay . . . Angry brute strength rose up in him as he saw her coming down the path towards him. She was completely naked, her slim body twisting and turning. Her arms were above her head as she moved rhythmically towards him. This was too much for any man. He dashed towards her with a roar and suddenly he crashed head-first over a deep ravine, his loud cries echoing through the woods as his heavy body rolled over and over down one hundred feet. From the bushes dashed a large yellow cat making straight for home, Marsh Cottage.

The news buzzed around the village and its neighbourhood like swarms of angry bees, from the farm to the coastguard's cottage, and back to the village into the shop-cum-post-office.

'Have you heard?' women whispered and nodded at each other. 'Last night it happened.'

Dennis the poacher had discovered Big Bill, down in the old gravel pit with both his legs broken. It was a miracle that he had not drowned, as the gravel pit was known to contain a great deal of water.

'Got hung up on a tree stump,' the gossips informed one and all.

'Dennis might never have heard him yelling if he had gone down deeper.'

'Drunk, I suppose.'

'You bet. He always is.'

'But that's not all. It's said he was up there with a woman and she pushed him in.'

'Who was it?' echoes of voices demanded. Villagers stared anxiously at their informer. Surely they would learn the name of the woman.

'It's the young hippy girl from London. Supposed to be old Clara's granddaughter.'

'Good God, what is the village coming to?'

The postmistress was a holy disciple, being a member of the Jehovah's Witnesses. She rolled her eyes to heaven. 'Dear Jesus,' she cried, 'protect us from this evil!'

'Better shut up,' cried one old lady, nudging her friend. 'Don't want to start her off.'

'Yes, it's poor old Bill and his mother that I pity.' This group of gossips dispersed but the speculation went on all day in various cottages.

Bill's old mother hung her head in shame while she was waiting at the hospital, and listened to her son roaring in pain as his legs were put in a plastercast.

Out in Marsh Cottage, old Clara was gradually getting used to her guest. She was not such a bad little girl, she told herself. Very free with her money, she was, and kind of funny. What fantastic tales she told of being burned as a witch. Too much imagination, Clara decided, but then Clara took it all with a pinch of salt anyway. And it was a change to have a bit of young company.

Clara was feeling uncommonly good today. She had no aches or pains and was bursting with energy.

At that moment Theodora was scrabbling about down at the bottom of the garden. Clara decided to see what she was up to. But now Theodora was returning with her skirt bunched together. It was full of rubbish and her hands were covered in clay. There was a strange triumphant smile upon her lips.

'What have you got there?' demanded Clara.

'All the ingredients I need,' replied Theodora. Her eyes shone and her face radiated happiness.

Old Clara stood looking at her in puzzlement for a moment and then, with unusual affection, she said: 'You are a funny little bugger. And what a mess you've made of yourself. And what with that dress being all you've got to wear.'

Theodora excitedly turned over the weeds and plants she had brought in. Clara noticed that she also had a big ball of clay.

'I don't know what you're up to,' declared Clara. 'You don't seem to be bothered at all about your appearance. I've never ever seen you tidy your hair.'

Clara undid the buttons at the back of the print dress and it slipped to the floor. Theodora stood there completely naked, but she took no heed and just continued to sort out her new treasures.

'Oh my gawd!' cried Clara. 'Mean to say you don't wear drawers?'

Theodora was quite unconcerned about her nakedness but she looked at the astonished Clara. 'Leave my dress alone, Gran,' she said. 'It will perish if you put water on it!' But she still made no attempt to put the dress back on.

'You are a rum one, and no mistake,' declared Clara.

'Now listen, Gran,' Theodora's sweet voice continued, 'I'll put my dress on if it offends you but will you go shopping for me?'

'Don't see why not,' replied Clara. 'There's only one shop and there ain't a lot of choice there.'

'This is what I want: candles, lots of them, and great big ones. And pins, lots of pins. Don't hurry back. Go and have a drink.'

Clara was only too willing to get out. She felt oddly restless, almost as she did when courting Pete all those years ago. The village shop was still buzzing with the news about Bill and the hippy, and with great religious fervour the postmistress was informing every customer – familiar or not – of the evil invasion of the village by hippies, drop-outs and flea-ridden, shoeless heathens. One was here already and more were coming any minute. Several stout women were hanging on to every word. Their presence almost filled the small shop.

With the sudden arrival of old Clara you could have heard a pin drop. She stood in the doorway, a shabby figure in her old cardigan but somehow much more upright than usual. Her teeth were in and her hair soft and white.

'Is that all you've bloody got to do, Daisy?' she addressed a harassed bystander who fled from the shop with fingers crossed. But another bolder villager said: 'I hear you've got your granddaughter staying.'

'Have I? Well, that's my business,' snorted Clara.

'I suppose you've heard about Big Bill,' said the

postmistress, her eyes round and protruding from behind those thick lenses.

'No, what about him?' demanded Clara crustily.

'Broke both his legs. He fell down the gravel pit.'

'Should mind where he is walking,' replied Clara. 'Blind drunk, I suppose.'

'No,' cried the postmistress. 'That hippy girl who's staying with you, pushed him.'

For a moment Clara looked taken aback. But then she quickly recovered. 'Silly lot of old cows,' she cried. 'Give me some candles and pins. I ain't got time to waste on you.'

'Thinking of a power cut?' asked the postmistress as she packed up the candles.

'No, I'm having a bloody wake,' sniffed Clara.

'Please refrain from swearing,' complained the postmistress.

'Swearing?' yelled Clara. 'I ain't even started yet, and the whole bloody village will hear me when I do.'

The postmistress raised her eyes piously toward the ceiling as if her friend the Lord lived upstairs.

'It ain't no good calling on Him,' cackled Clara. 'After the larks you got up to when them Yanks was here, it's going to be a long time before you get back in His good books!' Then cackling like a hen, Clara took hold of her parcel and left the other women standing in the gloom of the small shop.

'Ah!' she muttered gleefully. 'I wonder what Theodora did to Bill. Serves him right, whatever it was, serves them all bloody right.'

Feeling very pleased with herself, she went home to

Marsh Cottage. There she found the curtains drawn and a queer blue haze pervading the room. Theodora was still naked and she stood stirring a big pot on the fire with Clara's long wooden spoon.

'Phew!' exclaimed Clara as she put the bag of candles and pins on the table. 'What a stink!'

'It's quite all right, Gran,' said Theodora placidly. 'I'm making some wine.' Her voice seemed to drift up from the murky blue haze.

'Oh, you naughty girl, what are you doing to me gooseberry jam?' wailed Clara. 'And it's very dark in here,' said Clara, looking worried.

'Hush, Gran,' said Theodora. 'Give me the candles so I can light them.' She took the candles and lit them one by one, standing all ten of them along the shelf. 'We are going to play a nice game. You will like it,' Theodora's sweet voice continued.

Clara sat down in her chair but looked about her suspiciously. What was she up to? Funny sort of girl, never know how to take her. Clara did wish the girl would put some clothes on. All these thoughts tumbled through the bewildered old lady's mind but Theodora, flushed and smiling, brought her a little glass of liquid.

'Drink it up, Gran,' she urged. 'It's some homemade wine, and it'll do you good.'

'Not bad,' remarked Clara as she sipped the liquid appreciatively.

Theodora had lit the last of the candles. Now she was swaying and singing all the time. Clara began to feel very placid and sleepy as she watched her, and quickly dozed off peacefully in her chair. Through a faint faraway dream, Clara imagined that small animals came in to the room; bells jingled and danced. She remembered seeing that white body twisting and turning but it all seemed unreal.

She awoke in the cold dawn light feeling very rested, even though she had spent the night in her chair. There was no sign of Theodora so Clara made herself a cup of tea.

'Where is that bloody girl? Keeps disappearing like that.' Then Clara went out into the garden to feed the chickens.

Hanging in the orchard from a branch of the old apple tree was the body of a young man. His legs were hanging stiffly down as he swung gently in the breeze.

'Oh my God!' exclaimed Clara. 'It's poor old Doughy Meade.'

She went dashing down the lane to the vicarage where the old vicar was still in bed. He listened to Clara's story while in his dressing gown. He seemed very disbelieving of her but he did eventually telephone the police station.

For the rest of the day, Marsh Cottage became the scene of local interest. Children and adults gathered in the lane to watch the police enquiries taking place. The police sergeant, doctor and vicar went in and out of the cottage. Old Clara, very subdued, was constantly questioned: Had she heard any noises? Did she awake in the night? Old Clara confessed that she had heard nothing and seen nothing.

Doughy had been an odd sort of youth. He hardly ever worked, but just roamed the marsh fishing or collecting birds' eggs and ducks alike. He was the youngest son of the village baker. All agreed he was not quite right in the head, which was one of the reasons why he was nicknamed 'Doughy'.

His death was a sad affair and his parents were distraught. The last time he had been seen was at dusk when he had been standing in the lane stroking a big yellow cat and talking to it as he did to all animals. But why he should hang himself was a complete mystery. But a deeper mystery as far as Clara was concerned was the whereabouts of Theodora.

'Little bitch,' she muttered. 'She went off without saying goodbye.' She stoked up the fire angrily and sniffed at the big pot still on the top of the range. 'Don't it stink? I wonder what she was doing?'

Something then made her open the oven door and look inside. There on the shelf a little row of figures stared out at her. They were all fashioned in clay, and so neat that each little figure seemed to possess its own shape and personality. There were six boys in a row. One had a little piece of string about his neck. Clara shivered. An uncanny feeling overwhelmed her.

Clay figures? That was witchcraft, even Clara knew that.

Clara was afraid as she stood looking into her oven at that sinister line of brown clay shapes.

She jumped as a soft sweet voice behind her said: 'Oh, my little dollies. Are they done?' Theodora was back. She took the figurines out of the oven and lined them up on the table.

Clara watched, fascinated. There was the baker and

his sons, and one very fat one with a huge belly and thick thighs. Beside him, Theodora's gentle hands placed another. It was a woman, with Wellington boots and horns on her head like a cow.

'Do you like them?' asked Theodora, clapping her hands with glee.

But now Clara stared at them gloomily. Theodora picked up the figure with the fat belly. 'Now, this is the one I want to punish next,' she said. 'He did this, you know.' She pushed back her hair to reveal again the long scar at the side of her face. 'But I'll get him very slowly . . .' A hard note came into the soft sweet voice.

'How can you blame old Jed for that?' asked Clara. 'You had that bloody scar when you came.'

Theodora crouched by the fire, still caressing the little clay shape of Jed the landlord. 'It's difficult for you, Gran, I know,' she said reproachfully. 'I told you I lived here before you. You must try to believe me.'

'Believe yer?' snorted Clara. 'I don't believe a bloody word you say.'

Theodora stared up at her, her thick lashes flickering from over those strange eyes.

Clara shivered. 'All right,' she said, 'I believe you, but God knows why.'

Theodora nestled close to her feet like a kitten does and Clara put out a wrinkled hand and stroked the golden hair. A feeling of peace and tranquillity came over her.

'This is the third time I've been back,' said Theodora. 'It will probably be the last. At first I was a queen. Shall I tell you about it, Gran?' The soft, sweet, hypnotic voice lulled Clara into a cradle of memories of Peter her lover who left her the cottage. After bringing up eight children with a drunken husband, she had come to Pete. 'Snow White, with one extra,' the villagers had called him. She stroked Theodora's hair and imagined it was Pete sitting at her feet in the firelight.

'First time I was in the mortal world I was a queen,' continued Theodora. 'Sat on a golden throne with purple cushions and gem-encrusted slippers to match. Are you listening, Gran?'

'I'm listening, fibber,' said Clara in a distant voice.

'I was born very humble but was sold to a house of pleasure. I became a famous snake dancer, and sold my soul to the Devil. He has been my master ever since. I would like to be a queen again but that beast the innkeeper destroyed my beauty.' She touched the scar on her neck. Her voice changed suddenly as anger, bitterness and shrill curses came from that soft red mouth. 'I'll get him. I'll make him suffer.'

'Now don't get bad-tempered, Theodora. Go on with the story, it's more relaxing,' said Clara.

'I've had many lovers but my master wanted me to be queen so I married the King's son. I lived in a gold palace with mosaics and marble floors with a fountain and peacocks in the gardens.'

'Sounds lovely,' said Clara, 'but I feel sleepy, I'll go up for a nap. Got a drop of that wine left, Theodora?'

With her gentle hands, the girl held the glass for Clara to drink.

'It's very strong,' said Clara. 'But it gives me a good sleep.'

Theodora helped her from the chair and Clara went up to bed to dream strange unreal but lifelike happenings of when she was younger and in love with Pete.

With a strange smile on her face, Theodora lit a candle and placed it in the window. Her eyes closed and strange words came from her lips as she looked out into the night. With eyes still closed she stood at the window as though she was waiting for someone or something. Then there were footsteps down the path and a knock on the door. Swiftly she opened it, and on the doorstep was Peter, Clara's youngest son. He looked shamefaced and very apologetic.

'Is my mother at home?' he asked. He seemed a bit surprised to see the visitor in his mother's house.

Theodora held the door wide open for him to enter. 'Your mother is sleeping. Can I offer you a drink?'

Peter sat awkwardly on the edge of the chair twisting his cap in his hands. 'Thought I'd pop in. I was a bit worried about her having that bad turn last week.'

Theodora smiled sweetly. 'Your mother is fine. I'm taking care of her.'

'That's very good of you,' said Pete. 'I won't stay. Tell her I called.' He knew his wife would nag like hell if he was late home.

'Have just a small glass of wine,' urged Theodora, pressing the glass of wine into his hand. She stirred up the fire and the flames outlined her slim body.

Through the thin dress he could see the complete shape of her legs. Not a bad little bit of stuff, decided Pete as he sipped the wine. He always had fancied a nice blonde. But there was not much chance with old Bet chasing him.

The fire burned hot against his thighs. Why he put his arm about her waist he never knew, but he did know that she sat on his lap and entwined her arms about his neck. The rural henpecked husband was lost. They slid down on to the floor, her slim shape pressing against him. Theodora was whispering: 'Love me, Peter, I need so much to be loved.'

While Clara slept the sleep of the dead upstairs, her son lay beside the fire, Theodora's naked body beside him. Peter slept soundly, with a supremely satisfied smile upon his homely face.

A gale-force wind came roaring over the marshland. Trees were bent over with the force of it, the rain teemed down and black storm clouds tore across the sky. It was a weird night and all in the village felt that it was a wild evil night, and pulled blankets over their heads.

Through the night drove a car, headlights blazing as it travelled very fast, driven by a young man returning from a binge in town. In the back seat lay his friend, who had had one too many.

Along the wet, shiny, twisting road, they had passed the lane to Marsh Cottage. The driver suddenly saw a naked white body ahead of him. It was twisting and twining and singing in the wild evil night. Then a large yellow cat ran across the road. Startled, he swerved suddenly and crashed through the hedge into a cornfield. The car turned over and over until it came to a shuddering stop. The befuddled passenger crawled out of the wreckage to see the strange sight of a yellow cat that stood, back arched, spitting on the body of his friend, Bobby Meade.

Bobby was the second of the baker's sons to die that week. And Bobby's death was not the only event that night. At four o'clock, a red dawn streaked the sky. As Danny the herdsman went out to bring the cows in for milking, through the grey misty dawn a huge shaped charged towards him bellowing very loudly. It was old Jed's pedigree bull and sitting on its back was the hippy who was staying in Marsh Cottage. It charged madly past him, knocking him flat, and then rushed down the lane past Marsh Cottage into the village street. It charged the door of the Post Office to end up with its head stuck through the counter where it bellowed fit to wake the dead. Altogether, it was a tragic night and a tragic morning.

They say old Jed wept when they had to destroy his bull. A thousand pounds he had cost and Jed had been mighty proud of that pedigree animal.

The storm had flattened fields and ripped off roofs. It had been a very expensive night for old Jed, who owned most of the farmlands. He could not believe Danny's fantastic tale about a girl who rode the bull to his death. It did not bear thinking of. Old Danny must be going potty.

Then there was this nasty business of Bet Buckley, Peter's wife. She was nearly off her head with worry having run out in the storm to look for her husband. She beat on his mother's door but got no reply. Then she had gone down to the police station but did eventually find him sleeping by his mother's fire in the morning. Was she angry! She had beaten her husband all the way back home with old Clara's umbrella. Meanwhile, Clara was wondering why her cushions were on the floor and what had gone on the night before, and where was Theodora? She had vanished again.

Soon Theodora came in wet and dishevelled. She had a wild light in her eyes. Clara felt somewhat afraid. She looked different, like an animal at bay. The girl stood poised on the doorstep, her hair flying loose as if she had been running.

'What's your game?' demanded Clara, her courage returning. 'Why was my Peter here all night?'

But Theodora gave her an impatient push and went past her towards the fire. 'Peace, old woman,' she said in a shrill voice. 'I have great things on my mind.' She had taken the two clay figures of the baker's sons and crushed them in her hands.

But Clara was not easily quieted. 'You have been out all night, dirty little bitch. And what's going on with you and my Peter, eh?'

Theodora turned, her slim body taut. 'I needed a man, old woman. You had my man, so I took your son.'

Old Clara's mouth gaped open. She had dreamed of a big man who raped her. How did Theodora know?

Theodora burst out into peals of laughter. Clara rushed at her, her arms waving. She was screaming and shouting. There was a flash and the yellow eyes blazed fire. Where Clara had stood was a white bulldog with its nose on the floor. It whined and snuffled in a melancholy manner.

'That's better,' said Theodora. 'An old dog should be more use than an old woman. You will stay that way.' Then curling up on the mat, Theodora went to sleep with the white dog beside her.

It was now mid-December. Silver frost lay most of the day on the shrubs and reeds on the marshland. The sheep and cattle were protected from the harsh weather by being taken into winter quarters.

Since that dreadful wild night in November things had settled down in the village. The only real item of extra news was that the baker, Mr Meade, had taken his family to Australia. It was a very sudden decision but he and his wife were unable to withstand any more of the ill luck that had suddenly descended upon them – the death of their two sons, the bread that refused to rise and the plague of cockroaches in the bakehouse.

The elders in the village thought it a great pity. John Meade was a local man. He had been born in the village, his father and his father's father had been the millers in the old mill on the marsh that had ground the corn since the sixteenth century. Now he had left for a foreign land. Tears were shed and tongues wagged. The local newspaper gave him a write-up with a list of the unfortunate happenings that had hit the small hamlet recently. But life went on. Men went off to their daily work, and the women sat knitting and sewing and waiting for the spring to come round again.

Clara had not been seen in any of her usual haunts recently – not in the post office nor in Gallows End. Her cottage looked unkempt and her chickens roamed free. But everyone knew that it was occupied by that young girl and a huge white bulldog that ran swiftly over the marsh each morning savaging anyone and everyone who passed down the lane. At the sound of someone's footsteps, it came roaring out, snarling viciously, saliva dripping. Its viciousness guaranteed that no one hung around for long.

At Gallows End a big log fire burned and the Young Bulls sat around playing cards. Big Bill was there, out and about once more but he hobbled in with two sticks, his legs still encased in plaster.

Old Jed was very drunk. He was nasty, aggressive and insulting, as he leaned on the bar casting out remarks to all and sundry.

'Old Jed's gone tonight,' remarked Dennis of the woodlands.

'He's worried over sweet Violet,' said Yorky with his bright grin.

'Why, what's wrong? Not in the pudding club?' asked one wit. 'Don't tell me the old bull got her in trouble before he committed suicide.'

They all began to laugh, and old Jed snarled across at them.

'No, it's serious,' whispered Danny the herdsman. 'She's got something growing out of her head on both sides, they say.'

This comment added to their amusement and the old walls of the pub echoed with merriment at poor

Violet's expense. But it abated as the girl herself came into the bar.

There was definitely some change in sweet Violet. Her mouth dropped open in a most melancholy manner, and her whole face seemed to have assumed a downward look. A soft down covered her upper lip and her eyes showed a wide, round blank expression about them. On her head she wore a red woolly hat pulled right down over her ears, giving her an extremely odd look.

All heads went down and faces twitched. They knew they dare not laugh.

Old Jed said: 'Feeling better, my love?'

Violet moved her head from side to side and her voice had a deep hollow tone. 'No, Pa, the doctor don't know what it is. I got to go to hospital tomorrow.'

Jed was touchingly tender with his daughter. 'Go to bed, my love, I'll manage,' he said. He was very fond of Violet.

'Don't drink too much, Pa!' said Violet, and she wandered slowly out again.

The all began to discuss the girl in low whispers.

'Don't she look awful?' said the villagers.

'Wonder what it is?'

'Seems like a growth.'

All were sympathetic about this terrible illness.

'All right, you lot,' shouted old Jed. 'Don't make a bloody meal of it.'

Then the pub door opened and in waddled the white bulldog bitch followed by Theodora still wearing that same print dress over bare legs and feet. Cards dropped from work-worn hands. Feet shuffled. Eyes fixed on the doorway in anticipation of Clara's appearance but no one else came in.

'Jesus,' whispered Yorky to Danny. 'She still ain't got no shoes on and it's freezing out there. It's unnatural.'

'You might be right, mate,' said Danny. 'Didn't I see her with me own eyes astride that bull? I don't like it.'

It was time for Danny to go home. As he made for the door, the old white bitch growled and showed her teeth. From a seat in the corner, old Jack the shepherd raised his head. His old dog lay under his seat. Jack had not worked in weeks as his old dog had refused to go out on the marsh. Jack wouldn't have the animal put down so he was managing on his pension. But suddenly the old dog darted out from under the seat and the white bulldog flew at him, catching him by the scruff of the neck and shaking him like a rabbit.

The sound of the dog fight was terrifying with all the snarling, growling and barking. Chairs scraped back and everyone got to their feet, except Theodora, who just pushed the white bitch with her bare foot.

'Shut up, Clara!' she commanded. The bulldog immediately let go of the sheepdog and lay quiet.

Swearing and cursing, Jack the shepherd followed his cringing sheepdog out of the door.

'Vicious bloody old bitch you've got there,' grumbled old Jed.

'She would be,' Theodora replied with a sweet smile. 'It's old Clara.'

Everyone stared at her in astonishment. Had they heard correctly? They laughed nervously.

Theodora slid her slim body up on to the high stool and stared soberly into Jed's red-veined eyes. Drawn like a serpent to music, Jed kept his gaze on a focal point, the small pointed breasts which rested on the bar counter. Then he quickly pulled himself together and said: 'What's your order?'

Theodora placed her white arms on the polished bar and put her hands under her chin. Her golden hair cascaded down to her waist, causing the card players to hold their breath. Then Theodora's silvery voice rang out: 'I haven't got any money and I've no desire to drink. I only came to ask how your poor daughter is.'

Jed's large and blubbery mouth lolled wide open. He could not believe that someone was sufficiently interested in Violet to come asking after her health. 'She's rather poorly, love,' he said, pouring himself a large brandy. 'Here, have a drink on the house. It will warm you up, what with you having no shoes on in this cold weather,' he added rather kindly.

'Oh, I'm quite used to it,' replied Theodora. She moved nearer to him. Her scent overwhelmed him. It was unlike any he had ever smelled before. It seemed to be of honeysuckle and wild roses, and the woods in spring.

Jed held her tiny hand and said, 'What's up with old Clara, letting you run about half undressed in this weather?'

'I'm never cold,' said Theodora. Taking Jed's large beefy hand, she put it to her face on the spot under her hair where that big scar glowed an angry red.

Jed pulled his hand back quickly, as though he had had an electric shock. 'Blimey!' he said. 'Who did that?'

'Someone burned me,' replied Theodora in a pathetic voice.

'Oh, I'm sorry,' babbled Jed.

'Sorrow will not suffice,' Theodora said icily. 'This my earthly body is marked for ever. All the sorrow in the world will not take that away.'

Jed looked embarrassed as if he did not know how to answer. He just sweated and shivered. She was having a strange effect on him, this long-haired kid. 'Drink up,' he said, 'and have another. I feel like having a good time myself tonight.'

'I will give you a good time,' whispered Theodora.

Her fingers gently passed up and down his hairy arm until the hairs literally stood on end.

'All right,' muttered Jed excitedly. 'I'll see you outside and take you home. Where's old Clara?'

Theodora stared at the dog at her feet for a moment and then said: 'Old Clara has gone on a short holiday.'

'So you're on your own up there . . .' Jed's breath came short and sharp, his beady eyes gleamed greedily. 'Good, I'll bring a bottle and a nice bit of cold supper. We will make a night of it.' Looking craftily from side to side, he reached out and clumsily squeezed one of her small breasts.

'Here, see that!' whispered Dennis from across the room. 'That gel's got old Jed going.'

The others nudged each other and whispered,

casting lewd glances in Theodora's direction, all that is, except Big Bill, who dealt the cards slowly. His ears glowed red and his mouth was set in a grim line.

'Bloody little whore,' he muttered. Then he threw the cards down. 'I'm off. Who's going to give me a lift home?'

They rose as one man – three hefty fellows. Bill was their mate and if he was offended, so were they.

'Come on, lads,' they called. Off they went, out of the door without even a good-night.

As the old bulldog leaped up to snap and snarl at their heels, the Young Bulls rained kicks and curses on her. Bill hobbled out frowning. 'I'll do for that bloody bitch if you don't keep it in order,' he snarled.

Theodora swung round on her stool and stared at him with an odd look in those opaque yellow eyes. Bill turned away quickly.

Meanwhile, old Jed dashed about bolting and barring the doors to the pub. Every now and then he would shove one great hairy hand down the front of Theodora's dress and slide the other one along her thighs. 'Wait out in the lane,' he whispered hoarsely. 'I'll get the old jeep.'

Theodora remained passive, a fixed smile on her face as she glided out into the cold night, with old Clara waddling behind her.

Upstairs young Violet was brooding in her room. Suddenly she realised that the bar was closed. There were no sounds from below. All was silent. 'I wonder where Pa is?' she muttered quietly to herself.

Violet went to the window and was amazed to see

her father starting up the old jeep in the yard. Going out at this time of night? Her curiosity got the better of her and she pressed her nose to the window to get a better look. Then she saw Theodora. The moon was shining on her golden hair. What *was* Pa doing? He handed her a basket. Oh, no he couldn't! He was actually pawing that dreadful hippy who seemed to be backing towards the pond. Then she went out of sight and Violet couldn't see her any more. Nor could she see her father in the jeep revving the engine loudly. Then suddenly there was a fearful yell and a yellow cat leapt from the bushes on to old Jed who let the brakes slip as he fought with it. The jeep shot forward, roaring down the slope into the pond.

Violet leaned out of the window in great agitation. Strange noises came from her. The red woolly hat slipped off her head to reveal two distinct horns sticking out from each side of her head.

The jeep entered the icy water and came to rest in the middle of the pond, with the thick banks of reeds supporting it. Old Jed was up to his neck in icy water; with his face purple with fright, he yelled desperately for help.

The Young Bulls had deposited Big Bill at his mother's cottage and returned home past the inn just in time to hear the rumpus coming from the pond. Sweet Violet was leaning from the window mooing loudly, while Jed, who had almost gasped his last breath in the icy slimy water of the pond, was rescued with the aid of a rope and a heavy chain. Unfortunately, they lost the jeep which slid on down into the bottomless depths.

Jed was put to bed and the doctor arrived. The man would live, the doctor said, but the constant pulling and pushing by those hefty lads had strained his back and he might have to spend a few weeks in bed.

But as Dennis remarked on the way back home: 'It's funny how old Jed got in there. He said that a wild cat attacked him. I, for one, am staying away from that hippy, and I'm keeping me bloody fingers crossed whenever I see her coming.'

As a result of all those strange happenings, the village was becoming notorious. Visitors from far away began to come to have a look as word spread.

'Where is this godforsaken hole?' asked Jock McGregor, the photographer on the county newspaper.

'It's not far from here,' replied his young assistant Jerry. 'Plenty of news out there lately – suicide, bulls running amok and a lot of old twaddle about evil spirits. I know it quite well. I used to bike it to the marshes when I was at school. We'll take a run by there tomorrow night and get a few interesting shots.'

At that precise moment, someone else was asking the way to the village. He was fat and rather prosperous looking. He wore a long black cassock and a three-cornered hat. The porter who had hailed a taxi for him said: 'It's five miles as the crow flies and it's like no-man's-land out there.'

Monsignor Mortimer smiled benignly. He was in no hurry. After years of foreign service, he was taking a holiday with Arthur, an old university pal who was now the vicar of the oddly named village of Bel Uncle Halt.

When in his letter the vicar had mentioned Bel Uncle Halt, the Monsignor had been very interested as his family had descended from the old Mortimers who had ruled that part of the country in Elizabethan days. His hobby was history, so he had always fancied visiting this remote spot. When the taxi came to a stop outside the vicarage and Arthur appeared with his hands outstretched to greet him, he knew the long trip from Rome had been worthwhile.

Out on the marsh, Clara's cottage had become almost unrecognisable. Theodora had transformed it into a witch's den. The table was littered with herbs and weeds from the woods, and shells and seaweeds collected from the shore. A chalk circle had been drawn around the objects in the room. Chickens clustered about the fire and an old rooster perched on the table. Everywhere there were bird droppings. A box of toads sat under the table. Candle-grease and cobwebs covered the furniture.

Theodora was busy stirring the everlasting pot, and old Clara the white bulldog lay on her back, paws in the air, snoring loudly. A full extended stomach still contained almost all of the goodies that had been in Jed's supper basket the night before.

Theodora was stroking the belly of the clay figure of Jed. 'I'll never kill him,' she muttered. 'I want to make him suffer.' She picked up a long pin and stuck it into its belly and then another in its chest. 'That will do for today, old Jed,' she said. Suddenly, she stiffened and adopted a crouched position like a cat within the big chalk circle. Someone was at the window!

A pair of eyes peered in, and the lens of a camera could be seen quite clearly as Jock McGregor tried to take a few sly shots of the village hippy.

'Might catch her naked,' he had said to Jerry. 'That would bring in a few bob or two, a shot like that.'

But Jerry had not wanted to join him and now sat in the Gallows End while his mate prowled around Marsh Cottage.

Theodora's slim and graceful figure rose and went to the front door. 'Is anyone there?' she called sweetly.

Looking rather shame-faced, Jock rose from the bushes. 'Good morning,' he muttered, gaping at this beautiful girl with her perfect lines and her long golden hair. A mixed character, was Jock. Born in the Gorbals, he was an artist at heart. The human form, pure and simple without clothes really brought out his artistic nature.

'You want to take a picture of me?' Theodora asked gently.

Jock nodded dumbly.

Placing her arms behind her head Theodora gave her body a little wiggle. Her dress dropped to her ankles. There she stood in the cold light of day without a stitch on.

Jock rushed madly hither and thither, camera clicking, getting her in all positions fore and aft. Then Theodora dropped her arms and, with a smile on her lips, she called: 'Clara!'

Out of the door rushed the white bulldog. There was a ripping sound as the seat of Jock's pants came away and the man tore down the lane as though the devil was after him. But it was the old devil Clara and she would not give up until she had a trouser leg and a good nip of his backside.

Jerry was sitting comfortably enjoying his pint when the exhausted Jock burst in through the pub door. Only one leg remained of his trousers and nothing in the place where he sat. Young Jerry stared at him in astonishment. He could not believe that the arrogant Jock had been reduced to such a state of abject terror. Jerry went off into hysterical laughter.

It was Danny the herdsman who came to the rescue. 'Better come over the way. I got an old pair of pants in the barn.'

'Thanks, pal,' said Jock, slowly recovering his breath. He handed his grinning assistant his camera. 'Take care of that. Got some bloody fine shots of that bitch – till the dog came at me.'

Later they sat about a table in the bar, Danny and the two newspaper men. He loved to talk so he told of all the strange happenings in Bel Uncle Halt that previous month. They stoked him up with beer to keep him going. It proved to be an interesting tale. Jerry swiftly took shorthand notes as old Danny nodded his grizzled head and his wrinkled face worked up and down. Then he told them about seeing the hippy girl astride the bull, and the yellow cat that was on the scene of every accident. 'It's black magic,' he whispered. 'Always been about here, it has. It's like in days gone by,' he continued. 'Dancing naked on the marshes, me father has seen them, witches,' he declared dramatically as he guzzled his free beer.

'And where is old Clara?' he asked. 'Never left the village before, not in my time, she ain't.' And he then told them about how old Clara had died and then come back to life before all these odd things started happening.

A stranger had entered the bar. He sat drinking a glass of beer and listening intently to Danny's story. It was the stout Monsignor enjoying his first glass of English ale.

As Jock and Jerry drove back to town, they discussed the information they had gathered from the village. 'What a story! We will hit the headlines if this breaks. With my shots and your article, it will be worth the losing of my new trousers,' said Jock. 'With a bit of luck it will make Sunday's edition. I can see it now: "Who is Theodora? Has Witchcraft returned to our village?" ' Jock turned to Jerry. 'You get cracking on the article; I'll bring in the shots tomorrow.'

But next day Jock came in looking quite ill. His bald pate was wet with perspiration, his blue eyes looked miserable.

'What's up, mate?' Jerry asked. He was concerned. It was not like Jock to be so down.

Jock handed him the negatives and Jerry held them up to the light. He handed them back to the gloomy photographer with a puzzled frown. 'But she's not in them,' he said.

'I know,' sniffed Jock. 'Every bloody thing – the cottage, the chickens, the whole confounded scene – it's all there except the naked blonde.' He looked doleful.

'You are sure you got her?' Jerry asked quietly.

The veins in Jock's neck swelled in temper. 'I know I got her! She came out on the path without a stitch on. I got a good half-a-dozen shots and there's not one sign of the bitch. I just can't make it out.'

Jerry rubbed his chin thoughtfully. 'I'll tell you what, mate, it's no hoax. That hippy must be a real, live ghost.'

'Get away!' replied Jock in disbelief.

'I read it in a book on psychic phenomena. You can never photograph a ghost, just like they can't be seen in a mirror.'

Jock turned a sickly white. 'Well,' he said. 'What do we do now?'

'We will go back out there, that's what we'll do,' said Jerry, gathering his papers together.

'Can't go tonight, it's getting dark,' argued Jock as he remembered the dog. Now with this ghost, he was not sure that he fancied this assignment any more. It was a little more than he had bargained for.

'Come on, let's go,' urged Jerry, his long dark hair falling over his eyes as he went dashing out.

But Jock followed more slowly. 'If she is flesh and blood, I intend to find out,' said Jerry.

The van sped swiftly through the country lanes, only slowing down at the end of the lane that led to Marsh Cottage. It was very dark and a high wind whistled eerily through the trees.

'I'll wait here,' said Jock.

'No, you hide in the bushes halfway down the lane,' ordered Jerry. 'Get the flashlight ready. I'll try to persuade her to let us in.'

'All right, but don't be too long. This place gives me the creeps.'

Jock stood in the shadows while Jerry marched boldly up to the cottage and knocked on the door.

There was no sound from Marsh Cottage, but strange blue lights came from the window. Jerry waited for a few seconds, his fist raised ready to beat on the door again. But it suddenly and slowly opened and there, standing before him, was a wonderful apparition. Theodora was decked out with shiny glittering jewels. About her neck was a heavy collar blazing with precious stones, and ropes of pearls twisted around her lovely hair. Her small breasts were bare but she wore long filmy trousers that draped her slim legs. They glittered with gold and silver.

Jerry stood with an arm upraised as a sweet sickly smell overpowered him. His head swam as he heard her say, 'Oh! Justin, my love, you came to me.' Two soft arms folded over him and drew him inside. He seemed to be in a large room with a high domed ceiling, purple drapes and golden cushions on the floor on which he lay very willingly while Theodora stroked his long hair. 'My love, my long-lost love. How I've waited for you through many centuries!'

Lost in this unreal world, Jerry lay passively as her sweet-scented body overpowered him. Meanwhile, Jock was standing outside in the dark lane shivering. There was no sign of Jerry, but fear and the thought of that bulldog bitch prevented him from getting any closer to the cottage. He stood first on one foot, then the other, waiting and praying for Jerry's return. Then out of the back door waddled the white dog. She snarled when she saw him and Jock began to run. The dog came after him, teeth showing and growling fiercely but Jock leapt into the van and drove off in the nick of time. The dog chased the van for a while but then gave up and sat quietly by the roadside.

It was Friday night and the Gallows End was full of customers. One of the Young Bulls helped the mournful Violet behind the bar. The beer flowed freely as they all chatted about recent events. Violet's red woolly hat seemed to have stretched out even more. In fact, her head was a most peculiar shape.

From upstairs came occasional yells as old Jed got terrible twinges of pain. The doctor could not work out what was wrong at all and could only recommend aspirin.

Suddenly, into the midst of all this, dashed a very harassed-looking newspaper man, swearing like a trooper. 'I'll do that damn dog!' he yelled.

Realising that it was the bulldog bitch he was complaining of, the Young Bulls moved over. 'Come and sit down, mate,' said one. 'When old Clara finally comes home she will have it out of there. Hates dogs, she does, old Clara.'

'Ah!' sighed Danny. 'Is she coming back?'

Within the crumbling old walls of the vicarage, in a comfortably furnished room in which blazed a big log fire, two old men had dined well. The vicar had an excellent housekeeper who sniffed disdainfully at the rural folk in the village, but was happy to serve the vicar's guests. Now she cleared the table and the vicar and his holy guest retired to the fire with a bottle of port.

With an extended tummy and benevolence written all over his face, the Monsignor sat facing his friend. 'It is my opinion,' began the Monsignor in a ponderous manner, 'that you have an evil spirit here in the village.'

'The ghost?' returned his host rather mildly. 'That's good local gossip. There's a lot of history attached to this vicarage.'

'No, not this building. I mean the old rectory and the cottage next to it, the one on the marsh.'

Arthur, the vicar chuckled. 'Nonsense, my friend,' he said. 'I'm surprised at you, of all people, believing such things.'

The Monsignor looked slightly embarrassed. 'I know it's not exactly in keeping with my position,' he said. 'But I do want to do some investigating while I'm here. There's no harm in it anyway.'

Arthur nodded. 'It might be amusing. Well, you could look in my library. There are plenty of old manuscripts and papers there that I have never examined properly, papers relating to the village. There might be something there.'

The next day the Monsignor put on an old tweed suit and visited the graveyard. He walked over the marsh on his way back at dusk and saw a young girl and a white dog running together. The girl's long golden hair was flying out in the cold north wind. He stood still for a moment then put his hand inside his shirt to the large gold crucifix he wore, before returning home to the warmth of the vicarage. After dinner,

Arthur had shown the Monsignor his library and the papers they had talked about. The Monsignor was thrilled to discover that two of the previous priests had borne his name.

'There is an interesting paper here,' said Arthur. 'It's of a witch's trial here in Bel Uncle Halt. It was presided over, I believe, by one of your ancestors.'

With the aid of a magnifying glass, the Monsignor began to read:

In the year of our Lord 1606, I was present at a Witch Trial, of a young girl called Dora Buckley from this village, Bel Uncle Halt. They brought this young girl before me. I tried to reason with them but certain villagers were very incensed. I begged her to reject her vile ways to confess, but she bit and scratched like an animal. I had no option but to pronounce sentence on her. The Miller and his sons had trapped her holed up in a lonely cottage near my house on the Marsh. Having ordered the fire to be lit I left, having no heart to watch a female burn. Some boy from the village loosened her bonds and she broke free and fled to the pond where she drowned. Her hair was fair and she had a wound where the Innkeeper had struck her with a burning faggot. Her body was never recovered but peace came to our village once the evil force was destroyed.

James Mortimer, Priest of this Parish

The Monsignor sat back. 'The old rogue shut his eyes to pray so as not to see her burn,' he murmured.

'Yes,' said Arthur, 'they did dreadful things in those days.'

'Ah!' said Monsignor, 'but it is not unique. Quite often I've known this evil to return.'

'I doubt it,' said Arthur.

So the two old men sat into the early hours and discussed the forces of evil.

On that Friday evening, the black night had descended over Bel Uncle Halt. A pale full moon shone icily into the still waters of the pond, as Big Bill struggled along the path to Gallows End. Hobbling along on his crutches, with two legs in plastercasts, was a feat of endurance but come what may, he had to be with his pals for that evening drink. Slowly and laboriously he progressed. The casts were getting heavier by the minute and his temper more angry. He had reached the end of the lane that came out almost directly opposite Clara's cottage. He breathed a sigh of relief at the sight of the lights at Gallows End, then, looking towards Marsh Cottage, he muttered: 'I'll get you one day, bloody bitch. Wait till I get on me feet. I'll get you one night, bloody whore.'

Then feeling better, he continued on towards his good companions and the warmth of the inn.

Then suddenly out of the darkness, came the old white bitch bearing down on him like a tank once did in his Army days. Bill hobbled as fast as he could but could not outpace Clara. She dashed up, snapping and snarling at his legs. This did not hurt because of the plastercasts but having your best trousers ripped up is no joke. Bill lashed out with his crutches and lost his balance. One crutch spun away into the darkness and Bill wallowed in a muddy ditch. He clambered out but the next minute Clara was at him again, snarling and growling. Leaning against a tree stump was a large pitchfork left by some careless labourer. With a terrible curse Bill grabbed it and literally propelled himself at Clara who stood defiantly in front of him.

Bill lunged at the dog and shoved the pitchfork forward as hard as he possibly could. The pitch-fork entered the dog's side. There was a terrible scream, like a woman's rather than a dog's. Bill lost his balance and fell forwards on his front. He recovered enough to see the blood spurting from that white writhing body. With a feeling of great panic, Bill gave one terrific heave and hurled the dog and pitchfork into the pond. Then, hobbling with only one crutch he made his way into Gallows End, where Danny the herdsman, Dennis the poacher and Yorky the muscular tractor driver had been drinking with Jock McGregor. All these men were drunk.

Danny was clutching his rabbit's foot for luck as the door opened and a mud-covered Bill staggered into the room. 'Get me a drink, for gawd's sake,' croaked Bill.

They filled his glass with whisky and he took it straight down.

'What's up?' they asked in chorus.

Bill motioned them to be quiet. 'Hush. I don't want them all to know I done her in. She came for me so I stuck a pitchfork in her and chucked her in the pond.'

No one spoke, not even the half-dazed Jock. It was Yorky who recovered first. 'You're kidding, mate,' he said nervously. 'You ain't done that hippy tart in?'

'No,' roared Bill. 'Her bleeding dog, that's what.'

A great cheer went up and the men all began to laugh and celebrate. Everyone was fed-up with that old white bitch. Even Jock forgot about his friend who had vanished into Marsh Cottage.

They sang filthy songs and got disgustingly drunk and argued and sang till closing time.

Sweet Violet, looking very depressed, put a towel over the beer pump and requested them to leave. They all did, except Jock who was quite incapacitated, so they dragged him into the bar parlour, put Violet's goatskin rug over him, and went their merry way.

Bill was taken home to his ma, and as Danny deposited him in his front garden, he said that it had been a very good night. Unknown to them all, it was certainly to be a night to remember.

The next day was Saturday and the peace of the village was disturbed early by the sound of frantic activity. Police cars sped through the streets. The villagers darted from their beds to look out of their windows. Another police car sped by followed by a plain blue van. They were all going in the direction of the pond at Gallows End.

The villagers rose one by one and went out in the cold morning air to discover that a murder had been committed in Bel Uncle Halt.

'Oh, dearly beloved Jesus!' screamed the post-mistress looking even less attractive than usual without her spectacles and dressed in a long woolly dressing gown. 'I knew it,' she wailed. 'It had to come, we are being punished for our evil ways.'

But the more moderate thinkers just stood listening to Danny the herdsman in the forefront of the gossipers. He informed them that old Clara had been murdered and her body had been found floating in the pond by none other than himself. And a terrible shock it had given him, he told them.

'Got drunk and fell, I expect,' said the milkman.

'No,' replied Danny. 'She was all bloodstained. Horribly murdered, she was.' His voice dropped down. 'It's that witch what done it, mark my words!'

All eyes turned fearfully in the direction of Marsh Cottage. Then the villagers all stood in respectful silence as the plain van bearing the body of old Clara passed on its way back to town for the postmortem. Then nodding and chatting, they dispersed to go home to breakfast.

At Gallows End Sweet Violet was feeling quite worried. Her father had ceased roaring which was not like him. She was most concerned. To add to her troubles, there was this business going on downstairs, with the place full of cops and newspapermen, and that nosy lot from the village standing out there staring. She put her hand to her aching head. It felt so heavy with these huge lumps growing from either side of it. Oh dear, what should she do?

It served old Clara right, but she had distinctly heard Big Bill say that he did it.

'Chucked the old bitch in the pond,' he had said last

night. He had actually joked about it, yes, she had seen him come in all covered in mud. 'Please God, don't let them question me,' she prayed.

Downstairs in the bar parlour, Jock was very heavy-eyed and dishevelled, having just been yanked awake by a hefty constable.

'What are you doing lying there? Have you been out in the night?' the constable demanded.

Jock rubbed his bald path and tried to remember. It was then he remembered that Jerry was still missing, and he learnt that some old gal had been hauled out of the pond. So, that was what the fuss was all about. Should he mention Jerry? He was not likely to have bumped off an old gal, was he? Better shut up. You never know with these country cops. So Jock sat slightly stunned, waiting for something to happen.

The police had gone up to interview Sweet Violet. Within minutes the police car had been seen speeding towards Big Bill's mother's cottage to pick Bill up and take him to the station while further enquiries were made. With a heavy hangover and protesting loudly, Bill was bundled into the police car and his little old mum ran weeping to tell her friend the vicar.

Soon the religious fraternity had arrived at Gallows End – a small nervous vicar and his guest, the large, pompous Monsignor. On the way to the scene of the crime, the two men had listened to the villagers' various accounts of what had been happening.

'Strange business,' remarked the Monsignor, seating himself beside Jock.

'Could be right, sir,' replied the disgruntled Jock.

'Don't know whether I'm on me head or me heels sitting here hoping me mate will turn up.'

The fat priest looked very interested. 'Been gone all night, has he?'

'Yes, how did you know?'

'Where is he? In Marsh Cottage?' asked the Monsignor.

Jock looked very worried. 'Yes, how did you guess?' he whispered.

'Well, I have a theory about these strange happenings – the accidents, the death of the old lady and the disappearance of your friend are all linked to one thing: the evil spirit in Marsh Cottage.'

'Surely, Father, you don't believe in all that twaddle?'

But the priest looked very wise. 'In my line of work we come across many strange happenings. I trust, young man, you have been baptised and are one of my own?'

Jock looked embarrassed. 'Well, let's say I was brought up that way,' he muttered.

Suddenly a police sergeant returned to request that Violet go to the station with him and other witnesses he had collected.

Outside in the car sat Dennis and Yorky looking very disturbed but Violet set up a mooing sound and would not budge without the vicar. Eventually, the group all left for the police station, leaving Jock and the priest sitting in the bar parlour.

'That's better. Now we can start work,' whispered the old man to the amazed newspapermen. 'I trust you are prepared to help me.' He looked beadily at Jock.

Jock thought for a moment and realised that he couldn't go back without Jerry. He nodded.

'Good,' said the Monsignor. 'Now first to the vicarage, then to Marsh Cottage.'

'I've got the van,' offered Jock. 'We'll go in that, Father.'

First they went to the vicarage where the Monsignor dressed himself in his magnificent robes of office. He explained the theory to Jock all the while.

'An ancestor of mine was the priest here three hundred years ago,' he said. 'He left manuscripts that proved the existence of a witch who fled the fire and was drowned in the pond.' Still slightly shaky from the previous night's booze, Jock goggled at the old priest, who placed a crucifix about his neck and sprinkled him liberally with holy water.

'Now there is nothing to fear as long as you do exactly as I say,' the Monsignor informed him.

To Jock it all felt unreal. It was as though he were a boy again and getting ready to help serve the Mass in that big church in the Gorbals.

Now the Monsignor was busy with his beads, and then he was looking to the sun, his lips moving in prayer. The day seemed to be disappearing fast. A deep scarlet slash stained the horizon and the sun, like a shimmering orange, slid through a smoky haze. Then the Monsignor uttered a triumphant cry. 'Ah, the sun had reached the sea! At last! Off we go, we'll get there at dusk. You must try to be brave, young man. Think only on Holy Matters and pray fervently. Any little prayer will do, something you learned at school. Now, follow me.'

He stepped out, his robes billowing out in the breeze. Jock marched nervously behind him in a long white robe, his bald patch shiny with perspiration. In the one hand the priest held a huge crucifix and in the other a container and brush from which he sprinkled holy water all the way.

The village children tagged on behind laughing and giggling. At the end of the lane the two men met Yorky and Dennis returning from the police station after giving their evidence. Their faces were long and melancholy. Bill, they said, had been held in custody. It had been a great shock to his pals. And an even greater one for Bill himself.

Seeing the procession advancing, Yorky and Dennis went along with it, making for Marsh Cottage.

At the front door, the Monsignor came to a halt and burst into a frantic chant, his sing-song voice echoing out in Latin into the twilight.

The door came open gradually and Theodora stood there outlined by the candlelight within. Then her voice rang out, shrill with terror, as she saw the crucifix. She backed away, shielding her eyes from the sight.

'No, no, no! she screeched. 'Not this time, Father Mortimer, you won't get me this time!'

There was a roll of thunder from out of nowhere, and a dash of vivid blue lightning. A large yellow cat leapt over the head of the priest and dashed down the lane towards the pond.

The Monsignor did not flinch or stop praying. Holding the cross high, he walked into the dark cottage.

Shivering and shaking and muttering his Hail

Marys, Jock followed close behind him, while Yorky and Dennis gave chase to the cat.

'Get that bleeding cat!' yelled Dennis, waving his shotgun. He reached the pond first and took several pot shots at it. But the cat disappeared into the pond, letting out a great hissing sound as it hit the water.

'Just like a bloody squib being chucked in,' remarked Dennis as they watched.

When they returned to Marsh Cottage, nothing could have prepared them for the sight that met their eyes. They recoiled at the squalor inside, the mess, the dirt, the horrible smell, and the blood-stained table littered with bones and feathers. There was no sign of Theodora. There was a black kitten sleeping by the fire, and on the range was a huge pot from which came a smoky blue haze. On the wall by the fireplace hung a long carved wooden spoon. The Monsignor was marching around and around, sprinkling and praying, muttering and mumbling his prayers. Suddenly he swept everything from the table into the fire, including all the old parchments which crackled loudly as the flames consumed them. Smoke belched out as the men coughed and spluttered, unable to see each other for a few seconds. At last the smoke cleared and alongside the fire was Jerry. He was dressed only in his shirt and a wreath of leaves was entwined in his hair. He lay there with a stupid expression on his face, oblivious of all the world.

It was Jock who recovered first at the sight of Jerry lying there so peacefully. He aimed a hefty kick at him: 'Get up, you lazy tyke. You been lying in here all the time?'

Jerry sat up and looked about him in a dazed manner. 'Crikey! Been on a trip, I reckon. Where is that bird? Wasn't she a smasher?' He got up slowly, searching for his trousers. Finding them, he put them on.

The Monsignor seemed to have finished his task. He looked rather pale, as though he was under some kind of strain. 'Farewell, Theodora,' he muttered. 'I wonder if we will ever meet again.' He whispered the words so that no one could hear. Then he walked slowly from the cottage back down the path and past the staring children. He did not look in any direction until he was back in the warm sitting room of the vicarage.

Jock and Jerry sped back to the village, meanwhile, on the tail of Dennis and Yorky, heading for a final drink in Gallows End to compare notes and size up the situation.

'It's a funny business,' remarked Jock. 'Do you think that girl really turned into a cat?'

'I dunno,' replied Jerry. 'I can't remember it all, but I am sure I had a lovely time. I can see her dancing just like Salome, all beads and bare belly.'

'Shut up, mate!' demanded Jock. 'Don't confuse me any more. I just want to forget about the whole rotten business.'

And that brings our tale to an end. Theodora had avenged herself. Bill was convicted of the murder of Clara, and old Jed lay speechless and paralysed from a stroke for five years. His daughter Violet looked after him diligently and after his death she escaped with her strange-shaped head to a remote island off the West of Scotland. Jerry never forgot his night of passion with the beautiful Theodora but he was never able to find happiness with any other woman. He had four failed marriages. Jock was fired from his newspaper job for failing to produce any decent photographs for this assignment. He died young, a bitter and disappointed man.

The cottage – with the long spoon intact – was inherited by Clara's children who continued to squabble over it for years to come. And every now and then, ramblers in the local woods would report sightings of a large yellow cat darting across streams or leaping from tree to tree. They all commented on its evil expression and its strange opaque yellow eyes.

So did Theodora, as the cat, drown in the pond, as Dennis and Yorky thought? Or did she live on, waiting to wreak havoc again on Bel Uncle Halt at some other time in the future, on later descendants of these present villagers? Perhaps we shall find out in another story.

Do you wish this wasn't the end?

Join us at www.hodder.co.uk, or follow us on
Twitter @hodderbooks to be a part of our community
of people who love the very best in books and reading.

Whether you want to discover more about a book
or an author, watch trailers and interviews, have the
chance to win early limited editions, or simply browse
our expert readers' selection of the very best books,
we think you'll find what you're looking for.

And if you don't,
that's the place to tell us what's missing.

We love what we do, and we'd love you to be part of it.

www.hodder.co.uk

@hodderbooks

HodderBooks

HodderBooks